A Keeper's Country

J. K. STANFORD

A Keeper's Country

Illustrated by P. N. Stewart

°THE°
SPORTSMAN'S
PRESS
LONDON

First published 1968
© C.J.N. Stanford, 1989

This edition published in 1989
by The Sportsman's Press

British Library Cataloguing in Publication Data

Stanford, J. K. (John Keith), *1892–1971*
 A keeper's country.
 I. Title
 823'.914 [F]

 ISBN 0–948253–37–1

Printed and bound in Great Britain by
Redwood Burn Limited, Trowbridge, Wiltshire

*Any similarity or apparent connection between
the characters in this story and actual persons,
whether alive or dead, is purely coincidental*

For
Buffie

I

THE sun was dipping as Alfred Blowers came out and stood in the shelter of his cottage porch. Across the wind from beyond the High Wood whose beeches studded the skyline, he could hear faint reports of guns, one, three, five, six, ten, then a flurry of shots, then silence. That meant Duncan had just finished driving the kale half a mile beyond the crest. They would have to hurry if they were going to do the High Wood and the Laurels before the light went. A wooden bench with a bush of honeysuckle nailed behind it flanked the cottage wall. Alfred sat down and his white-muzzled retriever snuffled round the corner and lay down at his feet.

The man's grey eyes (faded now but still keen) were fixed on the meadow in front. The wood-edge, where the steep down flattened out, was three hundred yards away. Ah! here they came, a cock pheasant and two hens scuttling towards his garden. How quick some birds were to learn! It was only the second time over but he felt sure that that old cock with the pale wings had not been near a gun for three seasons. Every time they shot he was an absentee and hid neatly in Alfred's cabbage

garden, usually alone, sometimes with other birds. The dog
turned her head at their faint rustle in the neatly trimmed
quickset and thumped her tail. She knew as well as Alfred
about those refugees skulking into the garden but she would
not betray them. And the old man thought, 'I'm still a game-
keeper though I'm on my seventy-eight.' Preserving game in
his old age, not from vermin and poachers but from the gentry
with guns!

The wind blew keenly off the down. The pheasants came high
here, flushed out of the beeches at the top of the hill, and with
the wind as it was, Alfred doubted whether 'this lot' (by which
he meant the Colonel's current syndicate) would touch one in
five as they sailed towards the Pleasaunce behind him. Poor
birds! He could imagine them waiting for their evening corn,
worrying at the noise of shooting far away, ears and necks
strained to discover what was happening, and those that survived the flush having to roost in an unaccustomed place.

The grinding roar of a lorry, changing gear at the corner of
the road, meant the guns were coming round to their pegs on
the meadow in front of him. Far away he saw two dark figures
silhouetted on the crest of the down where the beech wood
tapered out in a huddle of young trees. Duncan's stops round
the west end were probably too late to stop a lot of birds running out to hide in the rough grass. Alfred himself after the first
time over had always said you wanted as many stops as beaters,
especially if you meant to kill your cocks. But Duncan was up
against it nowadays with only six grown men worth counting
on and the rest schoolboys.

The lorry roared past behind him up the lane and he caught
a whiff of cigar-smoke and high-pitched laughter from under
its canopy. It pulled up a hundred yards beyond and he heard
the rattle of the tail board and voices calling to dogs. Here they
came – Numbers Five, Six and Seven along the meadow past
his garden. Number Seven passed him without a glance or a
word, a short podgy man rendered even more round by
'elephant trousers'. Funny, thought Alfred, half of them never
seemed to wear proper shooting clothes these days!

Two taller men followed twenty yards behind. One called 'Oi, Richard', to the podgy figure and then, 'Duncan's shifting us all one gun down on account of the wind. You'll be forty yards beyond that last peg, and Charles here is at Number Seven.'

The dumpy man nodded and walked on. The other two guns turned and Alfred saw that one of them was Sir Henry Westleton from across the valley. He stopped and smiled. 'Hullo, Alfred, I didn't see you. How are you?'

The old man stood up and touched his cap. 'Very well, Sir Henry, thank you. And what sort of a day?'

'First-rate. Duncan's worked them beautifully though they played him up a bit before lunch. Wonderful show of birds. You'd better not be watching *me* here, Alfred, or I'll never touch a feather in a wind like this!'

The two men strolled on. The thinner one, Charles Turner, with a neat beard and the prominent eyes of an artist, murmured 'And who is that *extraordinarily* handsome old man?'

'Alfred Blowers, used to be head-keeper here. He's coming on for eighty. Did a lot for this shoot. Nigel wouldn't be doing this stand this way under Alfred's predecessor! He hated showing his birds properly, and liked giving us a poor day.'

The artist was not to be diverted from his theme: 'Dress that chap in a white collar and a dark suit and give him a bowler hat, and he'd make my Lord Richard' (he nodded ahead) 'and half the members of White's and Boodles and the Turf look like cabhorses! I wonder where he got those features from. I should like to paint him.' They stopped out of earshot of the cottage at Number Six peg.

'We've got five minutes yet,' said Sir Henry pointing up the hill. 'They bring all those laurels along the crest and the flushing point is up in the beeches *there*. You'll get some stinkers over you on this wind, all very high and sliding downhill.'

'I'm interested in that keeper's face,' pursued Charles. 'Always in these villages you find someone, a thatcher or hedger or cowman, with noble looks which put our so-called gentry to shame. Why? Were they illegitimate far back, offsprings

of the *droit du seigneur*, or what? Look at little Richard
Tinkerton, fourth generation at Eton and brother of a duke, yet
that old boy could beat him down the course for looks and
breeding. Tell me why?'

Sir Henry loaded his gun. 'I've noticed it meself a time or
two. Never asked the reason. Perhaps it's because those chaps
have never had to think or worry themselves. Same as a cow,
no worries, lovely eyes and a really likeable face. But *she's* not
very intellectual. . . .

'I'm a ninth baronet,' (he grinned all over his amiable pug
face) 'but the Lord knows it doesn't show in *my* features. My
wife swears our yardman in his Sunday clobber at the Flower
Show looks far more like the Lord of the Manor than myself.'

'Yes,' said Charles. 'You can't go by features, Henry. They're
most misleading. I make a brothel-keeper's income painting
lovely ladies, and then I look 'em up in Debrett and hear what
people tell me about them in the Three Arts Club, or the
Berkeley, and believe you me, Henry, if they've got ethereal
good looks, they've either no brains or no morals, sometimes
neither. The most likeable portrait I ever did was of an octaroon
whore in the Bag of Nails. I've never sold that picture and my
wife's insanely jealous of it.'

Sir Henry nodded. 'Come to think of it, I'm not so sure
about gamekeepers having no worries. My own chap is full of
gloom, night and day. Whole world is up against him! And yet
a few keepers are the laziest chaps I know, make their own
day's work, and no one knows what they're doing half their
time.' He broke off suddenly. 'Gallop on, Charles, to your peg,
like hell! Here he bloody well comes. My God Almighty, what
good is a cock like that to me!'

A hundred yards away the old man had risen and was leaning
over his garden gate. He had seen the pheasant, even with his
old eyes, long before Sir Henry had, a dark form on almost
motionless wings, outlined between the beech tops and the rosy
sky. Too good a bird even for Sir Henry, who was, they told
him, something at Buckingham Palace, and shot at Windsor
and Balmoral and Sandringham. He watched him fire twice

and the dark shape never flinched but disappeared far behind into the Pleasaunce, unscathed.

Beyond Sir Henry, Charles Turner, one eye on the hill, was ruminating. Like so many artists, he came from the eastern counties. There had been plenty of Blowers there and he now suddenly remembered one, a yeoman farmer who claimed kinship through his great-grandfather with the old family of Blore who held the Earldom of Peasenhall. He recalled rabbiting with Ernest Blowers at Dersham Hall and the old man, after three glasses of home-made sloe gin, saying with a twinkle: ' 'Though his Lordship wouldn't thank me for saying so, his great-grandfather was mine too. My great-grandmother was the then Lord Peasenhall's kitchen-maid, a very respectable girl too till *he* set eyes on her one day. Fixed her up when her time was near with this here farm and here we've been ever since. I suppose I've better blood in me than some gentry round here!'

But then the pheasants began to come and Charles forgot East Anglia and heredity.

* * *

The rise was over. It was nearly dark. A tawny owl hooted from beyond the wood. The old man had leaned on his gate immovably to watch it. Sir Henry hadn't shot badly at all, as well he ought to, getting all that shooting with royalty year after year, but there weren't more than twenty-five birds down all along the line and he'd counted over 120 cartridges fired. Lord Richard Tinkerton was kicking some of his neatly down a rabbit-hole like a terrier burying a bone in a flower-bed.

He lit a pipe slowly as the guns and beaters converged on the road. Tomorrow he would tell Duncan, who had plenty to do before it got dark, about that hen which had dropped on the rise near the Pleasaunce. She was stone-dead and there were no foxes to worry about. She'd be there in the morning. And he suddenly thought, 'I was thirteen and a nipper when I first went on a day's shooting, more'n sixty-five years ago. I've come a long way since.'

II

IT had been a long way to come. And his career had begun the day his mother died, in 1900. Alfred's father, the head horseman, had died when he was five. He was now thirteen, a gaunt and ravenous boy doing odd jobs after school hours with old Mr Flickerson's shepherd at three shillings a week. Nobody knew how Mrs Blowers 'managed' for there were no old age pensions in those days. Her eldest girl was housemaid at the Hall and the next worked in the scullery at Tibberton House. Alfred himself had been shifting hurdles all afternoon in a bitter wind. He had eaten two turnips, raw like apples, to 'stay his stomach', since his midday meal of bread and cheese, and was looking forward to his tea.

The news, which brought the rest of Emma Blowers' children hurrying to her bedside, had somehow missed Alfred in the turnip field. When he came home he clambered upstairs and looked at his mother, pale on her bed in her worn black dress. It was the first time he had ever seen her not look worried. Yet it gave him a shock because he had never seen a human being dead before.

Tom his eldest brother, now one of the horsemen at the Grange, told him the story. 'She was took poorly on a sudden just after she'd got the washing in. Mrs Pryke came in to borrow a saucepan and found her laid on the floor. . . . She was dead before I got here.'

They discussed it slowly over fat bacon and the last of Emma Blowers' home-baked bread and tea. 'You'll have to get a proper job, Alfred, du there 'ont be enough money for this cottage.'

Alfred never forgot the service in the little church with its round tower. Emma Blowers was liked by her neighbours and every pew was full. Reuben, another brother, who had been walking out for years and saving up for marriage, had paid for the coffin. Mrs Flickerson had sent all the autumn flowers she could lay hands on and come with her daughter. There had been a scare because old Mr Samson, the Vicar, had been 'taken poorly', on a Saturday too, with the gout. But Mr Flickerson, his Warden, not only conducted the funeral service sonorously and well but stumped up to the chancel and gave them all a piece of his mind about Emma Blowers for ten minutes.

'I reckon,' an elder said that evening in *The Crown*, 'our Master preached a wunnerful good sermon on old Emma Blowers. This poor woman, like the one in the Bible, he sa', *she hath done what she could*. And I reckon she had. She'd had ten and brought five of 'em up all proper and how she did it with only what she could arn arter Reuben died. . . .'

Mr. Flickerson was the undisputed squire of the parish. The two hereditary squires at the Hall and Tibberton House were absentees, one always down in Venice with an Italian countess, and one away digging in the deserts of Arabia. They left their parish to old Robert Flickerson and their estates to their agents.

And when the burial was over, a message came for Alfred through the shepherd, a crimson-faced sardonic bachelor who was said to have seduced most of the married labourers' wives in the parish, and was rarely seen in church. 'Governor he want to see you, Allfred buoy, tonight at seven o'clock time.'

Alfred scrubbed himself anew, brushed again his only decent suit which he had long outgrown, and presented himself anxiously at the back door of the Grange. Few people were sent for unless they had earned Robert Flickerson's disapproval.

'Come yew on in, Allfred,' said Mother Balm the cook. Her tongue and cooking were revered by high and low. 'And mind now, don't muddy my nice clean mat with your great boots.

Why, yew're all of a tremble, buoy! I'm sorry for your pore mother: she was a rare nice woman, though it's hard for me to say it, for she always spoke her mind. "Mrs Balm," she sa' to me, years agoo and I've never forgotten it, "if you talked less and ate less you'd be a better woman. I only eat what few vittles them poor children of mine leave on their plates." But she had a beautiful funeral, now didn't she, what with the Mistress's flowers and all. And the Master I reckon ought to have been a parson, rather than that owd fule of a vicar who's half of him in the tother world and what's left don't make sense to me. Goo you on in now and leave your cap here.'

Mr Flickerson had changed the black frock coat he wore for funerals for a dark velvet frogged jacket. His snowy hair and beard gleamed in the lamplight. Alfred had never been in that high dark room before, nor had he ever seen so many books, which rose all round him to the ceiling. (Emma Blowers' library had consisted of one book, The Good Book, as she called it, and that rested in her spotless parlour alongside her husband's photograph.)

'Sit you down, Alfred boy,' said Mr Flickerson. 'It's sad about your poor mother, she was a fine woman, as I said today in church. What age are you now?'

'On my fourteen, sir,' said Alfred, though he was barely thirteen.

'Can you read and write?'

'I can, Master, not too good, but I can't reckon.' Arithmetic had always been Alfred's stumbling-block in the village school.

'A lot of people can't reckon, Alfred, and what they learn in school they usually forget. The shepherd says you can count my sheep and know them well. What else do you know I wonder?'

The old man took down a huge leather-bound book from a shelf. He turned the pages and Alfred saw there were great coloured pictures on almost every page. Mr Flickerson sat down again. 'Come you round here, boy, and tell me what that bird is, now?'

Alfred looked. 'That's a King Harry, sir.'

'Right. What some of us call a goldfinch. And that?'

'Rose linnet.'

'And that?'

'That's one of them butcher-birds what comes in the summer.'

'Right again.'

Mr Flickerson turned the stiff pages for five minutes and seemed well satisfied with Alfred's answers. He had not known one of the names in the bird book but had given them all the correct local names, felfoot and green linnet, bottle-tit, wind-hover and hornpie. This scarlet emaciated boy with the clean-cut features seemed to know where they nested, what they ate, and the special habits of their lives.

He said at last, 'Well, Alfred, you've passed your examina-tion. I'll tell Mrs Rolph you've got to leave school to earn your living. I'm going to make you backhouse boy here at six shillings a week. That won't be easy. You'll have to look after the fowls and clean the dog kennels and help Harry Clarke with my two horses and do the odd jobs for Mrs Balm – plucking fowls, coals, wood and what she tells you. And come the summer you'll have to give a hand in rearing my pheasants and on shooting days . . .'

Alfred went away in a dream. Six shillings a week and a plate of vittles at midday! Why, his brother the horseman only earned thirteen and a bit of harvest money on top, and had to find every bite he ate. Mrs Balm said 'Well, Allfred, there's a nice bit of rabbit-pie for you in the scullery and a mite of cheese. The Master he said you mightn't have had much tea. Now eat it up and don't you leave any crumbs on my clean floor or I'll have your life. I never did hold with buoys.'

Hunger and fear ensured that Alfred did not leave a crumb. As he was rinsing the plate, he heard Mother Balm's voice, 'Master, he tell me I've got that dratted boy Allfred acomen' into the back'us Monday. As if I hadn't had three of 'em in the last twelvemonth and what's more, he ain't only in the back'us, he's got to help Harry in the stable and du the dogs as well. He'll always be on another job just when I need him, with dirty hands. If it warn't for his poor mother that's in her grave, I'd ha' told the Master. I doon't know what we're acomen to.' For those were the spacious days and even in the Grange, which was not a big house, there were four indoor servants and sometimes five when the Master entertained or had a shooting party.

Alfred met the shepherd in the lane as he was walking to *The Crown.* 'Well Allfred, buoy,' (for rumour travels fast in country villages), 'they sa' you 'ont be with the sheep come Monday. And just as you was learning which ewe was which, and beginning to be of some use to me. Well, buoy, I wouldn't be in your boots for a five-pun note. With old Mother Balm there's everlastin' bleating more than my four hundred ewes together. You'll be wishing you was back with me out in the open and eating raw tarnips before you're much older, I'll lay a shillun.' For the village regarded 'back'us buoys' as a very low form of indoor life.

III

B UT that year in the backhouse had started Alfred on his life's career. He was no longer an unknown village hobble-dehoy but 'that boy Allfred at the Grange'. Harry Clarke was only a part-time coachman, and an even more part-time game-keeper in the rearing season, but he taught him how to trap rabbits with wires and gins, and both waged war on the rats round the pigsties and the rickyard. 'And don't you dare, buoy, to touch an owl here or the Master'll skin you alive! They're working away for us at rats and mice all night long. I never could abide them little cat-owls what some Lord brought in from abroad, blast him, I don't trust them a mite, but some doctor chap opened up a lot of their stummicks and there was narthen in 'em only beetles and such. Now go you on and clean them kennels before Mother Balm starts howling again.'

Alfred scrubbed the kennels out and privately thought none of his predecessors could have done it for years. He combed the dogs' matted coats and gave them clean wheat-straw and even remonstrated with the kitchenmaid when he found tea-leaves and potato peelings or tomato-skins in the dogs' dishes. He took the three out for walks and tried to inculcate some discipline in them. He did not realize that he had 'a way with dogs', as some nannies have with children, but under Alfred's care their incessant barking stopped and all three watched him with adoring eyes as he hurried from woodshed to coalshed, from scullery to the stables and back again, in response to Mrs Balm's summonses and Harry Clarke's shout of 'buoy'!

Gradually Alfred mastered his round, and by dint of working on Saturday afternoons he chopped enough firewood to keep Mrs Balm's Grand Remonstrance at bay. It meant getting up at 5.30, as his mother had done for years, and he had often done a day's work before his second breakfast of tea and bread in the scullery at 8 a.m. His midday meal was a generous one: 'How you do eat, Allfred,' Mrs Balm would say, 'and how you do grow! You're twice the size of your poor father already.' And then she would rate the kitchenmaid, 'that fule of a Rose gal', for so obviously admiring Alfred's looks and size.

Dogs, horses, and the multitudinous chores of 'the backhouse' filled Alfred's day and he found no time to worry till he fell into bed, far more tired than the dogs. But perhaps the most educative feature of that year was learning to talk to what he called 'the gentry', on friendly terms. Other village boys, rude and tongue-tied as savages, could do no more than touch their caps and mumble askance if they passed them on the road. But Mrs Flickerson, and her widowed daughter, who lived at the Grange, often sent for Alfred for some job about the house or garden; and he learned to look them in the face, to answer their questions, and even to say something other than 'Yes, m'm,' or 'No, m'm.' When Alfred later had to talk with princes and peers, this knowledge stood him in good stead.

Mrs Watts, the daughter, started the process with this shy, handsome creature. 'You're not paid to cut wood on Saturday afternoons, Alfred,' she said kindly, when she found him busy in the woodshed, for there was no overtime in those days.

'Well ma'am, there was whooly a lot to du today and there, I never got round to it.' He looked at her, so quiet, so different from fussy old Mrs Balm.

'You've done wonders with the dogs,' Mrs Watts went on, 'they're looking better than I've ever seen them. The Master's very pleased.' They studied them together while the dogs wriggled and squirmed and gazed at Alfred in mute adoration, and Alfred was emboldened to speak.

'That one ain't right, ma'am, he's got canker or summat in his off-ear, and the little dawg tore his dew-claw ascrabben' after rats.' So what with veterinary talk and the possession of a store of medicines hoarded on a shelf in the kennel, and the fact that Mrs Watts shared with him a few secrets about Harry Clarke's dogmastership, he felt he was getting on.

But his great day came on the First of September, for 'The First' was always a festival at the Grange. Alfred rose even earlier than usual in the chill mist which presaged a hot morning and buckled on his father's gaiters and gave the dogs a run at six o'clock before the scullery chores. To his astonishment he was given at breakfast-time four great slabs of bread and cold beef with mustard and a hunk of cheese by Mother Balm to 'put in his game bag', and a cask of apple wine for the refreshment of the guns. He and Harry Clarke (no longer a coachman, for the yardman was to 'bait' the horses and the horses of the visitors) leaned on their long ash-sticks while the guns assembled, three bearded elders who had shot with 'old Robert' every first of September for twenty years. They wore thick Norfolk belted jackets with roomy game pockets, and leather gaiters and boots below their breeches. And their truculent dogs (there were no bitches in the shooting-field then) who barked and wanted to start fights and wound their leads round their masters' gaiters, were put to shame by the two Grange retrievers, who sat quietly at Alfred's feet and merely shuddered at these strangers.

Old Mr Flickerson, beaming in the September sunshine and not knowing that it was his last 'First', completed Alfred's delight by saying 'Let me have the old dog, Alfred boy, and you take the young one with the gentlemen,' for he was an old man now and while the other guns were tramping in line the dew-drenched stubbles and mangold-fields, it was Mr Flickerson's habit to stand quietly by a gateway in a field-corner, in hopes that they would put a covey over his head.

Alfred never forgot that baking day, his first shooting day – the line wheeling solemnly round the fields, the screech of partridges starting out of cover, the smell of powder in the air, and all the little birds of the farm, blackbirds and warblers slipping out of the roots, a woodpigeon clattering off an oak tree, a landrail in the seed clover. His mouth was dry with excitement and his boots were drenched with the water off the roots, but the day was a succession of triumphs for a boy.

The first came when he found a rabbit squatting in a wheat stubble and said quietly, 'Here a' be a raabut, sir,' to the nearest gun. And when it ran and was rolled over, Alfred was as pleased as if he had shot it himself. The second came when the three stranger dogs all failed at a partridge in high mangolds and one departed jubilantly after a hare in the process. At last a bearded elder mopped his brow with a red bandanna and said, 'Here, boy, you have a try now with the Master's dog.' And Alfred, his heart in his mouth, unloosed the cord off the shuddering young one and said quietly, 'Hie lost, Royal,' and waved his hand, wondering if he would ever see Royal again or if he would bolt to where the Master was hiding three hundred yards away behind his gate.

And oh, the joy when Royal stopped and turned his head stiffly and picked the bird and brought it, snuffling with pride, his mouth full, his eyes adoring, to Alfred's hand! And the elders said, 'Well done, boy,' though they qualified it by saying 'There's not a breath of scent today. My dog couldn't own it at all.'

But later in the morning when everyone was thinking of lunch (and there had been two halts for the apple wine), Alfred's triumph was complete. He was sent back for two partridges, one a bird which had towered and fallen dead just over a high fence and the other which had carried on

and collapsed several hundred yards away in the mangolds.
'We'll be at lunch in the Old Barn, Allfred,' said Harry
Clarke, taking the gamestick with the partridges. 'Now goo you
back and have a try with the dawg for them two.' And off
Alfred went, rejoicing that the ground had not been foiled by
the truculent visitors, who were by now too exhausted to do
more than glare at each other. Alfred had the good sense to
give Royal 'the wind' and to let him hunt quietly, and when at
last the bird got up and ran, clucking and dodging in and out
of the drills, Alfred joined in the chase and luckily none of the
faraway guns saw him when he fell on the bird, as he had
done so often with a rabbit in the harvest field, and ended the
hunt.

He gave the tired dog a swim in a hedgerow pond full of
green water and between them they picked the towered bird
which was not on the stubble but 'lodged' in the hazel stubs of
the fence. His whole being was triumphant as he reached the
Old Barn whither Mrs Watts in the dog-cart had brought the
lunch along a lane. 'That boy's been a long time,' he heard
Mr Cord from Lower Abbey say, 'I'll bet a florin he never got
either of those birds. Boys nowadays never learn to mark
properly.' And at that moment Alfred slid past the barn
entrance, looking for Harry Clarke round the corner.

He was summoned back into the cool interior. He took off
his cap, as they all looked at him. 'Well, Alfred,' said Mr
Flickerson, with his mouth full of pie, 'I suppose you didn't find
either of those birds?'

'Ah, Master,' Alfred blushed to his hair, 'leastways the dawg
did.' He decided to give the credit where it did not really
belong. 'We got both on 'em.'

'Well then, Mr Cord here owes you two shillings. He betted
you wouldn't find either of them.' And Mr Cord produced a
whole half-crown and said slowly, 'Well done, boy, here you
are. I suppose you didn't put down a dead one, out of that
bag of yours, for the dog to find?'

They were all looking at Alfred as he turned more and more
scarlet. For it was an old trick to put a dead bird down secretly

'to encourage' an unsuccessful dog or to keep up a keeper's prestige, even in days before field trials had been thought of. Alfred was scratching his head, and, pocketing his half-crown, he said 'No sir, that I didn't. I hadn't got no dead bird to put down. Mr Clarke took them all off me before I went.' There was a roar of laughter and Mrs Watts said, 'Well done, Alfred.' He slipped out, blushing and triumphant, to eat his beef sandwiches with Harry Clarke in 'the horse-shod' – to which Mrs Watts added two apples and a hunk of cake. He was dripping with sweat through his father's old celluloid collar, but entirely happy. Royal, whom he had helped so nobly and mightily refreshed in the green slime of the pond, had deserted him for the pickings he hoped to get from the shooters in the barn, and was shaking himself all over Mr Flickerson's lunch.

'That boy of yours, Robert,' a bearded elder rumbled, 'is coming on well. I've never seen that young dog of yours so biddable.'

And old Robert said, 'That boy's well bred on one side. He'll get on one day,' and went on munching.

The rest of that baking day was a blur to Alfred Blowers. His feet swelled and blistered in his soaked boots, and the celluloid collar seemed like an iron band round his scrawny neck. He plodded on in a dream, almost as tired as the elderly guns. His only respite was a plunge late in the afternoon into what was called 'those maize' – a two-acre strip higher than Alfred's head which was grown as cattle feed before the days of kale, and seemed cool and damp and dense as bamboo jungle. The maize was full of young pheasants and inevitably old Robert, walking on the headland, shot one by mistake for a partridge amid derisive cheers, for this had become a tradition at the Grange and the bird went down in the gamebook as 'a macaw'.

Everyone was glad to see the rickyard shining at the end of the last wheat stubble. It had been an early harvest and there was a settled benignity on the landscape, a hush of accomplishment with summer nearly done, and all the autumn ploughing, the threshing and the hedging still to come. The apples were

mellowing on the orchard trees, a turtledove still crooned in
the elms and sparrows were chattering in the ivy.

Tired as Alfred was, with three hares 'hurdled' on his ash-
stick and his clothes sodden with sweat, he turned to the multitudinous tasks which had piled up in 'the backhouse' during the
day. They had shot 21½ brace of partridges, well-grown young
birds, and before the guns went in to their tea laced with
'French cream', each presented Alfred solemnly with half-a-
crown and Mr Cord said 'Boy, you and that young dog did
right well. I don't reckon we've lost a wounded bird all day,'
which made the boy's soul swell with pride. Even Harry Clarke
said 'You ain't done too bad, Allfred buoy, seeing as how it was
your first time out! Now mind you see that Mother Balm gives
them dawgs a decent plate of vittles.' And Alfred, having
watered and fed them, instead of going to his own tea, spent
half an hour searching their feet for thorns and pulling burrs
out of their ears.

That was his first day's shooting, and it remained in his mind
for sixty-five years as a golden day when everything had gone
'as right as rain'. But such an idyll was too good to last. Mr
Flickerson was an ailing man, though only Mrs Watts noticed
it. His temper became most uncertain, and there was a dreadful
morning in October when he suddenly determined overnight
to shoot his first lawful pheasant instead of waiting as usual for
his birthday party in November. Nothing went right that dew-
wet morning, though they did collect a few partridges and
pheasants. Even Harry Clarke, who had endured 'the Master's'
cursing for years, murmured 'The Owd Man ain't hisself at all
today'. And soon the rumour was round the neighbouring
villages that old Mr Flickerson had been 'took wunnerful
poorly with his innards'. At the birthday party in November
he stood on his lawn while they drove 'those maize' and the
larches over the garden. He shot his last pheasant, and then
drove in his pony trap with Alfred in attendance all day and
watched the others shoot.

He died just before Christmas and Tibberton church, packed
with farmers and farm-workers to its doors, showed Alfred how

widely the old man had been respected. But it meant the break-up of a settled life which had endured for forty years at the Grange. The farm was changing hands in May and Mrs Flickerson and her daughter were going to live near Ipswich. The household staff were offered some of Mr Flickerson's belongings as a memento of 'the Master'. The gardener cunningly chose a mattress, and Harry Clarke, surprisingly for he did not read and could barely write, two books with coloured pictures of horses. Alfred himself, too shy to ask for the great bird book (which had released him from further education) had his mind made up for him by Mrs Watts who produced a shiny almost new 'safety bicycle', a thing then unknown among the farm-workers who either walked to their work or stumped, sitting sideways, on the slow plough-horses. 'Alfred,' she said, 'this is for you. I won't put it in the sale for it belonged to my brother, who was drowned. It'll help you to get to your work and if you're going to be a keeper you'll be able to cover your beat much more quietly.' And Alfred, after a day of wobblings round the stable-yard under the sardonic eye of Harry Clarke, and more days of envious jeers from the village boys as he passed them, realized that he had been given a new mobility and could cover the farm and see things over the fences which he had never seen before.

Mrs Watts did more. She procured him a job. 'Alfred,' she said in April, 'I've told the Colonel's agent you're getting too big to be a backhouse boy. He wants you to start next Monday helping Mr Mould, the head keeper at the Hall. It's a wonderful chance for you, for they rear a thousand birds, and you'll learn all the ins and outs of a keeper's job. You won't find it easy, I warn you, but if you'll stick to it one day you'll be a beat-keeper on your own.'

'Thank you kindly, ma'am,' said Alfred, though his heart sank to his boots. Bert Mould had chased him out of his coverts several years earlier, as he did every small boy in the parish, and he felt he was out of Mrs Balm's frying-pan into a raging fire. But in those days no village boy queried any job that was offered him. It was better than the Army or the Merchant

Navy. Alfred had a good bicycle, a suit of clothes and £4 stowed away. He was better off than most of his contemporaries, and had an enviable capital of health and strength and early rising on which to draw.

IV

'HELPING Mr Mould' was a hard apprenticeship to keepering, and Alfred looked back on the next two years as among the grimmest in his life. Mould's employer, Colonel Darty, was away, archaeologising in the Middle East, and his estate was in charge of an agent who was also a busy auctioneer. But pheasants were still reared and the Colonel's cousin came over from Yoxenford thrice yearly with a party of guns and shot as many birds as Bert Mould permitted them to do.

Mould was a huge menacing figure who wore a green velveteen coat and breeches above buff cloth-gaiters, a red waistcoat adorned with the buttons of the Dartys' crest, and a high square bowler hat. There was a legend that he had beaten a poacher so badly in his youth that he died. He hated boys, and his heavy stick had wrought havoc on them whether they were birds-nesting or picking bluebells, or after nuts in the hazel hedges. A succession of under-keepers had departed in tempestuous rage and few lasted many months, so Mould was driven to employ boys each season to help with the rearing and the spring trapping.

He lived in a tiny pink domed house by the Great Wood, round, thatched, and not unlike the old-fashioned bee-skep. In this his wife had miraculously reared a numerous family, all of whom had fled from the nest to escape the incessant wrangling of their parents. Mrs Mould, a harassed scrawny woman with fair hair wound in a tight bun, was reputed to be thrashed every Saturday night while Mould's cringing under-fed spaniels suffered on other days. Indeed, Alfred Blowers never forgot the unction with which Bert Mould once intoned the adage that

> A woman, a spaniel and a walnut tree,
> The more you beat 'em the better they be.

Alfred, fearing the keeper's temper and stick even more than Mother Balm's tongue, plunged, with earnest bewilderment and at nine shillings a week, into duties which seemed to have no end. He learned to set pole-traps round the rearing field, to bury the village cats which wandered into rabbit gins, and to swear that no cat had ever been seen on his beat. He learned to dig out ants' nests and collect their eggs for the young birds. And he helped the knacker in May to haul on to a great scaffold of poles the carcase of a foundered cow which festered in a cloud of blow-flies above a heap of bran into which maggots dropped ceaselessly for the pheasants. Part of the Great Wood, in early spring a paradise of bluebells, stank to high heaven all summer, but in those days no one thought such pollution unusual. Mould spent much of his time, after the collection of pheasants' eggs was done, in a shepherd's hut on wheels in the wood, just out of nose-shot of the cow's carcase, a hut with a boiler besides it in which he cooked the weird mixture of feeding stuffs with which young pheasants were nourished before the days of 'chick crumbs' and 'rearing pellets'. Mould was the high priest of a secret formula which he had not varied for forty years; custard, greens, rabbits, rice, chopped lettuce and artichokes, hemp, rape, groundsel, hard-boiled eggs and a dozen other ingredients, all went into the boiler, and the labour of collecting it was never-ending.

But Mould had one weakness, intensified by rheumatics and the ceaseless bickering at home. He spent hours in the Tibberton ale-house, a process which he called 'keeping an eye on them poaching beggars', for it was a tradition that the village poacher was always 'a sot' because he was unemployable on any farm. The local poachers speedily rumbled Mr Mould's weakness and having seen him comfortably installed in 'the snug' along with the landlord, made their raids almost with impunity. Indeed it was Alfred, on his bicycle, who interrupted two one October dusk, dragging a silk net over a wheat-stubble for jugging partridges. They disappeared on to the lane at speed on seeing Alfred but stupidly tucked their nets in an overgrown drain. Alfred after much search recovered them, and stowed them in his game-pocket.

He expected congratulations next morning when he produced the nets, but Mr Mould was angry and incredulous. 'Comes of leaving a duzzy buoy on his own. If I'd been there I'd ha' copped them two and no mistake. Who were they now?'

'One was Skipper White, Mr Mould, but the other I couldn't rightly see, a dark chap with a fisherman's sweater and earrings. I reckon he was from Misner. I don't know him but his name is Tom.'

'That couldn't ha' been Skipper,' said Mould. 'I was keepin' an eye on him in *The Crown*. What was it o'clock when you see'd 'em?'

'That was very near dark and I heard the church strike eight, just before I see'd 'em along by the pightle. I reckon they come up the back footpath from *The Crown*.'

'Oh,' sneered Mould, 'and if you don't reckernize the tother man, how do you know his name's Tom?'

This time Alfred let him have it. 'Because, Mr Mould, I was in the Barn spinney when they passed and I heard one say, "Never you fear, Tom 'bor, the old sod is safe there till closing-time".'

Mr Mould was very angry indeed. Alfred realized for the first time that 'truth is the last thing that can be spoken politically'.

But in spite of Mould's temper, Alfred began to like his life. He was free of the park, the woods and spinneys with all their wildlife, he could go where he pleased on the estate and talk to farm labourers on some headland without being accused of 'wasting his time'. They told him of stoats, jays, and rats they had seen, of the cat that had 'gone wild', of nests which they had 'happened across', of lurking strangers, all valuable information to a keeper, which nothing would have induced them to pass on to Mould. In the rearing season Alfred worked a sixteen-hour day. In the shooting season he began at six, had fed his pheasants by seven and at dusk was counting the cocks 'going up to park' or listening to the partridges calling 'cheap wheat' on the stubbles.

Shooting days in winter were always a trial. Mould got him out at dawn to patrol the fields round the Great Wood, to keep birds from straying, while he himself, as spruce in green and red and buff as any cock pheasant, breakfasted at leisure and then stalked about on the Hall gravel, waiting for the guns' wagonettes to appear. Every beat was done in the same way year after year, regardless of the wind, and the flight of the birds; and Mould brushed aside surlily all suggestions of change. 'Drive it *so* and my pheasants will go over into Wenham's and we'll never see 'em again,' he would sneer, or 'What use is it to do *that*? If they du come, your guns'll never hit 'em.' And Alfred never forgot a remark he overheard once after luncheon when the Colonel's cousin asked mildly, 'Where do we go now, Mould?'

'Where I told you this morning.'

A keeper so rude and surly and impervious to suggestion would have been sacked by any of the neighbouring squires but Mould, blessed with an absentee landlord and only the Colonel's cousin to deal with, knew exactly how much he could say with impunity.

But there came a day, in Alfred's third season, of howling East wind in mid-January, when everything went wrong and Mould, suffering from rheumatism and a severe hangover, had had enough long before lunchtime. 'Alfred buoy,' he said, 'you'll have to take on arter dinner. Say I'm down with this here fluenzy and have got to take to my bed. You know where to goo.'

And when the guns came out after lunch, it was Alfred, scarlet and embarrassed, who touched his cap to them. Six pairs of eyes seemed to be poring into him as the Colonel's cousin said: 'Well, Alfred, we've had a rotten morning, though it wasn't *your* fault. Where are you going to take us now?'

'Mr Mould said, sir, to do Scarlett's, then the Broom Piece and finish with the Hall Wood.'

'What about this wind?' asked the Colonel's cousin. It was a suggestion he would never have dared to make to Mould. 'Won't they all go back?'

Alfred had been thinking exactly the same while he munched his bread and cheese. 'It's whooly ablowen',' he agreed, with a circular glance at the weather. 'I was thinking . . .' He stopped. Mould had told him that 'boys were not paid to think'.

'Yes?' said the Colonel's cousin. 'Go on, Alfred.'

'I thought as how we might blank Scarlett's into the Broom, sir, with the guns and brushers all together like in line and then drive the Broom Piece back on the wind.' This would have been anathema to Mould, but Alfred found it came easier than he expected. He glanced up. In spite of the cold, a drop of sweat trickled down his ear.

'And a very good idea too, boy,' said the red-faced be-whiskered man who was known to Mould as 'the General'. 'Don't you agree, George? At any rate, whatever comes over us on this wind will be worth shootin', which is more than it will the other way.'

George nodded. 'And how many hens were there on the feed in the Hall Wood this morning, Alfred? We've seen a lot of hens today and only shot a dozen cocks.'

'I seen forty-seven hens, sir, at seven o'clock time,' said Alfred, feeling that he was revealing state secrets.

'Forty-*seven*? In that wood alone? Then we can safely shoot three hens apece this afternoon, gentlemen. Jim won't mind.'

Jim, the squire, excavating in the Middle East and up to his neck in sand, was not likely to mind but, Alfred thought, Mr Mould would, and Alfred himself would certainly get the blame, if not the sack, next day. But he collected his beaters without a word and stumped off behind the guns. And the beaters, usually as sardonic and independent as most Suffolk yokels, decided quietly that young Alfred needed their support 'agin that owd Mould' and backed him up nobly.

Alfred's heart was in his mouth as the line reached the up-wind edge of Scarlett's Copse, for not one shot had been fired. He could only guess how many pheasants had run ahead of them out across the open into the 'Broom plantain'. Was he, in this his first command, going to give the guns who had trusted him a blank afternoon, even worse than the morning? He led his beaters round to the far edge of the broom in anxious silence while the guns lined out on the edge of Scarlett's. 'Now you brushers,' he croaked, 'spreed you out middlin' thick and goo right steady.' He was thinking that with this gale any pheasants that flew would go right over Scarlett's and on to Lord Wenham's land, in which case they would be lost to the shoot for ever.

They were halfway up the Broom before a bird rose. Then two cock pheasants rose hiccupping from the rough grass along the rabbit-wire and set sail for the Copse. They rose higher and higher on the gale and Alfred thought despairingly, 'They 'on't never hit 'em.' Then he heard two single shots, saw two crumpled forms high in air and relaxed. In after years, like most keepers, he rarely felt he could trust his guns in a down-wind drive: they so often let him down or else the birds seemed to stream over the weakest, most flustered gun. But now, as bird after bird clattered out of the broom and the young larches, and took the same line on the wings of the wind, Alfred realized that the gentlemen were for once 'doing him proud'.

The beaters reached the edge of the broom, to see the six guns picking up in all directions. 'Well done, you,' said the Colonel's cousin. 'As good a rise of pheasants as I ever saw, though a lot were too fast for us. Take four of your chaps into the wood, Alfred, and hunt this end of it carefully along.'

The search was over at last. Alfred's soul was exalted, as he counted seventeen cocks and nine hens laid out in a line on the headland. The game-waggon, drawn by a Suffolk horse, creaked round the corner, its old pensioner, Bill Crane, carrying two more birds which had dropped out on the plough.

'Mould'll be whooly wild,' he grinned. 'Blast, I reckon that's as well he took ill when he did. You've saved the day, buoy, and no mistaake. Seventy-eight shots they fired, I counted 'em.'

But Alfred was thinking of Mould's wrath, if he discovered that any hens had been shot at all. Congratulations were showered on him by the other guns, all that is but the Vicar, Mr Samson, who had fired sixteen cartridges and somehow failed to score.

They ended by blanking the Hall Wood slowly as far as its upwind ride and leaving the guns on the ride behind the beaters. 'Two hens apiece here, gentlemen,' said the Colonel's cousin 'and try and kill as many cocks going back as you can,' and the day ended with sixty-six pheasants, of which eighteen were Mould's sacred hens.

'Give each gentleman three hens apiece, Alfred,' he was told, 'then you won't have to explain them to Mr Mould'; and while the guns were at tea, Alfred and Bill Crane were busy tying them up and hiding the evidence of that afternoon. And in the dusk Alfred had his hand shaken as if he was a real gamekeeper and three half-sovereigns pressed into it which he was enjoined to 'keep for himself', for everyone guessed that tips in those days never went beyond the head keeper and that Alfred would have to disgorge the rest in the morning.

He was up long before dawn hiding the tell-tale cartridge cases which showed where the guns had stood and luckily Mould did not appear till Monday.

But that afternoon taught Alfred two lessons which stood him in good stead all his life. He had never heard of 'Coke of Norfolk', or the manœuvres at Holkham which urged a thousand running pheasants into Scarborough Clump. But he did realize that provided you kept pheasants *on their feet* you could push them with beaters to where you wanted them and 'bring them back'. And he realized too that some of 'the gentry' did not worry about the bag and would far sooner shoot a dozen 'good birds' coming over them high and fast on the wind than three score of 'bad' ones, blundering head-high out of a covert. The easterly gale, which sent Bert Mould to bed and left Alfred in charge with only one alternative, had been a blessing in disguise. As he munched two kippers that evening and washed them down with mugs of strong tea, Alfred's wind-reddened face was aglow from inner satisfaction. Though he could not have defined it to himself, he had tasted power and responsibility and had won the approval of grown men. He was no longer, as he had been for years, 'one of them duzzy buoys'.

V

BUT next season everything seemed to go wrong from the start. Just as the spring trapping was finished, a plague of rats descended on the estate from outside and Mould's pole-traps had obliterated the local owls and kestrels which might have helped to combat them. The farmers' wives were un-usually difficult that year about broody hens. The partridges had suffered through a long winter, for Mould refused to waste corn on them and a lot of the eggs laid by famished birds were addled. The rearing-field, which had been in use for twenty years because it was convenient for Mould, suffered a bad attack of gapes and other diseases and the antique cures then in use kept Alfred busy. Rearing pens were unknown and each broody hen with a dozen chicks in a separate coop on soaking grass took an endless time to get round.

Mould's rheumatics and temper got worse, and his absences more prolonged as the rearing season wore on. Alfred could do nothing right. 'Don't you leave them birds on any account, buoy, and if anyone asks for me say I'm up the wood.' Alfred by now realized that 'up the wood' meant either up in bed or down at the *Crown*, but he kept Mould's secret loyally even when Mrs Mould herself, with a man's cap perched on her bun, came to the rearing-field to ask if her husband was there. '*I* can guess where he is, Alfred, and you needn't lie to *me*. And I suppose you ain't had your tea yet? That ain't right; and I'll tell Bert so when I see him.'

On some days Mould would slip away about eleven and not be back by dark when Alfred, famished and dog-weary, would shut up his coops and plod home. Only two things sustained him, the changing pageant of the summer woodlands around him, with its infinite variety of bird life, and the feeling that he was a real keeper at last, with powers of life and death over the whole estate. In a way loneliness was better than working under the lash of the head keeper's tongue. One day, Alfred vowed, he would be a beat keeper 'on his own', with dogs of his own to train, and no one to see what he was doing.

He hardly spoke to a soul in the day but one windy afternoon he glimpsed a figure slipping round the corner of the main ride and followed him quietly to the edge of the wood. The stranger turned with a start as Alfred came up behind him, and lowered his fieldglasses. Alfred saw a bearded face with keen brown eyes above a clerical collar, and a Norfolk jacket.

'And what are you doing here, young man?' asked the stranger haughtily.

Alfred held his ground. 'Beg pardon, sir, there ain't no road here.'

'Indeed? I've just seen Mould, the gamekeeper, and he said . . .' He paused artistically. Actually, he had given Mould a double rum in *The Crown* to complete his disintegration and had read considerably more meaning into Mould's tipsy mumble of 'Good health, sir,' than the old man intended. In any case, the stranger was well accustomed, as a parson, to brow-beat village yokels.

'What are *you* doing here, lad? Birdsnesting, I suppose?'

'No, sir, I'm under-keeper here,' said Alfred, promoting himself on that instant.

'Oh, indeed, and I suppose you're one of my friend Mr Samson's parishioners?'

Alfred nodded. Mr Samson was a poor shot, rather a joke among the village boys on account of his intonation and absent-mindedness. He had even brought his cartridges to the Hall in the string bag which normally held his tennis balls. Alfred's respect for 'the gentry' did not extend to the only 'reverend' he knew.

'Well, lad, you can get back to work. I shan't touch your precious pheasants and as I told you, I've just seen the head keeper . . .' Again he left the sentence unfinished. 'I suppose you and he have killed all the poor hawks and owls, eh?'

'No, sir, there's a few about.'

'Do you know of any nests?'

'No, sir.' This was untrue, for Alfred knew of a hawk's nest within two hundred yards of where they were standing. He had not climbed to the nest and was not too sure of the bird's species but he was quite sure it wasn't a sparrowhawk or a kestrel. He had watched the pair at dusk sweeping with long scythe-like wings over the corn where they were catching insects and buzzy-witches. He had not told Mould and as the birds were rarely visible before dusk Mould would hardly notice them.

'Very well, young man, I'm having a little stroll around. I shan't be here more than half an hour. Good afternoon,' and the parson nodded dismissal with a smile.

Alfred went back to the rearing-field thinking. He did not altogether trust 'The Reverend' in spite of his affability. Perhaps it was his brown beady eyes which seemed to miss nothing. Perhaps it was his bland assumption that he could come and go as he pleased in woods which were signposted at every gate, 'PRIVATE. TRESPASSERS WILL BE PROSECUTED.' Perhaps it was that the stranger had omitted to mention his own name. The countryman's innate suspicion was strong in Alfred.

He went about his tasks in the rearing-field and boiled up the evening feed. There was still no sign of Bert Mould and

Alfred was ravenous and longing for his tea. His stomach and the light told him that it must be seven o'clock. He decided to go round the nearer tunnel-traps and took his spade. Tucked behind a bush at the northern gate he found a bicycle. So that parson was still there! Five minutes later Alfred gently peered round the hazel bushes towards the tree where his hawks were nesting. The parson was seated on a fallen trunk on the ride's edge with his binoculars fixed on the tree. Alfred came up behind him, the spade on his shoulder, and a dead stoat in his hand. This time he was quite certain that the parson gave a start on seeing him.

'Well, it's you again, boy,' he said, getting up hurriedly. 'Still at it, I see?'

'Yes, sir, beg pardon, what is it o'clock?'

The parson drew out a watch. 'Bless my soul, it's half-past seven. I must be going!' Then as an afterthought, 'What hour do you have to start work in the mornings?'

This time Alfred felt certain he had to lie. 'Seven o'clock time, sir.' He had for years been up at 5 a.m. and in the rearing season was usually at work by 5.45.

'A long day, my lad, but that's the way to be healthy, wealthy and wise. Well, I must be off. Goodnight to you!' and he tripped down the ride.

Alfred, hungrier than ever, went back to the rearing-hut, hung the stoat on the gallows, and seated himself wearily on Mould's couch of sacks. He had missed his tea and it looked as if he would miss his supper, though his sister-in-law took compassion on him and always kept something in the oven. He felt like eating the pheasant-mash, he was so hungry!

He heard footsteps brushing in the grass of the ride and leaped to his feet. Bert Mould must be back at last! But a tall lean stranger in tweeds, with a heavily tanned face and neck, was smiling up at him. 'You'll be Alfred Blowers?' he said.

'Yessir.'

'Well, I'm Captain Darty, the Colonel's nephew. I'm just back from the Sudan. I expect you've heard the Colonel's very ill?'

'No, sir, that I ain't.'

'Well he is, and I'm at the Hall looking after things for a bit. Where's Mould?'

'I expect he's up at home, sir,' lied Alfred miserably.

'His wife says she hasn't seen him since ten o'clock. When did *you* see him?'

'Eleven o'clock time, sir,' said Alfred. 'Mr Mould went up the wood.'

'Well, we won't bother about that. Have you had your tea?'

'No, sir, I ain't.'

'Dam' nonsense! And how many coops are you looking after?'

'A hundred, sir.'

'Well, Alfred, you and I will shut up now and let the chicks be till tomorrow. I'm told you've had a poor season; is that so?'

'We've had proper trouble with the broodies, and gapes ever since.'

'Dam' silly! This rearing-field ought to have been shifted years ago. It must be as foul as could be.'

The Captain and Alfred spent half an hour 'shutting up'. He seemed to know all about Alfred and his past at The Grange. Then he said, 'We'll go back to the Hall. I hear you gave Uncle George a rattling good afternoon at cocks last season. And tomorrow you and Mould can dismantle all these pole-traps. Cruel things, they ought to be abolished by law and they will be one day. Just imagine your being an owl and fluttering upside down in those dam' things all night long!'

Alfred, though as insensitive as most country boys to blood and cruelty, said 'Ah' and nodded agreement. Even he had hated his daily job as executioner at dawn. The Captain poked each trap down with his stick and sprang it.

'Any strangers about today?' the Captain asked casually as they walked across the park, Alfred wheeling his bicycle.

'There was one, sir, a reverend with a bicycle, what told me Mr Mould said he could come.'

'Never trust a parson in May and June. They're nearly

always egg-snatchers!' was the surprising answer. 'If he comes again, turn him off and say it's my order.'

Alfred suddenly recalled the question which the affable gentleman with the beady eyes had asked, about the time he came on duty in the morning. He said nothing but determined to get to the Great Wood at 5.30 on the morrow.

They entered the Hall by a side-door and the Captain shouted loudly in a foreign tongue. To Alfred's astonishment a tall coal-black 'nigger' in a long khaki coat appeared, smiled with a flash of teeth at a string of orders, and led Alfred away down long stone passages to a kitchen where Mrs Jewell, the housekeeper, produced soup for him and a huge plate of cold mutton and pickles. Alfred was so hungry that, though scarlet with embarrassment in such surroundings, he made short work of the meal and received a message that the Captain would see him on the rearing-field 'in the morning'. He plodded home in a dream and fell into bed.

He was awake next day when the first blackbirds sang and pedalled down to the Great Wood after a hurried breakfast. He opened the gate to find the Captain leaning on a thumb-stick in the ride. He put a finger to his lips to warn Alfred not to speak and indicated a bicycle leaning against a beech tree a few yards from the ride. Albert recognized it.

'That your parson's?' whispered the Captain.

'Ah, and I reckon I know where we'll find him, sir.'

'Let's just make sure,' said Captain Darty and he unscrewed both tyre valves and slipped them into his pocket. 'Now lead on as quietly as you can.'

Alfred knew every yard of the Wood by now and led the way by a zig-zag route to where the hawks were nesting. The Captain followed him as silently as if he had not worn boots at all. They emerged on the ride twenty yards from the tree. A tall man wearing climbing irons was just coming down with a fieldglass case slung on his back.

To say that the stranger was surprised to see them was an understatement. He slipped down the last ten feet and landed in the bushes with a crackle. For a moment he looked as if he was going to run, but turned with a smile and said 'Good morning!'

'Good morning, and would you mind telling me what you are doing here?'

'Oh, I'm writing the County history of birds and I just wanted to examine that kestrel's nest before your keepers shot the wretched birds.'

A dark shape on scythe-like wings swept at that moment over the ride and the Captain after one brief glance said: 'That's a hobby, not a kestrel, so you needn't try to bluff me. I suppose you've pinched the eggs? Let me look in that case! Alfred, have your stick ready if this man of God tries to bolt.'

There was a hard menace in his tones as he opened the case. 'What have you left up in the nest? Bantams' eggs with boot-polish on, or water-hens' eggs? Alfred, you'll have to shin up that tree and put this clutch back.'

Alfred did so, glad to see for himself the interior of a 'hobby-hawk's' nest. It was a struggle to reach it. He left the two angry men arguing on the ground and heard only fragments of what followed, but a few sentences remained. 'I know dam' well what you gave my head-keeper to drink in *The Crown* yesterday because Bill Plaice told me last night. And I know even better than you how rare hobbies are in Suffolk. But I'll promise you one thing! I won't show you up to your Bishop because he'd do nothing, but . . . if ever you're found egg-stealing on this estate again, *I'll have your trousers off you*, and you can pedal home to Menhaston without any! Now, Alfred, show this, er, reverend gentleman back to his bicycle. Here are his tyre valves, by the way!'

Alfred did so in pregnant silence, and such was the power of the cloth that he even helped the angry parson to pump up his tyres. He was told venomously that he 'and that precious employer' of his would hear more of it 'in due course' but the months went by without a word.

Captain Darty was smoking a cigarette at the hut. 'Look, Alfred,' he said, 'I don't want any talk in the village about this incident. Keep it to yourself! I shall tell Mr. Mould that those hobbies are on no account to be interfered with and I'm trusting you to *say nothing at all*. Understand? And when Mr Mould comes, ask him to see me at the Hall at 9.30 a.m.'

Alfred kept his promise to the letter and it was a pale and deflated Mould who came back to the rearing-field. His prolonged visits to *The Crown* 'to keep an eye' on the poaching fraternity ceased from that morning, and Alfred got to his tea at a reasonable hour each day. And soon it was all round the village that 'the young squire knew what he was atalken about'.

No one was more relieved than Alfred. He was sent on his bicycle into the market town to be measured for a suit of real keeper's clothes in a good stout broadcloth and was immensely proud, though the village boys jeered at him and whistled as they had done when he wobbled past them on his bicycle. He was even given a retriever puppy to train, and his gratitude knew no bounds. Whether Mrs Mould was still thrashed on Saturday nights he did not know, but the spaniels in Mould's kennels certainly looked much happier and were even taken out on Mould's rounds.

The Captain and his wife frequently came down to discuss the keepers' problems on the spot. By that time the young pheasants had been 'put to wood', gapes nor no gapes, and Captain Darty was full of ideas for 'next season'.

'There's too much silly work on the rearing-field,' he said once, 'opening and shutting a hundred coops every day and all this business of boiling up their food. One day we'll have a dry mash which can be fed to young birds straight out of the sack: and we'll have movable pens with stretcher handles, so that they can run about on fresh ground every day or two. I'd like to start a company to make them, only my uncle would be wild at my being "in trade". And what's more, Mould, these chicks want grit. Partridge-chicks pick it up when they're a few days old. I've seen 'em. All game birds do.'

Mould was by now reduced to dignified mumbles, for he realized that open rudeness was no longer possible, but gradually the new suggestions were adopted for Captain Darty was forty years ahead of his contemporaries. The estate carpenter made some movable pens to hold twenty-five pheasant chicks each, and Alfred with eleven shillings a week, a suit of new clothes and an allowance for dog food, felt really started on a career.

VI

THOSE next few years, under the young squire, were the happiest of Alfred Blowers' life. Bert Mould, always a menace to an underling, was less formidable, for he alone knew how nearly he had been dismissed. He bullied Alfred as much as he dared, but Alfred was now raised to the status of under-keeper, he worked reasonable hours, his opinion was sometimes asked on a day's shooting, and to his immense pride, he was given the care of dogs. In fact, in Captain Darty's second summer Alfred was entrusted by Mrs Darty with no less than three Labrador puppies to train, and wherever Alfred went, they accompanied him, black, silent, adoring shadows who, after a week of struggle, 'dropped' when he told them and 'stayed put' as if Alfred had pegged them down.

Most dog handlers in those days ruled by fear. Starvation, beating, and rating for any misdemeanour were the methods used to bring home to a dog what it had done wrong and few dogs went out shooting unless lashed to their owners by a chain or leather leash. Truculent, monastic males, they were apt to fight when they met their rivals on shooting days. But now one of Alfred's new charges was actually a bitch and he realized she was the most 'biddable' of the trio and the easiest to train.

'That lessest one, Dinah,' he confided to Mrs Darty, 'she's whooly acomen' on and I reckon she finds more than either of the tothers; she've got a wonderful nose.'

So one week in early September, when the Annual Flower Show and Fête was being held at the Hall, Mrs Darty sent for

Alfred. 'Look, Alfred, I'm having some sideshows tomorrow besides the coconut shies and the greasy pole. And you and your young dogs are going to be one of them! I know you won't let me down. All the Captain wants is for you to work them on dummies in the long grass there. We'll rope it off and the crowd can see how well they obey your handling.'

So next afternoon Alfred Blowers, sweating with embarrassment in his best clothes and the bowler-hat of tradition, was one of the sideshows, before a row of chairs in which 'the gentry' sat under the lime trees. He walked out into the grass, his heart in his mouth lest his pupils should disgrace themselves, with the village watching. A silent and critical audience watched him drop his dogs, stalk out and fling dummy rabbit skins in the long grass. To the present generation it would be an elementary exhibition of dog-handling, but in those days it was new. Each dog was sent out while the others waited, trembling, for their turn. Behind the chairs Mother Balm was saying to a knot of women, 'Well, love me, if that ain't our Alfie, what was in my backhouse at The Grange. How he du grow and ain't he smart! If that ain't a masterpiece!' But the keeper from Weasenham Manor said, 'Cor, that's narthen only circus-tricks, I'd like to see them brutes out on a shootin' day!'

In fact, many in the audience were critical and assumed the performance was only put on because Mrs Darty hoped to sell her puppies. But when the little bitch, Dinah, was sent for two dummies in turn and far apart from each other and brought both back with a commendable swagger, an old gentleman in a deck-chair (who had been watching in complete silence with his grey bowler hat tipped over his eyes) said, 'Margaret, that boy of yours has the idea. When you and Charles come up to Glenovil, I hope you'll bring him as loader. I'd like him to have a go at my dogs on off-days. Old Sandy Macdonald in charge of my kennel doesn't know a thing!' Then he lowered his voice and looked round, 'He's a good-looking lad and I hope he won't make trouble with the shy damsels, who come out of the glen to my servants' hall!'

And before Margaret Darty could reply, another old gentleman, with a red and yellow ribbon on his panama-hat and an impressive moustache, leaned over her chair and said: 'I suppose, hr-hm, Mrs Darty, you wouldn't, er, care to part with one of those puppies? I'd, her-hrm, give you your price, of course.' And Margaret Darty said 'Oh, *no*, Colonel, it would break Charlie's underkeeper's heart to pass any of them on before they've had a proper season's work!'

The silent gallery behind the chairs were much impressed when they heard this, as no one had imagined in that era that any gamekeeper had any heart or feelings, and muttered 'Well, there!' in tones which expressed awe and wonderment.

When the prize-giving was almost over, Alfred, who had been drinking a glass of beer in the refreshment tent, heard a stentorian shout of 'Alfred Blowers'. And he had to put on his hat and hurry to receive an envelope containing four half-crowns from a Duchess's daughter at the prize-table, amid laughter because this time all three puppies followed him up to the table and insisted on being presented. And the Lady Elizabeth said some complimentary things to Alfred and gave him a sweet smile and patted the dogs, amid applause. And he even remembered to take his bowler hat off and call her 'M'Lady'. Alfred was getting on.

But about six o'clock with the gentry drifting away to their carriages, the turtledoves purring in the elms, the mellow sunlight over everything, and a German band playing 'The Boys of the Old Brigade', Alfred slipped away from 'the Feet', as everyone called it, and the congratulations which he felt undeserved. Even old Bert Mould, resplendent in red and green and buff, had muttered, 'Well young Alfred, your dawgs ain't shown up as bad as I expected,' which for Mr Mould was high praise. And just as Mother Balm and a handful of village girls, all 'in service' and in their best attire, were clustering round the tall young man, he slipped away on the ground that he had got to feed 'my pheasants'. What Suffolk called 'The Frolic' or 'The Feet' was still in full swing, but duty called.

His joy in his dogs' behaviour was short-lived. And he realized that a keeper's job was never ended. He kennelled the puppies, gave them a bucket of water from the pump, and then heard his brother Reuben's voice from the back door.

'Alfie,' he muttered, for his cottage was 'semi-detached' and one spoke low because of one's neighbours, 'I was up the Grange to bait my horses an hour ago and I see'd Skipper White and another man going up Toller's Lane behind *The Crown*. They fared right drunk. And there was the tinker's cart from Kelsall Green near the corner of the Wood when I passed. I reckon they're thinkin' you and Mould won't be there, what with the frolic and all.'

All thought of Alfred's tea was abandoned though he asked Reuben 'to tell Eliza them puppies want their vittles'. Then he was away on his bicycle, with a heavy 'ashen stick' in his hand. He had fed his pheasants (prematurely) at two o'clock but he had left them for over four hours! He pedalled up the lane between the high impenetrable hazel hedges. Mrs Mould, he knew, was at the Hall helping with the teas. Bert, he suspected, was either lording it over the neighbouring keepers or in transit between the refreshment tent in the Park and *The Crown*. The Captain, who would certainly have helped him, had been busy all afternoon with the coconut shies, the swings, the greasy pole and the children's sports, and was probably now entertaining the inner circle of 'the gentry', who had patronized 'the Feet', to drinks. On Alfred lay the responsibility. He must do whatever had to be done, alone and quickly.

Alfred hid his bicycle behind a bush and slid into the Wood by a path that he alone used. He crossed silently to the ride which led from the main gate. It stood open and backed into it was the square cart of Elijah Dow, the Kelsall Green tinker. Alfred saw a wicker basket on the cart. Towards it, staggering down the ride from the laying-pens with another large basket, came 'Skipper' White and the man he had seen once before, 'the man from Misner with ear-rings', whose name Alfred did not know.

As Alfred burst out of the bushes, the two dropped their

burden but, instead of running away, they advanced on Alfred with menace. 'Get you out of here, young Blowers, before I do you an injury,' said Skipper. Skipper had had a chequered career since Mr Flickerson had sacked him for what was called 'purloining', and had since been in the Army. Most of the village steered clear of him, for he had boxed for the 'Hoozars' and was quick with his fists.

Alfred was badly scared as the two came at him and somehow wished either the puppies or the Captain were there. As Skipper, with his fists held low and his rolling gait, came up, the boy struck out wildly with his ash-plant. By chance it landed on the kneecap of the 'man from Misner' whose leg buckled under him. He screamed that it was broken. Skipper's right fist landed on Alfred's ear, he ducked a second blow and struck again wildly at the bullet-head. Out of the corner of his eye he saw Elijah Dow, bearded like a prophet in a very old bowler hat, come up behind him with a heavy pig-whip. The butt caught Alfred across the nose and jaw and as he staggered, his stick somehow entangled in Elijah's legs and tripped him up. The whip fell in the grass.

Alfred, bleeding and weaponless, was about to run away when the tinker said, 'I'll cut your duzzy throat, young Alf, next time I meet you, you see if I don't.' And to his surprise the fight was over. His wild swipes had included not only the Misner man's kneecap but Skipper White's thumb. All three staggered to their feet, gained the cart and drove off at a gallop, swearing and shouting.

Alfred, with blood streaming from his nose and jaw and ear, found himself alone with the pig-whip and a basket full of squawking bantams (his precious foster-mothers), lying in the ride. His first thought was to restore the birds to their pen, his second was 'Them's evidence! There'll be a court case out o' this.' He put the heavy basket gently among some bushes, and mopping the blood on his face and clothes, pedalled back to *The Crown*. He called out Bert Mould and told his story.

For once Mould was only a quarter drunk and acted with promptitude. He sent a man off to summon the village constable from 'the Feet' and hurried Alfred to the Hall to 'get the squire'.

Charles Darty was not pleased at being called away from his guests to the back door but when he saw Alfred's face he listened in silence, smoking a cigarette and giving unintelligible commands to the Berberine henchman who was his butler and valet, to order a horse and trap and some hot water and bandages for Alfred's face.

'The Chief Constable's gone home but I'll get a message to him. Let's have a look at the scene of crime and Mould, you be off and tell Constable Young to come up to the Wood at once.'

It was after ten o'clock before Alfred got home. They had released the outraged bantams but the twenty pheasants from the laying pens had all gone and from the feathers left behind were probably dead in the tinker's cart. Alfred with plaster on face and ear was given the first drink of whisky of his life and received many congratulations. 'That first smack of yours was a jolly lucky one,' the Captain said. 'Otherwise with the three of them you wouldn't have stood a dog's chance. You've done well, Alfred, and I only wish I had been there. Remember the nose, the knee and the shins are what to go for to stop anything heavier than yourself, if you've got a stick. I've stopped even bulls that way.'

Alfred's head did not swell as much as some had expected from the publicity he gained on the day of the Feet. There were 'summonses' in due course and Alfred, no quicker in repartee than most of the village, had to endure an unpleasant twenty minutes in the witness box, from a local solicitor with black hair plastered across his bald crown. By the time he had finished with him it almost looked as if Alfred, after celebrating his prize in the refreshment tent, had stolen the birds himself and wantonly injured the man from Misner into the bargain.

'I put it to you,' the solicitor said, 'that my client, Mr Dow, did nothing whatever in this affair except to drive the other two men, badly injured by you, away from this brawl? He did nothing?'

'Narthen only this,' said Alfred mildly, caressing the scar on his cheek, 'with the butt of his whip, sir.'

'In defence of a badly injured man? Come now! He said nothing whatever?'

'Only,' said Alfred again, 'that he'd cut my duzzy throat next time he met me. But I ain't giving him no chance of that, sir.' He smiled.

The Bench, all game-preserving squires in those days, took a serious view of the incident however and imposed 'exemplary' fines and commended young Alfred for his presence of mind. Alfred, still raw after the cross-examination, and knowing that most villagers were secretly in sympathy with those who abducted their squires' game-birds, for ever afterwards hated to bring any case into court if he could help it. He realized that a keeper's job, like that of a policeman, is never done but that in both prevention is far better than cure. He also learned that it was just when things seemed to be going well that a keeper must look out for trouble.

VII

'BETTER you than me, Alfred!' was Bert Mould's remark when he heard his underkeeper was going north as a loader. 'A lot of bloody Scotchmen what talk to each other in foreign tongues, and narthen to eat only some swill they call purridge.' But Alfred guessed that Mr Mould was green with envy because his 'duzzy buoy' was leaving him to do all the work and had even been given lessons on the lawn in the art of changing guns.

Alfred had never left Tibberton or even travelled in a train, and to a country youth of those days a journey to Scotland by way of London was as grim an introduction to the world as could be imagined. In after years he thought of it as the nearest approach to Hell he had ever encountered. It was sultry September weather and what with the 'polyphanalia' of clothes, the dogs' requirements, and the Captain's precious guns, cartridges and fishing rods, he was 'in a muck sweat' before the journey began.

The atmosphere in the train seemed to grow more sulphurous as the train approached the grime and gloom of Liverpool Street and one of the young dogs was even more sick in the guard's van than Alfred felt. To think that decent human folks actually lived amid smuts and soot and no clear air all their lives!

The Captain, sensing his and the dogs' distress, packed them into an ancient four-wheeled cab for King's Cross, tipped the cabman liberally in advance against disaster and told Alfred 'Meet me by the booking office at seven. And put all those things in the cloakroom.' He left Alfred to his fate.

Centuries later the journey north began from the thunderous vault of King's Cross. The guard, primed by a half-sovereign from the Captain, had accommodated the unhappy dogs on sacks in his van. Alfred spent a sleepless night in his carriage, feeling grimier and grimier as the hours dragged past. He shared it with a very smart 'gentleman's gentleman' in a blue suit who snored and refreshed himself at intervals from a leather-covered silver flask of his master's, and a bony dog-handler from Norfolk in tweeds and a deer-stalker hat whose setters too were in the van. These seasoned travellers assured Alfred 'he would feel a lot better when he got to Perth'.

He paid a surreptitious visit in the small hours to the dogs who dozed in a despairing huddle on their sacks. And Alfred saw the dawn rise over a clean green fell-country, a land of sheep and shining waters and rain-washed slopes, a wilder place than Suffolk which seemed in that hour like Heaven's Gate. And at Perth he even got some breakfast and gave the dogs a run in a great park of grass near the station, covered with wind-blown gulls.

No need to enlarge on that slow journey, which was a commonplace in Edwardian days. They came at last to a great castle set amid pinewoods and rhododendrons and a long bothy Alfred shared with four other loaders. And he, having bestowed his dogs in kennels which would have held a pack of hounds, realized that for three weeks he could forget the purgatory of that transition.

Tongue-tied, as only a Suffolk yokel can be, among a posse of sophisticated loaders, Alfred learned to be, if not quick, at least safe in changing guns. His horizons were larger, three thousand acres to look out over instead of twenty, and he realized the huge 'lordships' of the local gamekeepers whose beats were six times as large as his own. He realized the art of driving grouse, and the thrill of seeing black dots on the horizon speeding 'straight as a string' to the hidden butts which had been there for fifty years. He met in the kitchen a shy rosy-faced lassie who called him 'Mr Blowers' and looked appreciatively at his height and thews. He cleaned the Captain's guns jealously in his bedroom for he realized that irreparable damage could be done when six men were all at once busy in the gun-room, brandishing barrels and 'anxious for their tea'. His dogs, once recovered from the journey, revelled in the keen air and the smell of grouse. And on off days, when the Captain was fishing, Alfred began to assert his nannie-like control over His Lordship's unruly kennel. His unaccustomed muscles ached as he walked up steep hillsides weighed down by the Captain's guns and cartridges and mackintosh, and sometimes, when he had seen to the dogs and guns, and greased the Captain's boots and filled his cartridge-bags for next day, he was almost too tired to eat his own ample tea.

But there were compensations. His own dogs, pegged down in the heather behind the Captain's butt, were as orderly as could be, what time their neighbours were whining and squirming at the din of shots going on around them. And one Sunday, after a drive on the Home Beat when the Captain had 'sworn himself silly' missing a succession of grouse which swirled downwind round a rocky face and seemed armour-plated, Alfred took his three dogs and two of Sandy Mac-donald's, and plodded up the hill. He had an inspiration and decided 'to give the dogs the wind' and hunt them not round the butts but three hundred yards behind. The result astonished him.

Captain Darty, in his Sunday clothes after church, saw Alfred watering his dogs in their kennel.

'I saw you coming off the hill, Alfred. Did you pick any birds?'

Alfred did not overstate it. 'Well, sir, the dawgs picked $3\frac{1}{2}$

brace behind your butt and another nine birds further down the hill. They was all dead birds but four of them wasn't no good. The crows had had 'em! They were a long way on the hind side of the butts. You didn't miss as bad yesterday as you thought.' He smiled.

'Well, I'll be damned.' Those four short words set the seal on Alfred's achievement, and the Captain was loud in his loader's praises at lunch.

'I've always said,' his host remarked, 'that where the guns are pretty good, there is, or there ought to be, a much *bigger* pick-up than where a lot of rotten guns are missing everything by feet. And those birds yesterday had a lot of wind behind them.' He passed the port decanter and lit a cigar. 'I *know*, Charles, I ought to have chaps with dogs lying out on the hill behind every drive. But it's getting harder and harder to find them, fellers who can be trusted not to spoil the next drive, and to mark birds.'

He paused. 'That's always our trouble here and it's going to be worse as the years go on. We've got to shoot our moors when the wind's right, and often with four days' shooting on end my keepers get no chance, as you do in Suffolk, of picking up next day. When Sunday comes they're too dog-tired to scramble up the hill as your lad, Alfred Blowers, has just done. But I remember now how Ian Malcolm, at Prosen, told me that a good dog-man behind the butts would put any day's bag up ten per cent. I never believed him but, after today, I will!'

And Alfred's assistance to the Glenovil moor was not confined to finding a dozen dead birds on the day after a downwind drive. One afternoon when they were walking down the hill, Alfred, with three dogs at heel, heard the Captain say over his shoulder,

'Alfred, what do you make of His Lordship's dogs?'

Alfred scratched his head and said 'I reckon they'd be a lot better, sir, with proper vittles. The shepherd . . .' He stopped abruptly. Could he possibly quote Colin Thomson, the tall young shepherd who acted as flanker?

'Carry on, Alfred.'

'Well, what he told me was that them sheep dawgs, and the shutin' dawgs too, gets narthen only flaked maize all their lives. And a sheepdog at them gatherings has to do thirty miles a day, uphill and down. So by the time they're four years old, the poor brutes are done for, so Thomson tells me. And I reckon it's the same with shutin' dawgs. There ain't an old one in the kennel, not to call old.'

Alfred paused. In the modern phrase he had 'said a mouthful', but here on the hill with no one else near he hoped he could say his say, unscathed.

'And they get no meat *at all*?' the Captain asked incredulously.

'Narthen only some owd ewe's afterbirth and they get a hiding for stealing that, so the shepherd sa', or a raabut what's been dead a week on the hill. That ain't right. A working dawg needs more than a lot o' maize.' He stopped again. There would be trouble if Sandy Macdonald, with his great white beard and lordly air, ever got an inkling of what he had said.

The Captain changed the subject though he was keenly interested. Like Orientals and Victorians, he had always treated dogs as unconsidered animals, polishers of plates, lickers of crumbs from the rich man's table. 'A dog's life . . . a dog's chance . . . a dog's dinner. . . . Fit only for a dog' – they were all contemptuous terms for unregarded beasts. There were, of course, lap-dogs, petted and pampered, but they were in a class of their own.

Margaret Darty, who had been walking behind, with her woman's intuition cut the corners. 'Are *our* dogs getting enough to eat, Alfred, up here?'

'Yes, ma'am, but . . .'

'But what?'

'I've got Bessie in the kitchen' (he blushed because Bessie was a secret ally and had even given him an early morning cup of tea in the gunroom), 'to boil me up a nice young raabut or a bit of soup with their biscuit. Ours ain't done so bad, though they look thin. They're growing.'

'Good for you and Bessie. Any more?'

'Only,' said Alfred, 'I hope, ma'am, you won't say narthen to His Lordship. I'm a foreigner here and I don't want to make trouble over other folks' dawgs. But that's how it strikes *me*.'

Alfred heard no more, but the Captain lost little time in telling the laird what had suddenly 'struck' himself about the all-too-short life of working dogs in the Highlands. And a month later venison scraps, broth, bones, and even rabbits were added to the kennel menu. Alfred, the tongue-tied foreigner from Suffolk, who had so often gnawed turnips to 'stay' his own stomach, may have done more for the working dogs in those savage places than he realized.

He came back to Suffolk with a new self-assurance, ruddier than before with the keen hillwinds, and with new muscles in his calves and thighs. He also had a secret understanding with Bessie Thomson, though neither would for worlds have admitted it. 'Walking out' with a view to matrimony was in those days an imperceptible process, taking years. A letter at Christmas which had taken Alfred eight hours to write and re-write enclosed his best wishes and a very bad Kodak snapshot of himself surrounded by dogs. The reply in February, much better written but equally brief, enclosed a postcard of Glenovil after weeks of heavy snow. Alfred kept both in his waistcoat pocket and read the letter four times a week till the paper fell to pieces.

VIII

THE next few years completed Alfred's education. Now that
he had qualified as a loader, Captain Darty took him out to
shoots within a twelve-mile radius of Tibberton and sometimes
further afield by train, where he met not only the keepers and
loader-valets of that epoch but the extraordinary medley of
demi-professional guns who composed 'the shooting-world'.

There was Major 'Coper' Copgrove, as his regiment had
called him, who had given up horses because of his debts and
was now without visible means of subsistence, though he ate and
shot his way from castle to manor house between August and
January and made enough to live on by side-bets with other
guns. Coper Copgrove's assets now consisted largely of his
marksmanship, his Purdey guns and three thousand cartridges
with which a ducal brother-in-law presented him yearly. (At
six-and-sixpence a hundred those cartridges were not such an
opulent present as they might have been today.) Coper was
famous in a dozen servants' halls for the richly starched dress-
shirts and ties which he insisted on being laundered and sent on
to his next port-of-call, though he often omitted to tip the
maids who 'did them'.

There was old Cumbernauld, the Law Lord, who had, so a
keeper told Alfred, 'shot someone every year of his life', al-
though his prestige, his landed aunts and his legal anecdotes
seemed to ensure that he was asked again next year. Lord
Cumbernauld clearly regarded mere beaters and beat-keepers
as expendable items which would 'get in the way' and their

protests when shot were brushed aside as brusquely as his Lordship had been accustomed to do those of junior counsel. Yet it was Alfred, very angry and with blood trickling down his face and ear and wrist, who for once bereft Lord Cumbernauld of words, after a certain partridge drive, by calling him what Samuel Johnson called 'a term of endearment among sailors' prefixed by the word 'dangerous'. Alfred later told Captain Darty that 'Lord or no Lord, *he* didn't ought to be allowed,' and was congratulated by the other loaders at lunchtime.

And there were other guns who came to rely on the tall young man with the quick eyesight, and the quiet dogs. 'Blowers,' they would say, 'I suppose you didn't notice that high bird of mine which carried on and towered?' or 'Charles, can those dogs of Alfred's possibly have a try for one I've got down in those thorns?'

And off Alfred would go and after a few lucky finds he earned quite a reputation and a number of 'crowns' and half-sovereigns to swell the hoard he kept in a cocoa-tin under his mattress. There was the famous Nigel Garamie, then only at the start of his career, who was reputed to do 'muscling-up' exercises in pyjamas each morning to fit himself for the day's slaughter. Nigel after a grouse-drive would sidle up, solemn and inhuman, and peer curiously into his neighbours' butts to estimate how many cartridges they had fired. Alfred's large feet often obliterated this evidence in the Captain's interests. And he saw the equally fabulous Gerald Withering who drank hard all the year round and yet in a gale could put himself a hundred yards downhill behind his other guns and 'wipe their eyes' at every stand.

And there were the keepers he met, of all types, over an increasingly wide area, first the 'gentlemen-keepers' who, in the Bert Mould tradition, left the dirty work to their underlings but, like bandmasters on a guest night, were summoned to drink a glass of port with 'the gentlemen' after lunch. They looked so dignified and impressive that few guessed their limitations. There were hard-working keepers who would uncomplainingly stint themselves of lunch to pick up, or 'get round' a lot of wayward birds, or 'bring in' certain fields to swell the next drive. And there were others, who starved or thrashed their unhappy spaniels and shot every bird with claws down to woodpeckers, and who assumed that if they could not see any partridges in July they were 'all safely in the corn'.

Alfred learned much about their methods of vermin-control but nearly all ignored the common rat which often swarmed in their ricks and hedgerows. They regarded the destruction of rats as beneath a keepers' dignity.

Alfred met, too, many dog-handlers. Foremost among them was Rex Dale, an immense bony man who had quitted keeping abruptly on the day when he had knocked down his employer for inexcusably shooting Rex Dale's spaniel in a rabbit drive. Forced to seek other occupations, Rex Dale now lived in Suffolk a more congenial life, as a loader, and a breeder, trainer or handler of gun dogs. He had talked with Kings at Sandringham and Windsor but had not 'lost the common touch', as was shown when he informed a Lord Mayor of London that 'he *had* seen people who shot worse but only two, and they were just bloody beginners!' Alfred learned a lot of Rex Dale's training secrets, notably how much patience and quietness counted with a bewildered young dog. 'You'll be good, Alfred, if you stick to it, and mark my words, there'll be big money one day in gun-dogs! And it's a wonderful moment' (his rugged face wrinkled into a smile) 'when a young dog suddenly realizes what you want him to do, just when you're beginning to think he'll never learn a dam' thing!'

So for several seasons Alfred's life flowed on, placidly but always increasing in interest. His yearly visits to Glenovil as loader continued, and his affair with Bessie Thomson ripened imperceptibly towards marriage. Once, in early October, when an ankle, broken while fishing, laid the Captain up, Alfred stayed on with him and learned the manner in which Glenovil settled down to the long unhampered winter months. Alfred went hind-shooting on the hill and learned to use a telescope and a rifle. The stalkers and keepers, thrown for months on their own resources, filled up their evenings by making their own boots and by reading books. They were often better read than their masters and thought much about what they had learned in the long empty days. And they were not afraid to disagree at times with the rich and the great who came up to shoot and stalk and fish. 'They tell me he's a Cabinet Minister, and a big name in the Privy Council. But he doesna know everything. A nice gentleman but not, by my standards, a brainy one!'

Alfred was twenty-six now, a tall, thin, rather handsome young man with brown hair. He had £50 in his cocoa-tin, and a fund of self-reliance on which to draw, and he could watch his contemporaries slumped sideways on their plough horses as they went to work. He was better-clothed, better-fed and in many ways better-educated than they and the Captain, sensing what Alfred was too shy to ask, had lent him books on shooting and natural history. Over these Alfred, by his sister-in-law's lamp, would pore – notably Richard Jefferies and the eccentric Charles Waterton's essays. He realized that these authors, like the Cabinet Ministers, did not know everything (though they could write vividly of what they did), and how full of errors were the bird-books of those days.

But though much of what Alfred read went over his head it improved his letters to Bessie Thomson, and he even tried to tell her some of his inner secrets – how he had revelled in flowering charlock against an August sky of summer clouds, or the feeling that the days were drawing in, when a mellow light hung over the unthreshed rickyards, and all things seemed to be preparing for the winter. His letters made no parade of sentiment though a line of crosses preceded the words 'Yours as ever, Alfie'.

But he, and all those of the 1913 shooting world, fondly imagined that that world would continue as before within 'the foreseeable future'. No one had even guessed at a world war, or syndicate-shoots, or the break-up of the great estates, or cartridges at three pounds a hundred. The old order had not changed perceptibly in the last twenty years. What was good enough for their fathers was good enough for them and seemed likely to remain so. They looked forward to shooting or fishing year after year on the same estates, a pattern altered slightly only when old So-and-So died or his keeper was retired, but in most respects the same.

'Alfred,' said the Captain one May morning in 1914, 'Bert Mould isn't well and he'll probably have to retire. When he does and that won't be till the autumn, I'm going to give you his job. You're young but I believe you'll do it.'

'Thank you kindly, sir,' said Alfred, 'but Mould he say it's narthen only fleabites on his legs.' For in those days phlebitis was almost unknown. 'He'll be himself come Michaelmas.' But his thoughts flew to the faraway Bessie Thomson, now second housemaid at the Castle and he wondered how in God's name she was going to make the journey from Glenovil to Tibberton, exchanging one 'savage place' for another, even as a headkeeper's wife.

'Of course,' the Captain went on, 'that's always assuming there's no war in Europe before Michaelmas. You remember General Towling who shot here last December? He says there'll be a war for certain, and it'll last three years and take every young man we've got in the country to win it.'

'Well,' said Alfred, 'if that ain't a masterpiece!' He could dimly recall the Suffolk Yeomanry Volunteers in their slouched hats and bandoliers singing

> *Goodbye, Dolly, I must leave you*
> *Though it breaks my heart to go,*

going to '*the Front to fight the foe*'.

But the Front was like Parliament or London, a savage place more remote even than Glenovil.

Then suddenly, just as the harvest was beginning, Alfred's world collapsed. The Captain went back to his regiment. Alfred had never heard of the Grenadiers and when he did, he imagined them hurling things like apples which went off with a bang. Alfred was called in before he left and told, 'Well, Alfred, I'm afraid everything's in the melting pot now and you'll probably have to go into the Army. If you do, take this chit to the Guards' depot. You're wasted in a line regiment.' And Alfred found himself in possession of a scrawl which ran,

'Dear Tiddley, Herewith my underkeeper, Alfred Blowers, whom you may remember loading for me at Billeaford. He should make an excellent guardsman after training, though he'll probably hate the birthpangs of becoming one as much as I do the prospect of this war! Yours ever, Charles.'

Rural Suffolk did not exactly leap to arms. In fact, the harvest preoccupied everyone, and Tibberton, which had never heard of Sarajevo, was none too sure whether 'these here Jarmans' if foiled in their attempt to pass through Belgium might not 'come around by us', for few had imagined the English Channel. Indeed, one neighbouring squire summoned his tenantry, explained that he was laying down his sons on the altar of war and invited the tenants to follow their example. Only one volunteered and he was the village half-wit, who rightly guessed that no doctor would pass him.

But soon the casualty lists rolled in and at Le Cateau hundreds of the Suffolk Regiment had passed into captivity, including three from Alfred's own village. Alfred wrote a long letter to Bessie, and begged her to wait for his return, and he consulted Mrs Darty who had already lost a brother and, dry-eyed and haggard, was convinced that she was going to lose her husband as well.

'You must do as you think right, Alfred, and I won't stop you. If you go into the Guards you'll hate every moment of it for the first six months but perhaps you'll be with the Major' (Captain Darty had been promoted) 'in France and can look after him. God bless you and your job will be waiting when you get back.'

So Alfred packed his belongings in an old wheat sack, put his savings into the Post Office and one day took train to London. He did not dare say goodbye to the dogs but Mrs Darty promised to take them under her wing and to store his bicycle. The village considered him 'a duzzy young fule just when he might ha 'stepped into Bert Mould's shoes' but when Alfred reached Liverpool Street and saw the posters with Kitchener's accusing finger pointing at him from every hoarding, he wondered not that he had been the first in the village to volunteer but why he had been so long about it.

IX

THE six months which transformed Alfred Blowers from a
Suffolk yokel into a foot-guardsman were far more savagely
testing than his prentice years under Mrs Balm and Mould.
Years later, when one of Alfred's employers had given him a
copy of Kipling's collected verse, Alfred was wont to relish
two lines from '*The Wonder*':

> *Body and spirit I surrendered whole*
> *To harsh Instructors and received a soul.*

and he would say ' "Harsh Instructors"! Lord, how I did hate
them all!'

It seemed so utterly senseless, the everlasting shouting and
sarcasm and reprimands, the meticulous stamping and dressing
and pirouetting, the realization that the so-called 'private
soldier' was the one being in the world without any 'privacy'
at all, his face, hair, teeth, toe-nails, clothes and slightest
movements at the mercy of tyrants' inspection and rebuke all
day long. Bewildered and scared, like a bullock at a fair or a
puppydog in a strange kennel, the patient Alfred longed to

5

run away, and he used to meditate desertion, by day in the roaring barrack-hut while he 'soldiered' his kit and rifle, and in the small hours when, as never before, he dreaded the coming of a new day. He thought longingly of a remote sandpit on Whistleton Walks where he could lie hid 'for the duration'.

Three unexpected incidents in the same week took his mind off desertion. Bessie sent him a parcel containing a cap-comforter and a photograph of herself taken in Kirriemuir. Mrs Darty sent him some chocolate and some snapshots of 'his dogs' and added: 'They miss you terribly but they have *not* forgotten all the *wonderful training and discipline* you put into them.' (If a dog can stick it, thought Alfred, so can I.) And next morning the Adjutant, a being as fearful and all-seeing as Jehovah, was inspecting the 'inlying picquet'; after looking Alfred coldly up and down for what seemed half-an-hour, he suddenly looked him in the eyes and: 'Blowers? didn't you load for Captain Darty at Billeaford last year? I'd like you to load for me tomorrow. We'll leave here at 8.15.' He passed on before the astounded Alfred could mumble 'Sir'. And the Regimental Sergeant-Major, a figure more terrifying than the Adjutant and Jehovah combined, made a note in his book and said, 'Blowers, parade 0730 tomorrow outside the orderly room. Clean fatigue with haversack and draw sandwich ration from the cookhouse. *And* get your hair cut!'

For the first time since he left Tibberton Alfred felt he had been recognized as a human being. He lay awake all night dreading lest it poured with rain, and was up at 4 a.m., among the curses of his drowsy hut-companions, putting a final polish on his boots and haversack buckles and clothes. But later he enjoyed a drive westwards in an open motor-car and a day 'at cocks' on the slopes of certain Berkshire downs, wishing that 'his dogs' were assisting him. He was also spoken to genially by several elderly gentlemen in worn tweeds who had apparently been guardsmen in their time, and to whom his employer, the Adjutant, was not Jehovah but answered to the name of 'Tiddley'.

'Tiddley' revealed himself as a friendly accomplice who could miss pheasants and swear at his misses. And that night outside the orderly room he gave Alfred five shillings with a 'Thank you, Blowers. Not a bad day, was it? I shall count on you for the same job next Saturday. And give my compliments to the cook-sergeant and tell him you haven't had your tea and it's up to him. Good night to you!'

Very suddenly, that day made Alfred abandon his plans for desertion. He realized that the Foot-Guards were not composed of monsters, whose minds were set on absurd details of saluting and drill and 'spit and polish', but that behind their inhuman façade they hid kindliness and consideration and knew a lot about 'man-management'.

In mid-February Alfred Blowers received a lance-stripe (' 'arf of nothing', as he learned later to call it with Kipling) and was sent on a course to Hythe as a potential musketry instructor. He shot on the range with zeal and increasing accuracy, and his training as a loader had already impressed on him the rules of safety which others ignored so light-heartedly. He also thought of Bessie Thomson when it came to resisting the bacchanal advances of the women who hung in those days round Army camps.

His reward came when a quiet officer in a Highland regiment, with a kilt and an empty sleeve (from which the fore-arm had disappeared in the first battle of Ypres) said to him, 'Didn't I meet you at Glenovil? It won't be long before they start asking for snipers in France. Would you like me to keep your name on my list, though they're mostly ex-stalkers?'

So Alfred murmured 'Sir', and attended special lectures which dealt with telescopes and stalking ritual and camouflage, in which the instructor had got himself up to look more like an 'odd-me-dod' or scarecrow than a soldier of the King. And Alfred lapped up what they told him, though privately he wondered what the Guards depot would say if they ever saw him with straws or bunches of grass in his service cap to conceal its outline. But the young officer had been among the first to see that Army traditions of smartness were not necessarily the way to win a World War.

Alfred was drafted to France in May 1915 and lost his stripe
in the process. He endured the rigours and boredom of trench-
life with the same fortitude (to the sensitive it seemed mere
brute indifference) which so many generations of countrymen
had shown. Even in water-logged trenches, his regiment
demanded an almost inhuman standard of cleanliness and
'turn-out', but they did far more than other regiments to
improve their habitations, and to see that their men got better
food and comforts, in and out of the line.

Alfred, who had attended with a boy's curiosity the ritual
pig-killings of Tibberton village and had, as a keeper, executed
a thousand trapped and suffering animals without a qualm,
found himself unexpectedly shaken by the slaughter of his own
companions. His cockney friends, whose mothers had crowded
to their doors to enjoy funerals, domestic fights, and street
accidents, had inherited a morbid curiosity at the sight of blood
and suffering. They could watch a man die with an interest
which they did not attempt to conceal. But in Alfred suffering
merely awoke a desire to 'get on with the war' and finish it.

He was in the historic counter-attack of the Guards at Loos
as a 'runner' to his company commander, too busy to worry
overmuch at what was going on around him. In fact, at one
moment he found himself in a battered trench with three badly-
wounded men, none of whom were in any condition to appreciate the urgent message that Alfred had brought. And he was
suddenly filled with wrath at seeing a cluster of grey-green
figures approaching over the skyline and managed to get off
a whole bandolier of cartridges before a gunner in the trench
behind called down several 'protective' salvoes all around
Alfred's head.

Alfred, with shrapnel wounds in his neck and shoulder, was
tempted, on his return after dark with one of the wounded
men, to address the gunner in the same terms as he had once
addressed Lord Cumbernauld after a partridge-drive. But to
his surprise he was whisked down to an aid post, given injec-
tions for gangrene and tetanus, and was later warmly commended for 'initiative in breaking-up a counter-attack'. And

after tea and a swig of rum, he was kept up by the sergeant-major till 3 a.m., restoring his kit, clothes, and rifle to a 'guardsmanlike' standard before he was allowed to turn in.

They gave Alfred a fortnight's leave in a rest-camp after Loos and later a medal for distinguished conduct. This Alfred felt he did not deserve because he had been 'shot by his own side' in the confusion and not by the enemy at all. But a General, who was also a Lord, said nice things to him on parade and there were letters from Mrs Balm and the Vicar of Tibberton and Mrs Darty, as well as a tear-soaked epistle from Bessie who said it was a crying shame that her 'darling Alfie' was not home for good after all that heroism.

Most unexpected of all was a 'buff slip' from Major Darty on a Corps staff. It began 'Well done, Alfred!' and said that he was 'trying to wangle' Alfred on to a Snipers' Course at Army Headquarters. This proposal was resisted by Alfred's Colonel who deprecated any attempt to turn a 'good guardsman into a second-rate poacher' and by the RSM who felt 'it would be the end of discipline, dealing with Grenadiers with straws in their hair'. But this struggle went on far over Alfred's head.

Major Darty won in the end and Alfred found himself in a motley group of 'specialists', which included Lovat's Scouts, stalkers weeded out of Highland regiments, a trick marksman whose targets had been bottles at a circus, and a 'white hunter' from Uganda. Roger Maurice had once been badly wanted by certain Colonial Governments for ivory-poaching on a lordly scale, but was now only wanted by an irate husband in London for wife-poaching. Intrepid as Mr Maurice had been when faced with charging lions, elephants, and rhinoceroses, he found the strain of waiting for this last assault too much for him and was dropped from the course as 'not likely to make an efficient sniper'.

Before he went back to his unit he confided to Alfred one evening that the aphrodisiac effect of powdered rhinoceros horn (that potion so beloved by Orientals from China to Kenya) was 'much over-rated'. This queer morsel of knowledge survived in Alfred's mind for the rest of his life.

X

ALFRED might have survived the war as a million infantry-men did, knowing nothing of what was happening on the other side of No Man's Land. 'The Foe' had been to nearly all infantry soldiers an invisible nuisance, or menace, behind his dark ramparts of sandbags and wire. The only sign of his presence was the crackle of shots by night, smashed periscopes by day, salvoes of shells which screamed at them from far away, and the everlasting flares which rose and fell all night.

As with rats and rabbits, a gamekeeper could see the foe's 'work', but nothing else of him, and unlike the humbler vermin with which Alfred had dealt at Tibberton, it was death to go near their holes or runs or to show yourself for a second above-ground. Most front line combatants shared the belief that the foe was a slightly superior being even if he was, in the Suffolk phrase, 'varmin'.

Alfred Blowers had much experience of 'varmin'. He had been brought up on two estates on which several thousand game birds and hares were menaced by a few score crows, rats, stoats, sparrowhawks and an occasional cat or fox, and 'good keepering', especially in the spring, could reduce all vermin to a controllable minimum. But 'these Jarmans' could not be so kept down. Alfred, after having at Loos got off 'eight clips' at figures approaching above ground and seen at least six fall, as oncoming grouse had fallen in front of the Glenovil butts, was suddenly seized with the wish to study his enemy and see what could be done by a marksman.

The officer in charge of the course had spent many years deer-stalking and after big game. He used to take his pupils from one to another of the few good observation posts, from which a view could be obtained over the enemy's hinterland. And there were other places, fosses and farms and rickety church towers and ridges behind the lines, normally sacred to the field-gunners, into which Alfred could crawl and see 'the foe' going about his daily tasks, the dust of limbers on a road, the smoke of trains, and, nearer, cautious stooping forms on their way to their latrines or sneaking down some trench. So Alfred watched 'them Jarmans' as a kestrel might watch them from the air. And on to the Sniping School lore he grafted his experience of keepering and learned, as the native jungle hunters had learned, to study his quarry silently and let it catch itself almost before it knew it was being hunted.

He was given a specially zeroed rifle with a telescopic sight and learned to use a powerful telescope. There were in those days no jungle hats or jackets, as in later wars, but Alfred was given an old leather jerkin, and was allowed to keep an older cap (known in those days as a 'Gor-blimey') from which all stiffening had been removed; and he converted a cap comforter into a face-mask. His course was taken to quiet sectors where 'live and let live' prevailed, until commanding officers protested that 'all these bloody snipers do is to draw fire'. There were few steel loop-hole plates in those days and Alfred had to camouflage himself with weeds and grass in his cap and lie for hours motionless as a poaching cat for some sign of movement on the other side of No-Mans-Land. The Foe seemed as limited as himself in observation posts commanding a field of fire, and slowly but surely he marked them down.

But it would be tedious to enlarge on Alfred Blowers' career, when he rejoined his Brigade, though it helped him later on in his gamekeeping career. A good many months later, snipers were considered obsolete, being replaced by clumsier and more wholesale methods of destruction such as bombs, trench mortar barrages, and creeping shell-fire. In time the sniper's art became as outworn as that of the duellist. But until the battle of the Somme, Alfred was wont to creep out before dawn into some shell-hole with what his Highland instructors called 'his piece' and a bottle of cold tea, prepared to lie all day in hopes of accounting for half a brace of 'them Jarmans'. When he succeeded he took his knife and cut a notch in the stock of his beloved rifle, as otter hunters do on their poles.

It was a lonely life with long hours of boredom and some times terror while whizzbangs screamed around his hole and it would be dark before Alfred could slink back to the safety of the trenches. His division, though no one guessed it, was being 'fattened up' for the Somme Offensive in a sector taken over from the French. There was one morning when Alfred's telescope spotted two 'cookhouse orderly men' in soft caps and fatigue overalls carrying on a pole a 'dixie' of food down a track towards the rear trenches. It was a tempting target but Alfred merely looked at his watch and refrained from firing. Next day they appeared again at the same hour and Alfred hoped that in the falling rain the gunner officer in the ruined farm behind him had not observed them. On the third day sighting for 550 yards Alfred shot one orderly and then the other. He waited with the same patience while the dixie of stew congealed on the ground, until a fatigue party came out from the front trench to see, as Alfred later told the company commander, 'what had happened to their dinners'. He saw yet another man fall and the party dispersed hurriedly. 'Them beggars never got no vittles that day' was all the comment he ever permitted himself in after years.

But Alfred's luck seemed too good to last. He enjoyed a roving independent life, exempt from the incessant fatigues and 'carrying parties' after dark. He was called the 'Old Poacher' and 'Deadeye Alfie' and other names of derision and respect by his comrades. But one day the brigade intelligence officer, after interrogating a prisoner from a Jaeger battalion, said to Alfred's adjutant, 'Your sniper chap had better watch out. He's been more of a nuisance to the Boche than I imagined. They've put a feller, a Förstmeister, on special duty to shoot him.'

This message was passed to Alfred by the adjutant in the evening at stand-to. He said 'Sir,' and then, curiously, 'What's a Förstmaster?'

'A sort of head gamekeeper, and probably a crack shot.'

'I'll watch out, sir,' said Alfred, thinking of head-keepers in terms of Bert Mould. He did not realize that he was being accorded the same attention as a man-eating tiger in India.

But he was not careful enough. The Förstmeister had sneaked out in the mist at 2 a.m. and was lying in a hole which commanded Alfred's chosen lair from an unexpected angle. He fired at a dark shadow creeping out just before dawn and his bullet drilled Alfred through the left biceps and grazed his shoulder blade. Alfred fell into the shell hole which was half-full of water, and there he lay all day, with his shoulder swelling and stiffening till he was fain to sink it in the water to stop its throbbing. He lay inert and thought of the pigeons crooning in Tibberton Park and of Bessie Thomson knitting away in Glenovil. He watched a pair of tree sparrows nesting, heedless of the war around them, in a shell-torn tree, and once a kingfisher appeared on the lip of the shell-hole within a few yards of Alfred's face. Half-delirious with pain, Alfred debated whether to wait till the Förstmeister came out to recover his body but he realized he could not lift his own rifle which had already been soaked in his fall. So as the pain got worse, Alfred crawled home in the dusk ignominiously and was nearly shot again by an excited sentry as he slid into the trench.

'You're a B.F., Lance-Corporal,' said the R.S.M., not unkindly, when Alfred at length arrived at battalion headquarters. 'We thought you'd cop it with thirteen notches on your rifle-butt! However, perhaps you're lucky. You'll miss this new offensive. That mess looks a proper Blighty to me.' Alfred was given rum and tea and later was punctured in the doctor's dug-out for tetanus and gangrene and given yet a third injection of morphia.

The doctor clucked over his wound and said 'How long since you've been hit? Eighteen hours? Good God!'

But the Colonel found time to come in and say 'Bad luck,

Blowers. I'm putting you in for substantive Corporal and ante-dating it a month.' Then, as he was leaving he said 'By the way, I've got bad news for you. Colonel Darty was killed two days ago. Didn't you work for him?'

'You mean the *Captain*, sir?' muttered Alfred.

'He was promoted last month to command a Kitchener battalion. A damned sniper got *him* too, near Hooge.'

'Well there!' mumbled Alfred and then the morphia over-came him. The rest of his journey was a blur of agony and evil dreams in which he was lying out in mud and rain to avenge his employer.

His wound was a 'proper Blighty', as the sergeant-major had predicted, and Alfred Blowers spent two months in hos-pital with tubes in his shoulder and then was given two months' sick leave. At Tibberton Mrs Darty said amid her tears, 'The Captain was very proud of you, Alfred, for being the first from the village to go. I can't promise to take you on here when the war's over. Two lots of death duties in six years . . . ! I've had to let the shoot to a syndicate and it looks as if the place will have to be sold. You'd better marry that nice girl, Bessie Thomson, while you're on leave and there'll be keepers' jobs after the war all over the country. I'm afraid this means the end of Tibberton Hall, at any rate for the Darty family! But I'll look after your dogs here as long as I posssibly can.'

Alfred spent an October day, as flanker and 'picker-up' with the syndicate, and did not like what he saw. They were a cheerful lot of middle-aged stockbrokers and business men to whom the War meant only an opportunity for making money. They talked of land as a speculation, they boasted what they had spent on their guns and cars, they made more noise, in Alfred's words, than a nest of crows. Also they spent so long over luncheon that the day's sport was poor. The 'guns' did not care. Shooting to them was an opportunity to meet their friends, to exchange the latest Stock Exchange stories and tips, and to raise an appetite. What went on on 'the place' for the rest of the year was no concern of theirs. They carried loaded guns from drive to drive, they shot with a callous disregard for beaters or stops or dogs, they had sweeps on every drive and it mattered nothing to them if old Bert Mould put his pheasants over them head-high.

All that day Alfred fumed quietly in the background and wished 'the Captain' was there to send them home. He spent an hour in the evening and more next day picking up wounded birds which the syndicate had blithely ignored. These on the Sunday he brought in privily to Mrs Darty's cook, knowing that to Bert Mould, now half-crippled with the 'arthur-itis', the day after a shooting day was a *dies non*. 'Take these and tell the Mistress,' he told her, 'they 'on't miss 'em. I doubt if they knew they'd wounded 'em. But don't you sa' narthen to Mr Mould, please!' And Margaret Darty and the cook hung all the birds in the larder and vowed the kitchen staff to secrecy.

It was Alfred's introduction to the post-war world of business, in which money was openly discussed. A new order had taken over from the old landed gentry. Other desirable things were being swept away, tradition and the responsibilities of land-owners and *tabus* of every kind. Alfred overheard two of the guns discussing what the Tibberton Hall estate was likely to fetch and the value of its standing timber. One said, 'I suppose we'd have to pull the bloody mansion down,' regardless of the life which had gone on in it for centuries. It left him with a lifelong distrust of 'them Syndicates'.

Mrs Darty gave Alfred several suits of her husband's clothes and two good mackintoshes, which took on a new lease of life and became him mightily. And she wrote a letter to Lord Inverarn at Glenovil which ended: 'I have persuaded my ex-under-keeper, Alfred Blowers, to go up to Kirriemuir and marry his girl Bessie Thomson. Poor dear, he's too inhibited for words but I can't believe Bessie will let him down. He's a Sassenach but he's served for her, like Rachel, all these years and Bill Lowther, his C.O., tells me he's made quite a name for himself as a Grenadier. Not bad for a yokel who began as a backhouse boy!'

So Alfred cashed his savings at the Post Office, and took the train to Forfarshire after due warning to Miss Thomson. And there he found to his surprise that 'the Lord' not only remembered him warmly but had arranged a *ceilidh*, with a lot of whisky and his own piper, to introduce Alfred in proper form to 'The Glen'. And while the wedding was preparing, 'The Lord' sent him out on the hill with Angus Ogilvie, the head stalker, to reduce the deer. And Alfred's wounded shoulder troubled him mightily so that he missed two good beasts which were quickly killed by Angus before they could move. And Angus, up on the heights of Carn Slamore, mumbled out of his great beard, 'Alf, you're a bloody Sassenach, but you're marrying on a nice wee wife. And believe me, a good wife is half the battle in a keeper's life. Your Bessie can cook and sew and bide her soul in patience while you're awa' on the hill. The careers I've seen ruined by wives! There's some canna get on with their neighbours. There's some worse than wild cats in the home when their man's come home wet and tired. And there's many keepers who don't realize that they have a verra great responsibility when the laird's away and they're in charge: salmon and deer laid on at their doors and no one to oversee them for months at a time. It's grand job, keepering, for an honest man *who's no afraid to rely on himself*!'

And when the wedding-day came, the Laird not only arranged a reception for his tenants in the Castle, but made a speech which caused Alfred and his bride to blush uncommonly. And he pulled strings by telephone with Alfred's depot and got his convalescent leave extended for three weeks, which Alfred and Bessie spent in the coachman's house above the stables, treasuring their brief interval of peace and, in Alfred's case, feeling like a rabbit that has escaped prematurely from the harvest-field and left all the other rabbits to be massacred. For a letter from his old battalion made it clear that half his old comrades had failed to survive the Somme. A and B and C had died and a dozen more, and even old D, Alfred's quartermaster-sergeant, who had seemed so settled and secure, had been killed one night coming up with the ration limbers, and half his drivers along with him.

One day a cousin of 'The Laird's', who was also on convalescent leave, came up to stalk and Alfred, in the shortage of
stalkers, was deputed to accompany him. His shoulder still hurt
him uncommonly but he managed to 'get' his gentleman 'into'
a goodish beast. It was shockingly late but the proper seasons
had gone by the board in 1916. Both knew it was a fluke
when they gralloched the stag and toasted each other in
malt whisky and the young man said: 'I never went a lot on
the Grenadiers, Blowers, too stuffy for me, but I'll take it all
back after today!' And then the injured warriors stumbled in
amity down the hill, dragging the stag, and were very late
home indeed. And the Scots Guardsman said, 'You'll be lucky
if you survive this war. I shan't. I know that bloody well.' And
Alfred, who had heard such forebodings among the Grenadiers
was emboldened by whisky to say roughly, 'Now don't you
talk like that, sir, it arn't right!' and was told, 'I feel it in my
bones. But we've had a wonderful day and my brother on
Deeside will give you a job if you want one after this bloody
show is over. I suppose your beat in Suffolk is about fifteen
hundred acres? I'd sooner look after fifteen thousand any day
even if there's damn-all but deer and ptarmigan!'

But when Alfred got home, his clothes slimy with peat and
rain, he found Bessie in tears, sure that her husband had been
lost on the hill. So he shelved the prospect of a stalker's life, for
there was obviously more war to come, and settled down to
enjoy his interlude from France as a married man.

XI

ALFRED BLOWERS came out of the war in 1919 as a sergeant. He had added a military medal to the D.C.M. he had won at Loos and on his sleeve were three gold stripes. He knew how uncommonly lucky he had been in the last two years and had spent six months in charge of the 'details' of a divisional headquarters, a motley collection of cooks, runners, mess orderlies, batmen, and signallers, whom Alfred had striven to weld into a 'defence platoon'. He was stiffer and greyer now and looked older than his years. He wanted nothing but a chance to return to Bessie and to some quiet cottage on a Suffolk estate where he could train dogs and rear pheasants, where life went on in the old routine in which he had not realized his own blessedness.

But one afternoon a staff captain spoke to him: 'I suppose, sergeant, after all this you're sweating on your demobilization?'

'Yes, sir, that I am, and no mistake.'

'And you don't want to soldier on and go back to guard duty at Windsor and Buckingham Palace? Bearskins and pipeclay and troopin' the colour and all that nonsense?'

'No, sir. I'd be no good at that.'

'Keeper, weren't you? Got a job to go back to?'

'No, I ain't, sir, and that's the truth! My squire, Captain Darty that was, he was killed and they've had to sell the place.'

'Got anywhere in mind?'

'No, sir, but I married a girl out of Glenovil and His Lordship did once say . . .' He stopped. Put not your trust in Princes, he was thinking, nor in Lords either.

'Well, most Sassenachs don't want to go to the Highlands. It's usually the other way on. But my uncle, who's a Lord Lieutenant up there, is looking for a youngish active chap for a special job. Didn't Major McLeod train you as a sniper once?'

'Yes, sir, he did. I did a bit out here before the Somme.'

'Well, now listen! My uncle's worried with poachers. They're a town gang which have made money in the war and they come up the glen by car at night and slaughter the deer with shotguns in winter, when the poor brutes are starving along the road. And in the summer they net or bomb the pools and take a lot of salmon. My uncle's only got one keeper left now and he's old. So he's got the idea of importing some outside talent to break the gang up. Your wife being a Highlander, you might get along in a place like Connich better than most. Would you like me to mention your name when I write?'

The young officer extracted from Alfred the details of his past and seemed well satisfied with the answers. So in February 1919 after the rites of demobilization were over, ex-Sergeant Blowers and his wife were given return tickets to Inverness. And a day later in a huge old house enveloped in pinewoods they were interviewed by a formidable old gentleman who had once been Colonel of the Scots Guards and who said: 'Blowers, I've heard about you from my nephew and also from Lord Inverarn, where your wife comes from. I must confess I'd sooner have had a Highlander on this place but you've got a very good record, if I may say so. My head-keeper will tell you about the job and you'll be everything under him, part-stalker, part-keeper, part-river-keeper. It may mean night work, I warn you, and as I'm Lord Lieutenant, I don't want to know too many details about what's going on. And you'd better pretend not to know too much yourself, as a Sassenach who's a bit out of his depth keepering up here. Got me? But . . . I'm startin' at the wrong end. Mrs Blowers would like to see her house. My factor, Mr Ramsay, has just had it done up with a new cooker, and I do hope she'll like it. First essential for any keeper is to have a comfortable base to operate from! Fix up the rest, pay and so forth, with Mr Ramsay and let him know if you'll come.' The old gentleman shook hands and bowed them out impressively.

By mid-March of 1919, Mr and Mrs Blowers were installed in the new house. It was a stone building, ivy-covered, sheltered from the north and east, with spacious kennels alongside and a deer larder. It commanded the river and the strath across the river and from behind the house Alfred could slip quietly up the hill and see over his beat for miles. He was given a good telescope, an old shot-gun, and a black retriever: 'hardest-mouthed brute in the county', the General grinned, 'but he's got a devil of a nose and is just the dog you want for police-work. I should train him never to take food from anyone except yourself.'

So Alfred brought up his belongings from Tibberton and settled down. Mr Ramsay lent him a dossier about the 'Kessock gang' which made him very angry. They had two cars, it seemed, with detachable number-plates, and in their midst was one underkeeper from the Connich estate who had been sacked for sloth. They operated over a huge area and seemed to know exactly how to time their raids. Alastair, the head-keeper, suffered from asthma and could not do much night work and had no transport. The gang were formidable. They had attacked one keeper in Glen Struy and thrown him in the river. They had spat at police constables who attempted to stop the van full of slaughtered deer. Alfred realized that they were a more astute and dangerous team to master than Skipper White and Elijah Dow and 'the man from Misner', and he suspected that if he 'put a foot wrong' he, as a Sassenach, would get no sympathy from the Inverness police. So he

confided in Bessie, who said 'Mercy me, now be careful, Alfie!'
and she took the 'bus one day into Inverness and returned with
a capacious vacuum flask which would ensure her husband
having hot soup or stew at any hour of the night. Nor, as a
good wife should, did she hesitate to lie on his behalf, when it
seemed desirable.

'The neighbours are aye enquiring after you and I said you
never went out at night on account of your war-wounds and
you were studying books to learn about the keepering. They
couldna mak' out why the Laird had given this job to a
Sassenach. They said he must be daft.'

'Let them,' said Alfred, 'the more daft they're thinking we
are, the better.' He had been on the hill all day after 'a heavy
vixen' and had shot her as she lay sunning herself in a peat-hag
near her den. It was a more merciful ending than a trap, some
of which were set three miles uphill from his house and visited
about once a week. Alfred reset them all quietly in places he
could 'glass' with his telescope from a distance each morning
and see whether they had been sprung.

One afternoon in late April he came in off the hill after a
day seeking hoodie crows, and found Bessie very agitated. 'I'll
get your tea, dear,' she said, though it was barely five o'clock.
'I think there may be trouble the night.'

'Trouble?'

'Aye, I feel it in my bones. There's twa girls gone up the
glen with a pack of camping kit on their backs. They said they
were from the South and they'd been told they could camp up
by the Long Bend, and they'll be away the morn for Glen
Monar over the hill. But I have my doubts they're from the
South. They asked for a glass of water and whether you were
the keeper and where you were.'

'What did you say, Bessie?'

'I said you were up the hill. And there's another thing.
Mrs Macdonald told me that a black car dropped them at the
foot of the glen and she heard them tell the driver, "See you
later".'

Alfred ate his tea, thinking hard. Two girls with a little

6

tent? No one had yet called such people 'hikers' nor were they in 1919 such common objects of the countryside as they became later. He slipped out after tea to his chosen point of vantage. The tent was there, pitched above the river, and Alfred could see one girl crouched over a stove cooking sausages. The other could not be seen.

Alfred's training had taught him to look all round the compass. He glassed the open hill to the north. The rain had ceased and it was a clear evening. Suddenly half a mile away and two hundred feet above him a movement caught his eye. At first he thought it was a stray hind feeding and then realized it was a young woman climbing the hill. He crouched lower behind a bush. She settled herself on a knoll and Alfred realized that from there she could look right down the glen, to a point where the river bent round, divided from the track only by a line of alders and rowan trees. She settled herself as if for a long wait and drew out a pair of binoculars.

Alfred watched her, as silently as a cat and thinking hard. She was not watching birds, that was clear, and she seemed to be looking for any sign of movement along the river. He decided to go back and warn Alastair. There were several hours of daylight and he did not expect any raid on the river would happen before nine o'clock. He slid down the hill and made his way through the birches to the track. He trudged slowly in case anyone was watching him and at last reached Alastair's dwelling behind the Big House.

The old man nodded. 'They'll be comin' the nicht. Last time they raided here, twa years back, there was twa wee boys who said they were Scouts lodged in a tent near the river but no quite so far up. It was my belief they must have signalled somehow that all was clear and I heard the bomb the gang threw in the water and when I got up, their cawr was coming doon without lichts. It nearly ran me doon and I couldna get the number. And when I got to the tent the bloody boys swore at me and said they were asleep. You'd best tak' your dog, Alfred, and a good stick, but be careful who you hit. I'll stay by the road and take their cawr number if they drive up the glen. But last time I took their number the polis laughed at Mr Ramsay and said there wasna sich a number.'

'Is it no good,' said ex-Sergeant Blowers, 'to block the road with a tree after they've gone up? And is there no one we can get to help us from the Big House?'

'There's a dinner party the nicht and I fear Sir Jocelyn would be wild. There's only his piper and the ithers are all Frasers or Chisholms and when they've tasted blood, there's no holding them. We must do this alone. It's a great responsibility. But I'll tak' an axe and see if I can fell a wee tree.'

Alfred drew out his watch: 'What's your time, Mr Macdonald? If it comes to a court case, we'd best agree on what time anything happened.'

The Grenadiers had taught Alfred to synchronize watches before an attack.

'I was thinkin' the same,' said Alastair, who had quite forgotten such precautions. 'But our job is to stop them, and no bring the case into court. It's prevention, ye understand, Alfie, which is better than cure.'

Alfred hurried home, changed his boots for some rubber-soled golfing brogues which had once belonged to Captain Darty and pulled an old stocking over his face and made Bessie cut a slit in it. He also took instead of a stick a heavy 'slasher', a curved blade on a long pole, with a vague idea of cutting down branches to block the road. Drifter, the hard-mouthed retriever, came with him eagerly.

'Bessie dear, if you hear a car coming up the road, slip down and take its number. But be sure you don't come out of the gate. I'll be all right. Don't worry.'

'But I *am* worrying,' she said. 'Mrs Fraser, the herdsman's wife, came asking for you an hour ago. Said she'd seen a fox and would you come and shoot it? It's near her hens.'

'If there's a fox there,' said Alfred slowly (thinking of 'them Frasers' and 'when they've tasted blood') 'it must wait. There's other foxes in the glen tonight. What did you tell her?'

'I said you were up the hill after a vixen away beyond the Lapaich.'

'Well done, Bess. I was watching a vixen but not the one she's meaning!'

Alfred took Drifter to his former vantage point. The light was failing but he could just discern the woman on her knoll. She seemed half-asleep.

He watched her with his telescope till dark. No bird watcher would have stayed there all that time, and the meal her companion had been preparing must have been ready long ago. There was no movement in the tent. Slowly the night came down, a greenshank called from the hill and he could hear an oyster-catcher trilling above the Long Bend where shingle banks enclosed the river. Was he wasting his time when it was obviously his job to watch the pools below the Long Bend? Then, in the dusk, he saw a spark of light from the tent. The other girl must have been watching the river. The woman on the hill seemed to wake and drew a torch out of her pocket and gave an answering gleam. Alfred sighed with satisfaction. He waited ten minutes and shifted his telescope down the glen. Nothing happened. Then a car crept round the bend, a mile away, almost invisible against the alders, and switched off its sidelights.

Alfred wriggled lower and turned his glass on the woman up the hill. She flashed her torch three times towards the place where the car waited. Alfred without his telescope could see the side-lights blink once and vanish again.

He wriggled down the hill into the birches and was about to cut down towards the track when a gun went off twice half a mile down river from where the car had been. Alastair must have heard it! Alfred, plunging downhill to his aid, suddenly stopped. In the war he had taken part in two trench-raids and two set-piece attacks. The Guards had taught him that, before any such 'show', there was a diversion, a lot of cannon-fire and noise to mislead the enemy. No one surely could be shooting hinds at dusk in April, especially on that stretch? Perhaps it was a 'feint' to draw any watchers in the wrong direction.

It took him ten minutes to scramble down the hillside to the glen road for he wanted to keep out of sight of the girl on the hill and to make as little noise as possible. He crossed the road and came out among alders at the lower end of the second pool which was known as 'The Pot'. All was quiet and once again Alfred wondered if he had made a mistake. Perhaps he should have gone lower down the glen from where the shots had come? Then he glanced down at the silent dog who was sitting beside him. His head was up, he was sniffing the air and as Alfred bent to caress him every hackle on his back was like wire beneath his hand. He was sniffing up-river towards the Long Pool and once he glanced up at Alfred and trembled with eagerness.

Not for the first time did Alfred bless the keener senses of a dog. Perhaps it was only those girls which the dog winded: perhaps not. The car he had seen at the road-corner could have crept up the glen without lights while he and the dog were coming down the hill.

It was five hundred yards by the fishing path to the top of the Long Pool and Alfred could hear nothing for the noise of the water in the shallows above the Pot. He hurried, the dog showing more and more eagerness. Alfred gripped his slasher, wondering if they would leap at him out of the trees, and hurl him into the river as they were said to have done with the keeper on the Struy.

At the bend where the Long Pool began, Alfred stopped and listened, the dog trembling beside him. A hundred yards away he heard a splash and then another, and then a low voice and the sound of nailed boots. Suddenly a white gleaming object floated down the river and Alfred saw it was the belly of a dead salmon, a fish of seven or eight pounds. There was a strange smell on the air. Alfred knew little of fish-poaching and imagined that it was accomplished with nets, or the crude explosion of a Mills bomb. He had never heard of the deadly techniques of using acetylene or cymag to wipe out every fish in a pool. He ran furiously along the path and heard nailed boots scrambling up the steep bank. Drifter departed into the darkness without orders, and he heard a worrying snarl. Above him he saw the outline of the girls' tent and three

shadows racing for a car on the road. As the last man dived
into the back seat and the car roared into life, Drifter leaped,
there was a scream of pain, the slam of a door, and the dog fell
back on to the road. The car roared without lights down the
glen.

Alfred stopped. Five years earlier he would have scratched
his head in bewilderment, but he was now an ex-Grenadier,
alone in the darkness with his 'responsibility'. The tent on the
bank was dark and silent. He had lost the poachers, he had
not taken the number of their car, and presumably with
miraculous speed they had absconded with their fish. The
angry dog was nuzzling a patch of soaking trouser-seat which
Alfred removed from his jaws and stowed in a pocket. He
coughed heavily and said to the tent, 'Are you there, miss?'

There was a feminine scream and a girl's voice said, 'Go
away, you disgusting man. If you dare to come in here when
we're asleep, I'll charge you with attempted rape.'

Alfred slunk off on to the road. He knew, from the dossier
Mr Ramsay had lent him, that a keeper in Glenisla had had
just such a charge brought against him years before by a hiker
in a tent and had had to explain himself in court before the
charge was dismissed. The tale still hung around his glen and
some of the mud flung that day had adhered.

Alfred sat on the road bank and wondered what to do. He
was not an imaginative man but he thought of Bessie alone in
her cottage, worrying; of how angry the General would be if
Alfred's first encounter with the gang misfired so badly; of the
soaking piece of trouser-bottom which was all the evidence he
possessed and which he could see some solicitor tearing into
verbal shreds 'in Court'. Ought he to go down the road and
find out how old Alastair had got on? If Alastair had felled 'a
wee tree' across the road, he might well have been assaulted by
the gang and be lying unconscious or in need of help. Alfred,
alone in the darkness, was perhaps letting precious minutes go
by.

Then two thoughts came to him: those girls in the tent with
their torches were obviously 'in it', and the fleeting glimpse he

had had of three shadows tumbling into their car had not suggested that they were carrying anything with them. They had been too keen to escape from the angry dog. Perhaps their haul of salmon was still about?

Alfred rose. Very quietly he stole through the birches down the steep bank on to the fishing-path. He moved slowly up-river towards the head of the pool. He had gone for fifty yards when he realized that Drifter had stopped, one forefoot raised, his head turned stiffly towards a patch of bracken above the path. Alfred slipped the mask off his face, dowsed the gleam of his torch with it and stooped to see at what Drifter was pointing. It was a green kitbag of Navy pattern and it bulged with dead fish. Doubtless the gang had dropped it or stowed it there when they took alarm or because they knew someone would come and claim it later.

With infinite stealth Alfred hauled the heavy bag up the bank and hid it twenty yards higher on the other side of the road. If those girls came seeking for it they would have a job to find it! He brushed away the trail he had left in the bracken. He slid down to the fishing path again and along it to the top of the Long Pool. Salmon-parr, dead and belly upwards, floated on the edge of the racing stream. In the tent Alfred could hear female voices muttering and Drifter again stood stiffly pointing at the tent. Alfred silently moved up, his hand on the dog's neck till he was fifty yards above the tent. His torch disclosed the wheelmarks where the gang's car had turned on the road.

He crept along the road till he was fifty yards below the tent and settled down to wait all night. He was tired and sleepy and soaking-wet with dew, but that was nothing strange. Drifter lay at his feet, also soaking wet but wrapped in his Labrador fur, and Alfred trusted to Drifter's ears and nose.

After midnight he was conscious of a spark of light in the tent and a murmur of female voices. Drifter cocked his ears, and then, unpredictably, rose on his haunches and gazed down the glen road. Alfred put a hand on his back but his hackles had not risen. His broad stern waved in the dust. A light step

came towards him and then a dark shadow. Alfred rose, his
'slasher' at the alert, and a faint shriek was his answer. It was
Bessie.

They clung to one another in the darkness. 'Lord bless my
heart alive,' he whispered; then, 'Whatever are you a-doing
here, Bess?'

'Och, my darling, I was so terribly worried. I heard the car
go down the glen, with no lights, and I made sure they'd
murdered you. Are you all well?'

'I'm all right, Bess. You shouldn't have done this but bless
you for doing it . . . !'

'I've brought you some hot stew and a spoon.' She fumbled
in Alfred's own game-bag and produced her new thermos and
half a loaf of bread and a bottle of warm tea.

Alfred wolfed his meal hungrily and wondered how many
keepers' wives would have faced that lonely road at night. How
right old Angus Ogilvie at Glenovil had been about keepers'
wives, and his experience had all been in the Highlands!
Somehow he could not see old Bert Mould at Tibberton lying
out all night for poachers, nor Mrs Mould bringing him hot
food at midnight down a lonely lane. He clasped Bessie's hand
tightly at last and said, 'Thank you, lass. That whooly did me
good,' which was as high a meed of praise as any Suffolk man
in those days could compass.

'What are you waiting for here?' whispered Bessie. 'They're
awa' doon the glen and home by now.'

'Some of their fish are still here, lass, and I'm thinking they'll
be back in another car, maybe, to fetch it. And them girls were
signalling to them just when it got dark. They're all in it.'

Drifter, on whom Alfred had bestowed a crust richly dipped
in stew, and who had been curled contentedly at their feet,
suddenly rose and sniffed the air. Alfred again saw the faint
gleam of a torch through the tent. The two watched the torch
gleam wavering along the river path and heard women's voices
as they searched for the bag which Alfred had removed. They
were obviously puzzled and angry and Alfred expected them
at any moment to emerge through the trees on to the road.

Then the light burned in the tent again and Alfred heard the purr of a primus stove.

The night was cold and endless. A wind blew off the snows of the Lapaich. A tawny owl called down the glen. Alfred heard the delicate bark of a fox far up the hill. He took off his tweed coat and wrapped Bessie in it and said, 'I must wait here. Will you not go home, my dear? It'll be perishing cold before sunrise.'

'No me,' said Bessie, 'I'll bide here. You're no safe alone, my man, with them women in that tent, even with the dog.'

In later years Alfred often recalled that vigil which seemed so pointless at the time, guarding a stable door from which the horses had long vanished! He was dog-tired after a hard day up the hill and the stew had made him even sleepier. He had no one to advise him, but years at Tibberton and in the Guards had given him obstinacy when alone. He would hang on and see what happened, even if Bessie caught her death of cold! So many long nights had he endured in trenches but then there had been the rustle of working men, the chink of spades, random shots from either side, a few heavy shells sliding across the stars, and the everlasting rise and fall of the Verey flares.

Bessie was asleep at his side and Alfred was in a doze when Drifter woke him by sitting up, and looking down the glen. Alfred glanced at his watch. It was nearly half-past two. He bundled Bessie and the dog quietly into the trees above the road as a large dark car without lights came up the glen and turned where the other car had turned. It stopped on the road beside the tent and Alfred heard low voices. 'Bide here, Bess,' he whispered, 'and don't move!' He hissed Drifter to heel and started towards the car. He lay prone on the verge, his hand on the dog's neck and saw three black shadows dragging a sack out of the tent and lifting it into the car. Then a man's voice said, 'Give me your torch, lassie. I'll look where the other one is. Now back to your tent and go to sleep. Donald will be at the bridge the morn to lift you home.'

Alfred lay beside the road, scarcely breathing while the

torchlight wavered down the bank, the girls retired to their tent and pulled the flaps to, and Drifter under Alfred's hand rumbled like a cat purring. Alfred was about to follow the torchlight down the bank when he thought: 'The fish! They're evidence.' He crept up to the car and with one heave removed the sack and staggered with it up the hill where he dumped it in the bracken. Then he sped down to the Long Pool. Drifter left him suddenly again. The torch on the path went out, there was the same worrying growl and a splash in the pool.

In the next ten minutes Alfred, whose rubber-soled shoes had slipped on the stones, ducked the man heavily and then hauled him, half-senseless, to the bank and squeezed the water out of him. He strapped his arms with his own belt, removed his braces as he had done with German prisoners aforetime, and dragged him to the road.

'Now,' he said, 'you'll drive me to the Castle and we'll see the Laird.' There was no sound from the tent but the triumphant Drifter stiffened and waved his stern at someone beside the road. It was Bessie, sitting hunched in Alfred's coat and her voice showed that she was shivering with cold. 'Alfie,' she said, 'where were your wits, man? And you a Guardsman! I've got the switch-key, and I've let down the back tyres. This car will stay here till the morning.'

It was dawn before Alfred had stowed away to his satisfaction the two kit-bags of fish. It was after dawn before he was satisfied that only superhuman efforts could remove the car. It was 7 a.m. when, after two cups of scalding tea at home, he had packed Bessie off to bed, and called on Alastair Macdonald with his shivering prisoner, whose charges of car sabotage, attempted murder by drowning, assault and battery lost nothing in the telling.

It was 9 a.m. before Sir Jocelyn Poynter, called from his porridge to the business-room, had heard his story. And it was 9.30 a.m. when, just as they were parading the sacks of fish for inspection, two furious young women arrived to add to the indictment with charges of 'attempted rape and improper suggestions' towards innocent campers. The General listened gravely. Then he said, 'Of course Miss Fraser, I'm only Lord Lieutenant and have no judicial status. But . . . if your story is true (and I would not suggest you're lying) do you really think that my underkeeper would come out at night to attempt rape on you, *accompanied by his wife*? There will, I fear, be two witnesses to rebut your story.'

For Alfred it meant a visit to Invergordon to identify the Naval kit-bags which held the fish. It meant interviews with the police and a rabid garage proprietor in Inverness who wanted to know by whom a potato had been stuffed into the exhaust of his best car. Alfred did not know, but Bessie later confessed that it was her idea. Women, like elephants, rarely forget and though Bessie had never driven a motor car in her life, she had once been told how to hamper their running.

Alfred reluctantly buried the two sacks of fish for in those days it was believed that they were dangerous to eat, though they had a market value in Inverness. The General said little but seemed well-pleased and told Alfred one day that he had acted 'in the best traditions of the Brigade' and that the gang was unlikely to come again. 'But I don't pay your wife, Blowers, to tackle poachers. Remember that!' And how could Alfred admit that Bessie had been a volunteer, who had disobeyed his explicit instructions to 'abide where she was'?

*　　*　　*

A fortnight later a fishing crony said to Sir Jocelyn: 'I'm bursting to know, Jock, what happened that night of your dinner-party when Alastair Macdonald came round just as we were all leaving. I've heard all sorts of yarns.'

'Oh that,' said the General. 'Well, I'm Lord Lieutenant for my sins and never know what goes on, but between these four walls . . .'

'Of course, Jock. Not a word!'

'Well, it was that infernal gang from Kessock raiding my water again. They led Alastair astray by firing shots down the glen and later nearly ran him down when he tried to stop their car. . . . So he came up and I telephoned the Chief Constable and they had a police patrol out to meet their car. Three men soaking wet but not a fish. However . . .'

'Carry on, Jock. This is fascinating.'

'My new keeper, though only a Grenadier, seems to have behaved well. He got their fish – about ninety pounds of decent fish all killed with some new dope, and nearly drowned the little swab who came up after midnight to fetch them, and put *him* in the bag as well.'

'Good for him!'

'Not bad for a Sassenach? And what's more, he had his young wife out to help.'

'His *wife*?'

'Yes, but she's a Highland girl out of Glenovil, Bessie Thomson. Ian Inverarn says she was his shepherd's daughter. And while Blowers and that wolf-mouthed Labrador of mine were half-drowning the chap in the Long Pool, she, if you please, was putting paid to the car. Know whose car it was?'

'Can't guess.'

'That old Rolls which Hamish Mackintosh sold in 1914 as an ambulance. It's been through several hands since, but it cost 'em forty pounds to get running after Bessie Blowers had had a go at it. . . . Now remember this is all highly confidential! There've been charges of attempted rape, murder, assault, sabotage, and God knows what, but I don't think they'll be pressed. And I hope we've heard the last of the Kessock gang in my glen and yours.'

'Well, well!' said the other man. 'I don't know many keepers' wives who'd help take on that gang. Who wrote "*The female of the species is more deadly than the male*"? Kipling, wasn't it?'

XII

FOR months after 'the Kessock lads' had been worsted, Alfred enjoyed peace. The gang had lost their fish, a loaned car had received expensive injuries and one raider had tooth-marks in his gluteal region which caused him pain and were an embarrassment for his wife to dress. Though they had sworn revenge, legend in the glens had endowed Alfred with super-human strength and ferocity.

All May and June Alfred was learning the work of a fishing-ghilly but he spent some time on the 'high tops' from which he could survey all the kingdoms of the earth, and study ptarmigan and dotterel and the rare snow-bunting, and watch the stags lying out on the unsullied snowdrifts of the Lapaich like flies on a window-pane.

One incident only marred that summer. Glassing the higher corries from some peat hags on a stony ridge, Alfred met a tubby man with a pink face searching the ridge not far from him. He greeted Alfred genially and said he was 'just botanis-ing'. Alfred steered him away from a stony area of moss and lichen for he knew there was a sitting dotterel nearby.

They sat down on the edge of a hag and the stranger said, 'You're no more a Highlander than myself. What part of East Anglia do you hail from?'

Alfred told him. 'Indeed! I'm Rector of Bildenhall.'

'Ah,' said Alfred; suspicion rising in him. Captain Darty had said, 'Never trust a parson in May and June. They're nearly always egg-snatchers.' He had never forgotten the parson who had so nearly pedalled home without his trousers after robbing a hobby's nest. This one did not even wear a clerical collar.

They sat among rocks and chatted about Suffolk and this village and that squire, and Alfred after twenty minutes was emboldened to say, 'Did you ever, sir, come across a reverend, name of Blaxall from Menhaston?'

'What, dear old "Soapy" Blaxall? Of course, a grand feller, but retired now. We were in the same rural deanery for years. He's Chairman of our Society.'

'Oh ah,' said Alfred, with the wooden face of the Grenadier. 'And what may that be?'

'Oh, we study birds and things . . . and of course, flowers and plants, *my* speciality.'

'Ah. I only met the Reverend Blaxall once.'

'Shooting, I suppose?'

'No. Climbing.'

'Charming chap, didn't you find him?'

'He'd charm a bird off a tree.'

'Well, well, what a small world!' The stranger looked at his watch. 'I must be off; in my hotel at Peffercairn they have high tea at six-thirty. Don't worry, keeper, you can trust me *implicitly*! I'm only here botanizing after sub-Arctic plants.'

Alfred's eyes were fixed on the stranger's binoculars. 'I didn't know botanizers needed them things.'

'Just to admire the views, my man, wonderful, wonderful. Do you realize you can see thirty peaks of over two thousand feet from here? You can't do that in East Anglia! What a pleasure to meet someone from dear old silly Suffolk!'

He held out his hand but Alfred said, 'Well, Reverend, I'm goin' your way. I got to look at one of my traps.'

Better see the fellow off the hill! Alfred steered him along the mossy stones of the ridge.

All might have been well, had they not stumbled, at the edge of the scree, on another dotterel's nest of which Alfred did not know. As the sitting bird scuffled and ran like a rat off the eggs, Alfred caught a gleam in the stranger's eye. 'What

beautiful little eggs! And what do you say they call the bird,
keeper?'

'Dotterel, sir. They ain't common here. And there's a lot of
beggars after them, so the General won't let 'em be touched.'

The stranger took a long look at the eggs and then a quick
glance round. Then he said, 'Turn your back, keeper, for a
minute, and there'll be a five-pound-note for you.'

'Oh,' said ex-Sergeant Blowers, 'it's that way, is it? Then you
can be off down that hill whoolly quick before I do you an
injury.'

Alfred did not know that the Highlands were full at this
season of such kleptomaniac marauders. The generation before
them had boasted that 'with a bottle of whisky and a kettle of
hot water' they could possess themselves of any rare eggs, eagle
or dotterel, greenshank or Slavonian grebe or crested tit, that
they fancied. They had no mercy on birds which had been
sitting for weeks, and were a standing temptation to any stalker
whom they met. Five pounds was for Alfred Blowers more than
a week's pay. He was paid to guard the deer and salmon and
the gamebirds. Anything else was apt to be 'vermin'. But his
dislike of the Reverend 'Soapy' Blaxall of Menhaston Vicarage
had survived the years. The stranger realized that he had given
himself away. He said haughtily, 'There's no law of trespass in
Scotland and I've as much right to be here as you have. I'm
off to Melvich tomorrow but I shall report you to your employer before I go for threatening me.'

Alfred watched him go. Had he made another Sassenach
bloomer? It seemed anyone could walk anywhere in Scotland
and indeed fish for trout almost without interference. When
he was a dot in the distance Alfred came down the hill, brood-
ing. That afternoon patrolling the river path near The Pot,
he encountered the General himself, who had been fishing.
He was sitting on a wooden bench smoking a pipe and putting
on another fly from his hat brim. 'Well, Alfred, how goes
it?'

'Sir,' said Alfred, and reported certain events of the last ten
days, this fox and that vixen, the fire which someone had

started in the heather along the road, some broods of grouse and blackgame, hinds calving on the hill.

Then the General said, 'By the way, Alfred, I had a complaint about you on the telephone this afternoon. What caused you to threaten a botanist with assault on Ben Bonach? Come on. I want your version.' He smiled his kindly smile.

'He warn't no botanist, General. That was just his cammyflage. Did he tell you he offered me a five-pun note to turn my back while he took some dotterels' eggs?'

'Good Lord, no! Come on, Alfred, I want the whole story.'

Alfred told his tale and added a bit about the parson's friend, the Reverend 'Soapy' Blaxall in Suffolk and how Squire Darty ('what I was with before the war') had threatened to make him bicycle home without his trousers.

The General laughed loud and long, then packed up his rod. 'Good for the Grenadiers,' he said. 'I'll go back and have a word on the telephone with the Chief Constable. You say he's staying at Peffercairn and going on to Melvich? Someone ought to put a spoke in *his* dam' wheel tomorrow. Anyway he won't trouble us here any more.'

But Alfred was not sure about that. He said nothing, but after his tea he asked Bessie to put him up 'a piccc', as he had to be up the hill again 'after a fox'. Bessie sighed. She was getting used to evenings and sometimes nights alone, which was the inevitable lot of Highland keepers' wives. 'You keep the dog here, Bessie, and let him lie in the kitchen. If anyone comes, you'll feel safer.'

At eight o'clock Alfred took the long path up the burn. It meant an hour and a half's steady climb and he was already tired after a day which had begun at 5 a.m. By careful glassing on the top he satisfied himself that both dotterels were sitting peacefully on their eggs and he settled down at dusk among some rocks fifty yards from the second nest. The wind was keen up here, and he put on a khaki sweater from his game bag. The moon rose gloriously and the rocks threw inky shadows. Alfred fought down the sleep which was overwhelming him. Mist gathered along the crest and for two hours there was not a sound, except once the coughing of a stag, and once the queer froglike croak of a ptarmigan.

Had Alfred been a fool? Probably the little parson was safe in bed at Peffercairn and Alfred thought of Bessie in their own warm bed and wished he was with her. What a life it was, this keepering, incessantly waiting for something which might never happen! All the sane world was in bed that midnight and he, with only suspicion to keep him company, was wasting the summer night in moon-drenched mist on the most inhospitable section of the forest. A shadow grew slowly out of the mist, became a hornless stag and then clattered off along the ridge, winding him. He wished Drifter was with him, with those superhuman ears of his and a nose to back them. He looked at his watch, 1.15 a.m. He would 'eat his piece', and in another fifteen minutes get off down the hill. He waited and suddenly a golden plover called somewhere down the slope. Alastair had told him that as long as you had curlews and golden plovers on any moorland they were as good watchdogs as any if a fox was about. Then, very faintly, he heard a clink on stone, then another. Alfred lay flat among his rocks and wished again for the dog. Then nearer came a sound, an indeterminate sound composed of heavy steps and heavy breathing. Ah!

Alfred wriggled noiselessly, as Alastair had taught him, towards the dotterel's nest. He had no wish to disturb the bird for he doubted if he (someone had told him the male dotterel normally brooded) could find the nest again in the dark and if disturbed, the eggs would surely be chilled before dawn. Another shadow loomed up on the ridge and he heard a cough as if someone, overdone with climbing, had stopped to find his landmarks. A torch gleamed for a moment and went out. The moon came out in majesty and illuminated the hill. Alfred found himself within five yards of a tubby figure which wheezed as it leaned on a stick. Something inspired Alfred to say in the broadest of broad Suffolk, 'Oh, that's you agen, the Man of God. Now do you get to hell out of here. I told you that afore. You said I could trust you but I larned my lesson about parsons fifteen year agoo. Now goo!'

7

The shadow gasped, turned and flitted downhill. There was a slithering sound of stones and loose scree and then a crash. Strange, unecclesiastical words came from below. Alfred, though not wishing to pursue, found himself bending over a dark writhing form which said, 'I've sprained my ankle. Don't you dare lay hands on me, keeper, or I'll have the law on you.'

'I hope you will. I met some chaplains in my time in the Brigade and they was right good chaps, brave as lions and you could reckon on what they said. I 'ont touch you, though I'd like to, surelie! And whatever pore bird you're arter at Melvich tomorrow, you leave it alone, du you'll be in trouble. Now goo!'

The shadow rose and limped out of sight, leaning heavily on a stick. Alfred waited, huddled in the lee of the rocks. It would be light in another hour and he would just make sure the dotterel was all right. Far down the slope where the heather began, he could hear cock grouse calling: they were always among the earliest birds to wake before it was light.

Alfred, stiff and tired, reached home at 4.45 a.m., was greeted with a 'woof' of joy by Drifter, made up the fire and put the kettle on. He drank two cups of tea and an hour later Bessie found him asleep in a chair. He ended his story, 'Now mind, Bessie lass, I don't want this to get about. Otherwise that little varmin will say I pushed him down the hill and broke his ankle. I reckon he'll have had a job to get to Peffercairn by breakfast time.'

* * *

But it was Sir Jocelyn who came round and invaded Bessie's parlour. He said, 'Alfred, the police have been making inquiries about your parson and he's still at Peffercairn and laid up. Are you *sure* you didn't manhandle him yesterday?'

'I never put a hand on him, sir, either time. He fell down them screes in the dark and hurt his ankle.'

'In the *dark*?'

'Ah, I thought he'd be back again, so I sat up under the moon last night and he comed up, about half arter one, for them eggs.'

'You *don't* mean it?'

'Ah, and when I spoke to him he runned away and slipped on all them loose screes, and fell good tidily and damaged his ankle. I never put a hand on him: he said he'd have the law on me if I did. He went off down the hill and he was whooly lame. I reckon he's boogus.'

The General looked long at Alfred and then at Bessie. 'Mrs Blowers,' he said, 'I knew I hadn't made a mistake when I took your husband on here. I rather hope that parson *will* bring an action. We'll have some fun with him if he does. I'm very grateful.'

*　　*　　*

Alfred heard no more. But Mr Ramsay, the factor, carefully briefed on the telephone, rather fancied himself as a detective. The Reverend Aubrey Melon, of Bildenhall in Suffolk, nursing his swollen ankle and a grievance that evening on the veranda of a Peffercairn hotel, was accosted by a stranger in worn tweeds who invited him to join him in a drink. They had a dram together and the stranger said, 'I hear you're a botanist, sir? I wonder if you could tell me what this plant is?'

He produced a withered stalk of herbage wrapped in toilet paper.

The Reverend Aubrey looked at it, sniffed it, turned it over and said, 'Well, I'm not good at plants, to tell the truth. Birds are more my line.'

Mr Ramsay sighed with relief. It had been one of the commonest but least conspicuous hedgerow plants he could find. Blowers had not been wrong when he thought this parson chap was 'boogus'.

'I see,' he said, 'you've had an accident. Bad luck. How did it happen?'

The Reverend Aubrey was tempted to say that a keeper had assaulted him. But he was a stranger in a strange land and decided on half the truth.

'I slipped last night coming down Ben Bonach in the dark.

Had a terrible time getting back. It's most painful, but the doctor says I haven't broken anything.'

Mr Ramsay, reassured that no charge was likely against his keepers, said, 'Birds are my speciality too. I suppose you've heard of the ospreys nesting on Loch Harmidale?'

'No, really, do tell me . . . I'll keep it entirely to myself . . .'

As he drove away, the factor thought that he had sent the Reverend Aubrey, if his leg ever got better, on the wildest of wild-osprey chases into a region where no osprey had been seen since 1850. He reported to the General next day.

'I was a bit doubtful of Blowers, sir, but I believe his story. There won't be a charge. It must be a temptation to a keeper to turn down five pounds as he did. Most keepers I know would have said, "Well, birds are nothing to me, unless they're game".'

Sir Jocelyn grunted and said no more. But one afternoon, Lady Poynter's car arrived at the house and she said, 'Bessie, they tell me you're expecting a baby. I'm delighted to hear it! We hope you'll accept this gramophone to while away your time this winter and here's something the General hopes you'll spend on the records you want. And if Alfred wants any books from our library to read, he's only got to ask.'

Old Alastair Macdonald, like other inhabitants of the glen, had been wont to spend his evening hours making himself two pairs of boots for next season. For reading matter he had been wont to read six months issues of *The Times* from cover to cover. It had given him a contempt for the prognostications of politicians and leader-writers, but, once read, these newspapers went under his mattress and added to the warmth of his bed which grew yearly in thickness.

But Alfred, whom the Grenadiers had taught to 'read books', took Lady Poynter at her word. So evening after evening while the gramophone played *If you were the only girl in the world* and *Keep the Home Fires Burning* and *Memory Street*, and Bessie knitted for the unborn child, Alfred was deep in books: Scrope on the stalking of deer, the *Badminton Library*, Eric Parker, the Duke of Portland's *Memoirs*, and selected novelists from Charles Dickens to Owen Wister. Much of what they wrote was above Alfred's head, but they were all serious men who had written down what they saw with their eyes and not spun fancies out of their heads. Alfred's education was proceeding apace.

XIII

LOOKING back later, Alfred Blowers realized how often his fate had been sealed by the sickness or death of his employers. At Tibberton first Mr Flickerson had died, then Mr Darty, the squire, and then Colonel Darty had been killed in the war, so that the prospect of becoming the youngest head keeper in Suffolk had abruptly vanished.

He had been lucky in getting an equally good job 'with prospects' in the Highlands, and now this was suddenly threatened just as he was beginning to master it. Sir Jocelyn, while fishing a neighbour's water, had a disabling fall among some rocks, cracked a rib and caught a chill. His wife decided to take him for a sea voyage to the Caribbean. The stalking and fishing was to be let.

The head-stalker and Alfred waited anxiously to know their fate. There would be so many gentlemen Alastair would have welcomed in the glen as old friends, but, 'The trouble is, Alfie, there's a' the young men in this country have no money now or are too busy up at London trying to make some more to keep their places going.' Alfred had heard tales from Suffolk of

good land going back to 'breck', and of rich farmers giving up
the struggle to grow corn or sugar-beet. And now to their
horror they learned that the new tenant was not only an
American, but actually a woman, a Mrs Skutz from Chicago!

'I don't like the sound of it, Alfie, it's no' the type of gentry
I've been used to. Mr Ramsay says she's a verra' good shot and
has had the head of every beast in Africa. But I'm too old to
lead a wumman round the tops. She'll never stop talking, and
I'll be forgetting my manners. It'll be as bad as Breanie!'

Alfred grunted. The impoverished laird of Breanie, badly
wounded in the war and faced with death duties, had let the
stalking to a syndicate of greyhound owners in Carlisle. They
wanted not sport but venison as dog-meat in quantity. After a
tramp or two in the strath by the lodge they complained that
there 'were no deer' and refused to believe there were plenty
of good beasts two miles uphill in the mist and rain.

'It's just flesh they want,' the ancient stalker had complained
one day to Alastair in Dingwall. 'They'd sooner get a lot of
hinds up against a face and blatter at the puir beasts rather
than crawl for a stag. And they wound half of what they shoot
at. It's butchery! It's no' what I've been used to with any of
my gentlemen for fufty years. But the laird was canny: he was
too good for them!'

The laird, who had charged the greyhound syndicate a
swingeing rent for the season, listened carefully to the com-
plaints of 'no deer'. He then suggested that for a further £1000
he would have the forest properly stalked by his own men and
would send the resulting venison to Carlisle by train. The
syndicate had got its dog-meat, the forest was rid of a lot of
'rubbishy beasts' and a few friends from the laird's regiment
had had some unexpectedly cheap stalking.

But Mrs Skutz was in a different category. A fair rosy-
cheeked woman, the only daughter of a rich meat-packer, she
had shed three millionaire husbands in six years and had since
become the bane of white hunters in Tanganyika and Kenyanga. To her, a genuine white hunter was as valued a trophy
as a white rhinoceros and rather easier. She now installed

herself, her armoury and her current boy friend in the Big House.

Alfred at their first interview was aware of keen blue eyes, under yellow waves of roached hair, staring at him from head to foot. He felt oddly as if he had no clothes on.

'So you're Alfred, the under-hunter here, they tell me. Where are your kilts?'

So might Eve have asked Adam where his fig-leaf was. Alfred blushed to his ears and said, 'I'm a Sassenach, ma'am. I'm not entitled to wear the kilt. It's a Highland dress.'

'You'd look cunning in kilts, Alfred. I'm always telling Mr Shulmann here' – she indicated the current boy friend on a sofa with his cigar – 'to wear them up here. His grandmother was a Mackenzie. Now tomorrow, Alfred, you're taking me up the hill and going to get me the very best stag in the forest? Okay?'

'I'll try, ma'am. There's some nice beasts on the hill but we may never see one.'

'We'd better, Alfred, if you want to keep your job.'

And she nodded good night with her eyes on his lean frame.

Alfred went home. 'She's not the type of lady I've been used to,' he told Bessie. 'I reckon she's got everything she wanted all her life.' He thought miserably of Mrs Flickerson and Margaret Darty and Lady Poynter.

'Never heed her, Alfred,' said Bessie, stirring the hot-pot. 'Tak' the woman the hard way up to Slomach and perhaps she'll not be too full of energy and sin when you get her there.'

The boy friend, whose penchant for 'Scotch on the rocks' outweighed all ideas of a royal on the hill, kept to his bed next day. Mrs Skutz, as inexhaustible as ever, was bristling with vitality and tested her rifle against the 'iron stag' in the quarry behind the Big House.

For two hours Alfred led her up the hill, choosing the steepest tracks of all. He dropped Hamish, the pony-man, at a spot where he could observe their stalk with his glass. Rather to Alfred's surprise, when he had finished his spy from a vantage point much higher up, there was a decent eight-pointer lying below them.

'There's hinds to the west of him, and more beyond him but I think we may get in if we're careful.' He tested the wind and took the rifle, for he did not trust 'a foreigner' carrying even an empty rifle trained on his own stern while he was stalking.

It was a long and rather difficult crawl, fifty minutes of slithering mostly down hill and Alfred was conscious of nothing but eddies of wind, a blur of mist and rain, a few suspicious hinds, occasional gasps from the lady behind him, and an over-poweringly rich perfume which made him wonder why every beast in the corrie did not leave it. They lay at last panting in a peat-hag and very slowly Alfred peeped up and saw the stag within sixty yards. He loaded the rifle and handed it back. 'He's lying down, ma'am, nicely. I'll roar him up when you're ready.' He uttered a strangled roar such as Alastair had taught him. The stag rose slowly and before Alfred could say 'Now', there was a thunderclap within inches of his eardrum, the stag took two slow steps forward, buckled at the knees and collapsed in the burn. 'Jesus, darling,' said a voice in Alfred's ear, 'I *got* him! Call that nothing?'

Alfred had never been called 'Darling' except by Bessie and that very rarely. He said, 'It was a good shot, ma'am,' and strode down the hill.

The meat-packer's daughter, who had presumably wit-nessed the methods by which her father's company earned its living, did not blench while Alfred bled the stag. She obviously thought that the Highland ritual after a stalk was woefully inadequate. Her Bavarian ancestors had knelt by their quarry and been ritually blooded and heard the time-honoured '*heil*' intoned above them. Mrs Skutz produced a camera from Alfred's game-bag and insisted on being photographed with one foot and the rifle butt on the dead beast, as she had so often done in what she called 'Tan' and Kenyanga. Ecstatic and garrulous, she watched Alfred as he took off his coat and gralloched the stag. Privately Alfred was thinking that he was

a nice beast though beginning to go back. He and the General
had been close to him the year before above the snow on the
Slomach march, but the mist had robbed them of their shot.

'My white hunter in "Tan" used to leave all that to his
niggers,' he heard, and a moment later, 'That's the hardest
stalk I did in years, Alfred. Why, in Kenyanga we were often
within two hundred yards of the truck. You boys certainly do
it the hard way here.' So she prattled on, the keen blue eyes
fixed on Alfred's sinewy fore-arm, Alfred still with the uneasy
feeling that he had no clothes on.

At last all was accomplished, the gralloch buried, the stag
ready for the pony, and Alfred said, 'You'd best eat your piece,
ma'am, by those rocks. They're out of the wind.' He climbed
higher up the slope and, after glassing Angus and the pony
(both munching quietly below) he waved a red and white
kerchief to and fro and at last saw Angus start to come towards them.

Alfred took his own 'piece' out of an inner pocket and sat
down fifty yards above his employer, who was showing a good
deal of shapely leg and was busy 'making her face'. In Alfred's
world the gentry lunched apart. It was an understood thing
even in the close companionship of a day's stalking.

Mrs Skutz lacked understanding. To her, Alfred was just
another 'white hunter', a very good-looking young man whose
shyness must be overcome. She was still garrulous and ecstatic
at her success and wanted to go inch by inch over the stalk.
She summoned Alfred to sit beside her, offered him a dram, and
overpowered him with her perfume which had lost nothing in
the renewal. As Alfred sat beside her, munching in silence and
crimson with embarrassment, he heard, 'Jesus, Alfie, they told
me you'd gotten yourself medals for valour, but you don't earn
any here, boy! I'm so happy. Kiss me!'

Alfred always drew a mental veil over what followed. He
had contended in his time with Mother Balm, with Bert Mould,
with drunken and dangerous poachers, with venomous young
women who had accused him of rape, with Guards sergeants
and sergeant-majors galore and even with an ex-Prime Minister.

But now, surrounded by thirty thousand acres of deer-forest, he felt with this amorous lady like an eagle in a gin-trap. Her avid lips, her electric eyes, her over-powering perfume and her certainty that this 'nice guy' was just another 'white hunter' too eager to be 'made', filled him with disgust. Into his mind came the memory of Mr Flickerson's shepherd, that crimson-faced bachelor, reputed to have seduced a dozen wives in lonely cottages while their husbands were at work. But he had been surrounded all day with four hundred ewes, which never saw a ram except for six weeks a year.

Alfred broke away angrily from that encounter, wiped a smear of lipstick off his cheek, and felt like Joseph who fled from the wife of Potiphar. He said, 'Angus will be here in a moment' and looked wildly down the hill. He could just see Angus's ancient cap and the back of the pony plodding out of a dip half a mile below. It felt like the Relief of Lucknow.

When he looked down again, the violet eyes had hardened, the shapely white leg was tucked under the skirt and a cold voice said: 'Okay, doughboy, you win! I was going to buy you a tuxedo and some decent clothes and take you out to "Tan" this fall as my private white hunter. But not now! You're the only man that ever passed *me* up!'

Poor Alfred did not know that Helen Skutz had read, in Paris, the unexpurgated French edition of *Lady Chatterley's Lover*, which years later was to make a sensation in the High Court, bishops and schoolgirls alike hailing it as 'a work of art'. Perhaps in that misty moment on the hill, Helen Skutz had seen herself as a Lady Chatterley, if not perhaps to the extent of being pursued, unclothed, up a woodland ride by a brawny game-keeper.

It was lucky for Alfred that at that moment it began to pour with rain. Mrs Skutz said briefly, 'I'm going home,' and set off down the hill. She paid no heed to Alfred's injunction to 'keep west a little, ma'am, and you'll strike the path'. Alfred, perplexed and miserable, waited for Angus and the pony. They loaded and lashed the stag, turned up their coat-collars, and set off for the Big House.

When the stag was in the larder, Alfred sought out Alastair. The old man put down a four-months-old *Times*, took off his spectacles, and smoked in silence, listening to Alfred's tale.

'And dae ye mean to tell me . . . ?' he said at last, like Jove emerging from a cloud of shag.

'It's the truth, Mr Macdonald, and I'm thinking that Mrs Scuts will be getting me the sack.'

'The abandoned wumman! I've never heard the like in a' my life. And to think of her wantin' to take you out to Africa and buy you evening dress and all. Did you ever hear tell of Malcolm Watters that was at Conon one time as second stalker?'

'No.'

'Well, some rich gentleman, just like this wumman, took Malcolm out to foreign parts and gave him braw clothes and made much of him in the verra' same way. It was the ruination of him. He learned to drink and spend money like water and he kept a wee photograph of himself in his braw evening clothes in his house. He got a job beyond Attadale with a great responsibility and a laird away for seven months a year, with stags and saumon laid on at his door. And the polis found him in February, you ken, with five stags in a van, so his laird had to sack him. He's just a crofter now, poor fellow, and far gone in drink! He was as fine a man as you, Alfie, once. It's pitiful. But, by what I read' – the old man waved at the stacks of *The Times* in the corner – 'there's been what they ca' a "general loosening of morrrals". They're in rut as badly as October deer!'

He re-lit his pipe and puffed another fierce cloud and said, 'I'm glad you told me, Alfie. I'll have a word with Mr Ramsay if there's any question of your getting the sack.'

'I don't want to take the hill with Her again,' said Alfred fiercely, 'and that's a fact. And I don't want anyone to sack me not for what I did but what I didn't do. I don't know what to tell my wife.'

'If it was me, Alfie, I'd no say a word. Wummen are aye suspicious.'

Luckily what saved Alfred was the migratory habit of the rich who find it hard to settle in one place for long. On reaching the Big House, Mrs Skutz was annoyed to find her boy friend asleep in bed, with an empty bottle of Glen Grant beside him and in no condition to render her the aid and comfort which she needed. She packed up in a temper, wrote a scorching note for the boy friend when he awoke, and departed by car for Cannes, and the glen knew her no more.

Alfred breathed a deeper sigh of relief than anyone.

XIV

WITH the departure of Mrs Skutz and the General away, the glen settled down for the winter. Alastair retrieved from the Big House a vast bundle of old copies of *The Times* for his winter reading, and passed on to Alfred another earlier bundle. Alfred in his timeless existence did not mind that this 'reading matter' was well over a year old. He had little time for reading till his day's work was done, the cow milked, the chickens shut up, the dogs fed and bedded down, and supper eaten. But an occasional snippet of what had been going on in the great world 'up at London' made him feel that Ross-shire was not too far out of that world.

Once his eye caught a headline: *Clergyman Fined for Egg Collecting.* It was his old acquaintance, the Rev. 'Soapy' Blaxall, who had been fined £1 for stealing eagles' eggs in the Hebrides. He had, it appeared, asked a laird for permission to take certain unprotected eggs of the commoner birds and had readily consented to keep away from the corner of the island which held the eagles' eyrie. On the night before his departure the reverend gentleman called on the laird, stayed to supper, and rose at 3 a.m. next day to remove the eagles' eggs before leaving. He made a spirited attempt in court to blame the laird's own keeper, and seemed to have got off very lightly.

Alfred found his contempt for these kleptomaniacs in Holy Orders rising. In the old days he had accepted them as 'gentry' and therefore unpredictable. How could the Church hold such specimens whose duty it was to instruct their parishioners in honesty and fair dealing? Alfred knew what to do if he met in future years any clergyman on his beat.

The hind-shooting was over. The winter promised to be long and severe. Alfred watched the scattered grouse on the low ground assemble on some young heather which was blown clear of snow and twice parties rose in air and moved off purposefully towards the South at a considerable height. He noted these facts in his diary. It was Bessie who brought him one day from Dingwall a stout cloth-covered book and said, 'Alfie, my man! Why don't you transfair those notes from your wee diary to a proper book?'

Alfred did not understand, but his Bessie was in earnest. 'You're what her Ladyship called in a unique position here. There's no a keeper or a stalker for miles with your learning and the gentry themselves are never on the hill or by the river, except for the shooting and fishing. You're here the year round, and what you see may be no one else will for a century. Write it a' doon and maybe there'll be value in it one day.'

Alfred did not guess that Lady Poynter had been talking to his wife. She took a keen interest in her employees. This unusual young guardsman, with his zest for reading, his memory, his keen eye, and his unrivalled opportunities, might be a second Gilbert White or Charles St John, with greater chances than those worthies ever had.

So night after night, Alfred, ruddy and wind-whipped, would clumsily transcribe into the cloth-bound book the notes made over the years in his little pocket diaries. No one, he felt, would ever read them but what he had seen others had probably never had the luck to see, the movements and nesting habits of grouse, the ways of deer, the crop-contents of ptarmigan, the mating of the dotterel, and the rare glimpses of eagles and falcons taking their prey.

Then the winter shut down relentlessly. The starving deer in the two glens, which met below the Big House, broke down the fences to get at the ricks and Alfred took the hill ponies laden with hay bales to feed them lest they should do lasting damage to trees. The snow was poached with mud by their feet, and they beat dark paths along the hillsides. Alastair, whose rheumatism now worried him, hirpled out to watch them, and was despondent.

'The puir beasties! Those that dinna hunger awa' before spring will blaw their bellies in the first flush of young grass in May, and that'll be the end of *them*! This winter will harm the forest more than three seasons of staiking.'

Alfred realized how Man had forced the deer up beyond their normal feeding limits to a cold white world where there was only subsistence for them in summer. He tracked down in the snow and marked 'for future reference' the dens of local wild cats and hill foxes. He could have trapped them easily to a baited gin, but he hated the thought of such animals struggling, fearful and angry, in the dark, with the last night they would ever see growing colder and more menacing around them until Nature dulled the pain in their mangled limbs and they sank lower in the snow into oblivion and death.

The rest of the glen had no such squeamishness. It had a long tradition of hardship and inhumanity, of hunger and cold, and merciless killings from Glencoe to Culloden and the Clearances. To them, the sufferings of a fox or cat were only what such 'brute beasties' deserved. Some of Alfred's neighbours across the hill would leave traps out all winter and if they 'accounted for' anything before they were frozen, well, that was a bit of good luck, often only realized in the spring.

So during the winter evenings Alfred learned a good deal, which he digested slowly by rumination on the hill. He was free of the library in the Big House and liked to annotate his notes on birds and beasts with what others had observed years before. His own notes were followed by brackets ['see Harvie-Brown in Sutherland in 1886'] or ['C. St John observed this in Morayshire'] or ['see Mr A. S. Leslie in The Field 1912'] for Alfred was no pioneer of knowledge and what other men had recorded in print was to him Holy Writ. He did not dream that one day a generation of young scientists would arise, phoenix-like, from the ashes of their unscientific forebears, and dismiss all that had been written long ago as 'amateur guess-work, unsupported by evidence'.

Once a letter reached Alfred at Christmas from a Guards officer who had stalked with him as the guest of the General; he hoped he was well, and his family, and ended surprisingly: 'You told me once you had a few hundred pounds put away. I am now, as you will see, a partner in a merchant-bank and if you would care to entrust your savings to me I think I could invest them safely for you, and they would double their value in five or six years' time. Think it over carefully and *talk to your wife before you decide*.'

Alfred consulted Bessie. 'He's a nice gentleman and he trusted me when the wind was wrong and there was hinds everywhere and mist ablowen'. I feel I could trust *him* but he says here to ask you.'

'London's a wicked place,' said Bessie, 'and we'd never know what they'd be up to there. And a nice gentleman like that is just the sort they'd skin. But I'm thinking of the wee boy. Perhaps . . . I'd no pit a' your eggs in the one basket. Keep a hundred pounds in the post office.'

So Alfred laboriously counted not only the balance in his savings-bank book, but a lot of crumpled treasury notes and silver stowed away in an ornate chocolate box. (This had been sent one Christmas by the Queen to every man in the Brigade of Guards.) To his surprise they came to over £513, so he sent 400 guineas to London and hoped for the best.

And as the winter dragged on, Alfred, indoors more than usual, had time to appreciate his own wife. She was always cheerful though she never seemed to stop work, cooking, baking, mending, knitting jerseys and stockings, and forever making some improvement in the comfort of her spotless home. Her cheeks and hair shone with health, and she never had that worried, fretful look which he had seen on the faces of his mother, Mrs Balm, Mrs Mould and other 'housewives' he had encountered. If Bessie was tired or irritated or flustered, she never said so and Alfred realized his luck, and how much 'a good wife' who did not nag counted in the life of a game-keeper.

He had known, ever since the Tibberton days, of game-keepers who wrangled unceasingly with their wives, or whose wives could never 'get on' with their neighbours in the village. Some keepers were always changing their jobs, because 'the wife' could not 'settle down' or hated the house she was living in.

In front of Alfred, who had little time for reflection, life seemed to stretch for ever in the same rustic backwater, eventless, as devoid of incident as that of a sheep or cow. He did not mind. He had helped to make history long ago as a Guardsman, but now was well content to let the main current sweep by, to watch young Ian growing up, every day stronger and more self-reliant.

XV

BUT Alfred's eventless life was soon to end. Rumours drifted round the ice-locked glens, of a new gang that was living by poaching over an immense area. They were more formidable than the Kessock Gang, whom Alfred had routed, and contained one of its old members. Somewhere on the Moray Firth was a gloomy building in which they converted their venison carcases into dog-meat. But the gang themselves lived, among fellow clansmen, in a hamlet commanding the few roads running west from Dingwall and Inverness; they used three motorvans equipped with skid-chains and spotlights and had repeating rifles, some even said a Lewis gun; and they ravaged the starving deer from Aultbeg to Lochearn.

Tales reached Alfred's ears, of hinds butchered, half a dozen at a time, at night along the roads, of stalkers and constables cowering under a sweep of machine-gun bullets, of police-patrols laughed at when they stopped vehicles for inquiry. There was at that time no close-season for red deer and its preservation came under no Act of Parliament.

Nobody knew where the next raid would fall. The gang

struck without warning, lay low for days, then struck again thirty miles away. They left behind grisly relics of their passing in badly wounded hinds, forlorn yearlings or calves, and un-buried limbs and grallochs. A tale drifted round of a hill-farmer being shot at at night when he came to his door to see what was happening. The gang boasted that it cleared £150 a week but its members drove their cars into Dingwall to draw 'unemployment pay'. Nobody outside the glens seemed to know or care, and it was whispered that the police, or petty officialdom, must be in league with the poachers. Alfred felt that if only the 'old General' was back, instead of recuperating in Majorca, something would be done.

'Mind, Bessie,' he said, 'if there's shooting at night in *this* glen and I'm out, you'll stay snug in the house. As the General said, you're not paid to go after poachers.'

Bessie's lips set. 'It's no right, Alfie, and it's a sin and a disgrace, such goings-on! I'm thinkin' of the puir beasts, starving and bleeding in the snow.'

'We'll get them,' said Alfred valiantly, though without con-viction. 'They'll be sorry one day, like them rogues from Kessock.'

Months went by after the tales had swept the glens before anything was heard locally of the Ardfin gang. Indeed, Alfred began to think he had taught the Kessock men such a lesson that they were unlikely to come back for more, even with other companions. But all one day he felt uneasy. An iron-grey snow cloud hung over the glen, the east wind whipped viciously off the frozen hills, and there was menace in the air. He put down the hay for the deer in sheltered places hidden from either road but he was still uneasy. He had often had such a feeling in the war and he felt sure wild animals had similar forebodings of trouble to come. He had watched from afar an old stag lie day after day on the same sheltered slope but on the morning Alfred took 'a gentleman' after him, he would have moved elsewhere. Alfred had never been taught anything about telepathy but it was as if his own thoughts about that beast had somehow been transmitted to the deer's mind.

That night after tea he put on a great black duffle coat, put a torch in his pocket and kissed Bessie.

'I'm away up the other glen. Now if anything happens you abide in here. I don't think they'll come and surelie they'll never dare take the road past this house.'

She looked up at him and said: 'You'll tak' the old dog, Alfie?' Her brown eyes were anxious.

'No, he's cut his off-fore badly on the ice. He'll be whooly lame if I work him with a foot like that.'

Alfred went down the glen, past the Big House policies and over the stone bridge up the other glen. He looked at his watch, nearly eight o'clock. He would wait among the young trees in the 'new plantation' for a couple of hours and then go home to his bed. Bessie would be there soon, with young Ian warm already in his little room alongside. Alfred suddenly found himself wondering if Ian would ever become a gamekeeper, a thankless, lonely, never-ending task which took you out at all hours and in all weathers, watching your 'responsibility' while more sensible folk lolled at home. He climbed the wire into the young plantation, and sat on his game-bag under a great rock round which the deer had beaten a path through the snow. The snow cloud had passed on and it was a brilliant night of stars. Below him on the road he could hear the click and rustle of passing deer and he knew by the sounds that others were busy at the hay above the plantation fence. They were too hungry to mind if they winded him. Every sound was magnified in the stillness, from the sigh of a fir branch as it released its load of snow, to the nibbling of a vole in some cranny behind the rock. An owl called forlornly from the beeches behind the Big House.

The clock in the stable yard struck ten. The Ardfin gang would never come tonight – twenty miles or more on snow-bound roads. He would wait another half hour and then go home, have a sup of the hot stew Bessie always left for him, and creep beside her into the bed she was by now warming. His cheeks burning in the intense cold, Alfred wrapped his cloak more firmly about him. His eyes almost closed. He pulled himself together but soon nodded off again.

He woke with a start. The sound of a shot away to the east was followed by the half-hour chime of the stable clock. Then a fusillade of shots rang out a mile away. They came from up the other glen, beyond the Big House, beyond his own cottage. The beggars! They had sneaked up the other glen after all, under what should have been his own nose! Another four shots rang out in quick succession.

Alfred could hear the rush of deer above him, as he seized his game bag and stumbled through the snow, slipping and swearing on the icy road. He crossed the bridge and looking up the eastern glen could see half a mile or more up, a spotlight directed on the hillside. That meant the gang had done their slaughtering and were guiding their comrades as they dragged the deer carcases to the road.

Hot with rage, Alfred stumbled up the road. He heard a sound and stopped. Something was approaching. He flashed his torch and a wounded stag with its broken fore-leg swinging across its chest stopped and limped aside into the alder, its blood staining the snow. Even in the dark, Alfred could recognize that switchhorn, an ailing beast which was so badly bullied by its peers that it spent its time round Alfred's tiny croft.

Alfred marked the spot where it had disappeared and hurried on up the road. He heard a shot and then another. A car with dimmed sidelights was racing towards him. He stood in the middle of the road, wondering if they would run him down or shoot him and leave his body in the snow. Instead, the car swerved abruptly into the open gate of the Big House and roared down the back drive, which wound through acres of rhododendrons and emerged half a mile on by a lodge on the Dingwall road. Perhaps the gang had been lurking there while Alfred was walking down to the big bridge two hours before, or 'those Frasers' had let them in later.

It was useless chasing the car. Alfred, hot and angry, stumbled on. He reached his cottage-gate at last and saw lamplight behind the thin curtains. Thank goodness, Bessie had stayed inside! Behind the house Drifter was barking furiously. Alfred pushed the gate open and suddenly tripped over something. Cursing, he raised his torch, as he sprawled. Bessie lay on her face beneath him with a dark pool spreading over the snow from her throat.

Alfred turned her over. He had seen too many dead people in the war to make any mistake. He lifted her body and forced his way into the house and laid her gently on the tattered sofa. His mind had totally ceased to function. All he could think of was that she had disobeyed him and had come out to take the number of the marauding car. At long last a poaching gang had had their revenge on Alfred.

XVI

THE rest of that night was a blur to Alfred, even in memory. He recalled afterwards a few things like moving a saucepan of stew which was boiling over on the stove, and thinking with a pang that his Bessie, whom he had imagined to be lying warm in bed, had really been dressed and preparing food against his own return. If only . . . but if only was no good now! Bessie had rushed down to the gate to take the number of that accursed car and walked into a stray bullet.

He looked at young Ian, still rosily asleep, took his torch, released the raging Drifter from his kennel and started down the glen for help. Alastair had been asleep long before the firing started and was not easily woken. But he clumped down the stairs at last, a towering tousled figure in home-made slippers and a vast coaching-coat which had belonged to the Colonel's grandfather.

'Deid?' he kept muttering: 'the poor wee woman, I never did!' and he looked incredulously at her blood on Alfred's coat.

'She's dead,' said Alfred grimly, 'and their car went away through the policies down the back drive. It's that bloody murdering Ardfin gang and they'll be in their beds by now. We must telephone the police from the Big House.'

At last they awakened Murdoch, the aged boiler-man who slept in the basement, and after a struggle they got through to the police on the telephone and sat down to wait for an unending procession of motors into the quiet glen, police and a police-surgeon from Dingwall, an ambulance, the fiscal's clerk, even

a reporter, and finally the Chief Constable himself. (Alfred
had not known such a commotion since a day when he had
been loading for Captain Darty, and the local member of
Parliament had shot an Earl painfully amidships, and had
gone to unparalleled lengths to avoid publicity.)

But now he himself was 'mazed' in a stupor of sorrow and
bewilderment, which no sympathy could lessen. He answered
questions mechanically, signed his name to a police statement,
and bore the wondering Ian, wrapped in blankets, to the house
of the herd's wife, where there were children of his own age.

The Chief Constable, who arrived after dawn, turned out
to be a close friend of Sir Jocelyn and an ex-Seaforth Highlander. He was unexpectedly kind and helpful. 'I'll cable the
General,' he said, 'I'm sure he'll be very sorry indeed, but he
ought to know at once. And if I were you, Blowers, I'd get your
little boy away from here for a bit,' and after questioning
Alfred, he promised to telephone Lord Inverarn at Glenovil
and arrange for Bessie's married sister to come over and take
Ian back to Glenovil.

It was 2 p.m. before Alfred was free, and then he remembered the wounded stag, the switchhorn with the swinging
foreleg, which had crossed the road the night before. Poor
beast, he could hardly have gone far in that condition! Alfred
took his rifle and Drifter, and together they followed a blood
trail for three hundred yards into the thickets beside the river.
They found the stag at last, couched miserably beneath a tree
and Alfred killed him mercifully as he struggled to rise from
the blood-stained snow.

Alfred dragged the carcase to the roadside and then followed
the gang's wheel-tracks up the glen. He found where three
deer carcases had been towed down the hill and slung into the
car. He found another hind limping miserably uphill in a
stupor of pain with three bullets in her flank and belly and
shot her, while his wrath against the Ardfin 'butchers' rose to
the boil. If one of them had appeared in the glen, Alfred would
have killed him without compunction and risked a hanging.

In the last of the light he tramped uphill and sprang a line

of fox-snares, for he would have little chance to visit them in
the next few days, and, though a gamekeeper, he was unusually
humane even to vermin.

And then in the dusk he came home to find that the herd's
wife, Mrs McLean, had cleaned up the bloodstains on his
floor and made up his fire and even milked the cow. Alfred
shut up the hens, fed Drifter and resolutely faced the dreadful
emptiness of the house. And all the time his thoughts were of
Bessie, his rosy-cheeked Bessie, who had loved him and cared
for him day and night for years, lying now, white and stiff
on a slab in a mortuary, peered at by doctors. Alfred had all a
Suffolk countryman's innate reserve about death. The Celts
'waked' and paraded their dead to the last minute. They took
a weird pleasure in the sight of a body. But Alfred in the War
had seen much death and buried too many men darkly at dead
of night. And his mind flew back to Tibberton Church and
'old Robert', stumping up the chancel to give the village a
piece of his mind about Alfred's own mother: 'She hath done
what she could.' Bessie, his Bessie, had also done what she
could, and it was much more than she need have done, and
now he had to 'face the naked days' without her.

The inquest was over at last and Alfred turned a guardsman's
wooden face towards the sympathy of the fiscal and his jury.
Bessie's death had created widespread indignation in the glens
for though no word was said above a whisper about the Ardfin
gang, everyone knew of them and disliked starving deer being
butchered in winter by the roadside. There was even an editor
at the funeral, from Dingwall, and a young detective in plain
clothes (though he looked every inch a policeman) and a huge
wreath from the General and Lady Poynter, with a card which
made Alfred blink and which he abstracted and hid for years
among his intimate belongings. The whole glen came to the
funeral, even 'those Frasers', one of whom, Alfred felt certain,
had been secretly in league with the Ardfin gang.

Then at last Alfred returned to the drear cottage which had
once been his cheerful home. He put old blankets on the floor
and promoted Drifter from the kennel to be his companion.

For the first time he realized all that Bessie had been to him and also the truth of what Angus Ogilvie had said years before about 'a good wife being half the battle in a keeper's life'. For a keeper's work was never done and to come in, cold and wet, after a day on the hill, and find the fire out, the chickens unfed and the cow unmilked, and to restart from scratch his domestic life which had gone so smoothly, was a burden he felt he could not face.

So Alfred sold the cow and the hens and decided to lay in a stock of tinned stores and flour which would only need renewing every six months. The stalkers and shepherds on outlying forests far up the strath, sometimes twenty miles from a village, prided themselves on being independent of shops. Cut off for weeks by heavy snow or other calamity, they were secretly proud of their isolation and to 'run short' was a confession of weakness. Knowing these things, Alfred took three sacks and arranged with the factor to 'lift' him in to Dingwall one day.

By chance he did not put on his best keepering clothes but a dark tweed suit which Mrs Darty had given him, and some brown shoes, and in these and a tweed cap he looked, except for his weather-beaten cheeks, most unlike a keeper. He bestowed his sacks in the boot of the factor's car, and dropped into a small inn for some beer and bread and cheese. Nobody in the little ale-house gave the tall man a glance, for he was obviously a Sassenach.

The only occupants of the bar were two men, a tall Aberdonian and a shorter man, who were talking to the shirt-sleeved barman. Alfred, munching his bread and cheese at a table in the corner, heard the barman say 'Hamish? Aye, he was in the morn, to draw his unemployment pay.' He said this with disdain. 'He looks ill, and I'm no surprised. He's never been the same mon since last month.'

'And sairve the wee bastard richt,' said the Aberdonian. 'I couldna thole wee Hamish boasting of his making fufty pound a week, and hiding his cawr when he sneaked in to draw the Dole.'

'They're a daft lot on the Council.' The other man might

have been from Glasgow, 'they're like the Arrmy, never let their richt hand ken what their left is daein'. And dae ye mean to say wee Hamish was luftin' fifty pound a week oot o' *them*?' He pointed to a stag's antlers on the wall.

The barman gave him a warning circular glance which embraced the corner where Alfred sat, munching, with his cap over his eyes but all ears. 'Aye, but last month frichtened them badly. They're a' unemployed now and a good job too, though it's bad for my trade.'

Alfred had listened keenly though with his wooden mask on and his eyes on the ceiling as he munched. But his mind was alert. The only person he had ever visualized as 'lifting £50 a week' was Mrs Skutz, and she, so Alfred had been told, was a meat-packer's daughter. He waited to hear more but the other men in the bar turned the conversation to shinty.

Later that afternoon the factor, as they drove home, said, 'I had a talk with the police inspector today, Blowers, about your, er, case. They haven't got much farther with the investigation. They're pretty sure the man who fired the fatal shot was a small man called Hamish Macbean, but he disappeared for three whole days from his village and they could pin nothing on him. One thing we can all be thankful for! That Ardfin gang's had a fright and closed down for a bit.'

Alfred said nothing though he was thinking hard. 'Wee Hamish'. So that was definitely his name! Alfred would have liked to put a curse on him, as a 'wise woman' in Suffolk had once done on young Jimmy Norton. (They had asked Mother Owles to investigate a case of 'perloining' wheat from the granary and, after a suitable retirement and the recitation of magic runes, she announced that the thief would have 'a horn agrowen' out of his skull' within a week. That was on Monday. On Wednesday morning Jimmy Norton, ashen-faced and trembling, had confessed about the thefts to the farmer. There had been no horn visible on his head, but he could 'feel it agrowen'.')

Alfred was not vindictive in the ordinary way. But now he found himself hoping that Hamish Macbean, nursing his guilty secret about Bessie's death, would have a horn, or a cancer, growing out of him somewhere, in that miraculous way in which a stag's antlers sprouted from zero in the summer. He said nothing, but hatred consumed him. He spent night after night lying out on the hills in the hopes that the Ardfin gang would make another raid. If they did, Hamish would find someone waiting for him.

XVII

THE winter wore away gradually. The grouse came back to the low ground and at the end of March the first greenshanks. Alfred watched one morning a skein of greylags gabbling over towards Sutherland high in air. Once he would have looked forward to the summer and noted down all these events in his journal, but with Bessie's death the spring in every sense had gone out of his life. So many things no longer seemed 'worth while', and he went about his tasks with a set, stricken look, though he was as conscientious as ever about them. Beneath his malaise was a rankling hatred of the Ardfin gang and their leader, the trigger-happy Hamish Macbean. The gang had gone into retirement and there had been no word in the glens of further raids. But everyone expected that they would start operations again, as soon as the salmon were running in the rivers south of the Kyle.

Alfred plodded on, rising at dawn to cook his breakfast and eating a supper out of tins long after dark. The General came back, his rib healed, his cough gone, though he looked older and frail. Neither he nor Lady Poynter said much to the tongue-tied Alfred though they asked many questions about him in the glen.

One evening Alfred was called to 'the business room', told to sit down and given a dram. Then the General suddenly said, 'Alfred, I feel you've, er, got rather a dislike of this, er, place, and I don't blame you!'

'Well, sir, it ain't been the same to me since last February and that's a fact!'

'Exactly! I can understand. And there's another thing worrying me. If ever those Ardfin chaps turn up again, I'm scared of what you might do to them!'

There was a grim smile on Alfred's face. 'I wouldn't be whooly sure meself, sir!'

'Just what I guessed. Now, I'm Lord Lieutenant and I can't afford a killing by one of my own employees on my own land, however well deserved. See?'

His eye, kindly but firm, rested on Alfred.

'Sir.'

'I got you up here for a special job and you've done it most ably. And it might be two years before the Kessock lot, or the Ardfin lot, or whoever the beggars are, worry us again. But would you like a change? I'd give you a very good reference and explain why you were leaving. What about Lord Inverarn at Glenovil?'

'I'd be thinking too much of Bessie there, General. We met first at his Lordship's and we was married there.'

'You're probably right. Anyway, I'll make you out the character and Mr Ramsay will send an advertisement to *The Field* and *The Scotsman*. It's the wrong time of year for changing keepers but you never know who may want one. Goodnight, Alfred, and cheer up!'

In a week two advertisements appeared in print inviting replies to a box number and stating that 'An able-bodied keeper seeks single-handed post. Excellent references.' There were only two replies because the first of February was the traditional Scottish date for changing keepers and stalkers. To one reply, from the estate office of a nobleman in Morayshire, Sir Jocelyn said firmly, 'No! I wouldn't recommend my worst enemy to go there, Ramsay. He's been on the bottle for years and the place is in almost as big a mess. It wouldn't be fair on Alfred.'

But over the other reply, typed from a hotel address in Peeblesshire, whose owner wanted a grouse-keeper, Sir Jocelyn thought hard and sent for Alfred again.

'It's not exactly what I'd hoped for you, Alfred, but you'll be on your own and independent. This gentleman runs a shooting and fishing hotel on the Tweed, and his biggish grouse moors are quite well-known, the Brinewell moors, seventeen miles away from him. I used to know his father. He's almost the first chap in Scotland to provide shooting and fishing for paying guests. There'll probably be big tips in the season and you might have some chance of training dogs, but you'll probably have a rum lot of guns to compete with.'

'And why,' asked Alfred, 'is the job going at all, sir, at this time o' year?'

'Well,' Sir Jocelyn peered at the letter through his spectacles, 'I'd say his late keeper either went in a hurry, or got the sack. Mr Henderson'll pay your expenses down for you to have a look at each other and you can see what you think of the place. And remember one thing: a hotel job is a frontier show, and to run a frontier show you've got to have your resignation in your pocket the whole time!'

So after a journey south and three nights in Peeblesshire, Alfred agreed to 'take on' as keeper with Mr Colin Henderson. Mr Henderson was a very fat man of about fifty with heavy ears, small eyes and an inquiring nose. He had spent ten years in Burma with a teak firm, and seemed to his contemporaries to have passed most of that time shooting big game or fishing for mahseer. Then his father had died and Colin succeeded to his hotel. A friend in the Burma Forest Service, who had noticed Colin's resemblance to an elephant, had nicknamed him 'The Hathi' which had been corrupted into 'Hearty' by those who knew no Urdu. 'Hearty Henderson' and his foibles were now a byword among scores of fishing and shooting guests from England and the Continent. 'He's just like an elephant,' the forest officer had once said, 'you never know when he's going to charge.' 'Or what he's going to charge you with,' put in his wife, mindful of past squabbles over bills and dogs.

Alfred's interview with the 'Hearty' took place on a Sunday, in a very small office which Mr Henderson seemed to fill. His black-haired wife sat in a corner rather consciously posed sideways, as someone had told her she had a good profile. Henderson studied the letter of reference again and again, as if it was Greek, rumbling and grunting to himself.

He looked up suddenly and in a throaty voice said, 'This is a very good testimonial, Blowers, from Sir Jocelyn. What went wrong?'

'Nothing, sir!' said the startled Alfred.

'Well, nobody gives anyone a character like that *unless he's very anxious to get him out of his cottage or off the place.*' He turned his little eyes on Alfred again as if about to charge.

A slow flush rose on Alfred's wind-reddened cheeks. The wording of the reference was too good to be believed! Alfred was not going to curry sympathy by mentioning Bessie's death. It had never occurred to him that people ever gave a man a good character *in order to be rid of him.* He said slowly: 'I got on well, sir, with Sir Jocelyn and also with Her Ladyship. We never had a cross word and they trusted me. If yew think that letter is more than the truth, you'd best ring them up and ask!'

Alfred was aware of a pair of bright dark eyes regarding him from the corner where Mrs Henderson sat patting her hair. She said with a queer enunciation: 'You are not then married, Mister Blars? Were you wonce?'

'Once, ma'am.'

'And where is your wife now?' The accent was so ladylike that even Alfred felt instinctively this was no lady.

'In her grave, ma'am.'

Most of the few women of Alfred's acquaintance would have mumbled an apology for putting that last question but not Mrs Henderson. To her, Alfred was 'staff', or at least fodder for staff, and as such unworthy of normal consideration.

9

They discussed the conditions of Alfred's service. He was to be in charge of 12,000 acres single-handed with a cottage, a suit of clothes, so much coal and an allowance for dog meat and cartridges. Nothing was said about transport, for in those days a keeper was expected to get about his beat, however extensive, on his feet or a bicycle. Equally, there was no question of overtime, or help in heather-burning.

Alfred went back to Ross-shire to collect his belongings. He spent £70 of his savings on a 30 cwt. truck with skid chains, though he was more than doubtful if Mr Henderson would recoup him for his petrol, and still more doubtful if he himself could 'stand it' for more than a season. But he was sure that an unmechanized keeper on 12,000 acres was inefficient, especially if there were poachers.

He soon realized how little his predecessor had done in the last year. There did not appear to be grit on the moor, no burning seemed to have been attempted that spring, and the butts and paths to them were in all stages of decay. Crows were everywhere and Alfred could only guess at the foxes on the moor. He settled down dourly to overtake the arrears of keepering which his predecessor had left. His efforts were not helped by Mr Henderson who, being a late riser and of a suspicious nature due to the fact that he was his own best customer in the bar, would ring him up after breakfast and wonder darkly all day why Alfred did not reply. As Alfred had usually been on one of his beats since 7.30 a.m. and occasionally earlier still, Mr Henderson's suspicions were apt to swell uncontrollably.

But Colin Henderson was usually too busy fishing in summer to pay surprise visits to the moor, and between mid-November and mid-July he left things largely to nature and his keeper. Having sent over two young Labradors for training, Colin thought he had done quite enough to ensure the success of the next grouse-season.

One visit Alfred did receive, on a June evening, was from Mrs Henderson. She had been lunching in another glen and instructed to leave Alfred's pay packet and a message on her way home. Alfred had been for eleven hours on the moor and was not best pleased at finding her waiting there when he came home.

'Oh, there you are, Blars,' said the stilted voice. 'I've been here half an hour. Mr Henderson was trying to telephone you all morning.'

'I was away at half after six, ma'am, and I ain't been home since.'

'Indeed! Where?'

'On Wanlokelaw. I been butting all day.'

The dark eyes peered curiously into the back of Alfred's truck. It held the two puppies, some fencing posts, a dead fox-cub, Alfred's gun, a spade and other tools. Alfred felt instinctively that both the Hendersons suspected he had been away to Edinburgh or roystering in some inn. He unlocked the door and said, 'Go in, ma'am, if you'd care to. I'll just get these puppies into their kennel.'

He was tired and hungry and the puppies were too. Damn all employers and their wimmenfolk! was his unspoken thought.

When he got indoors, the fire was stoked up, the kettle was on and Mrs Henderson was examining Alfred's photographs on the dresser. The dark eyes seemed everywhere.

'How do you keep such a good fire when you've been out all day, Blars?'

'Mrs Scott next door comes in and makes it up for me every day about five o'clock time. I don't usually get back till six.' (Alfred thought: 'That's huffed you, you nosey besom.')

'Oh, how nice for you and of her! I hope you'll make me a cup of tea, Blars. I've had *such* a long drive.'

'Why surelie, ma'am, but I'll just ha' to feed my young dogs first. They ain't had anything since sun-up and they're a-growen.' Alfred turned imperturbably to this task.

He came back from the kennel. The lady was peering into a cupboard which held a teapot and crockery. 'What a naice pattern,' she said patronizingly. 'Where did you come by it?'

'Lord Inverarn gave it to us as a wedding present.'

'What, old Smiler Inverarn? You were under *him*? When?'

'No, ma'am, I went to His Lordship's to load for my Master before the war and met my wife who worked for him.' Alfred knew he was saying too much. With every word he was giving ammunition to this dark-eyed creature, whom he instinctively distrusted as a dog does a cat.

'Your wife died, Blars? What of?'

'She was shot and killed, ma'am, by deer-poachers. That was in the papers. I don't care to talk of it, even now.'

(Shut up you bloody fule, you, an inner voice in broad Suffolk warned Alfred. She don't know narthen, and them wimmen can always get a thing wrong arterwards. The next you'll be hearing is that you shot your own wife.)

The curiously unemotional dark eyes bored into him. 'Tell *me*, Blars. I would not repeat it to a soul.'

'I'd rather not, ma'am,' and Alfred buried his face in a tea-cup firmly.

There was a silence. Mrs Henderson rose. She was not used to such obstinate young men. She said, 'Here's your wages, Blars, and how did you break the door of that stove?'

This time, Alfred let her have it. 'That, ma'am? Why, that was done afore ever I come here and you promised me to have it mended months ago.'

'Did I? I don't remember.'

No, you wouldn't, thought Alfred. He rapidly turned over the notes in his wages envelope. 'And,' he added, 'Mr Henderson promised me the very same time he'd let me have £5 towards the cost of my getting down here. I ain't seen that yet.'

'I know nothing of that, Blars. You'd better speak to Mr Henderson personally.'

'I wouldn't ha' worried you, ma'am, if I hadn't spoke to him twice, *and* no result.'

Mrs Henderson did not exactly flounce out but Alfred's keen eye noticed that her breasts, in his own words, were joggling up and down beneath her thin frock. With her it was a sign of indignation but Alfred, the unlettered guardsman, was reminded of two ferrets fighting inside a bag. He went indoors to finish his tea, sure that he had said too much and got nowhere; nor would he have been comforted if he had heard Mrs Henderson's account to Colin on her return.

'That young Blars may give us more trouble than he's worth. His cooker door is badly broken and he had the cheek to say it was done *before* he arrived.'

This took time to get through the 'Hearty's' ear-drum into his brain. Luckily he had among other elephantine qualities an elephant's memory, and he never forgot anything that could be used to other people's disadvantage. 'I told you,' he rumbled, 'to get that bloody thing mended before he came. Why wasn't it, Lobby?'

Lobelia Henderson was near to tears. 'You men *always* stand up for each other!' she moaned, 'and if it comes to that, Blars swears you promised him a fiver towards his expenses in getting down here?'

The 'Hearty' rumbled. 'I believe I did,' he grunted at last. 'Tears were the strongest gun in a woman's battery' so someone had once said, and counter-battery work was indicated. 'But *you're* supposed to keep my wages' book, Lobby. Look it up, can't you?'

At that moment the telephone bell rang. Someone was arriving within an hour to buy a dog and in the thrills of this transaction Alfred's £5 and his cooking-stove were forgotten by both combatants. In fact Alfred only got the latter mended much later by meeting in the local inn a travelling plumber, at work on the cooler of a neighbouring farm-dairy. Having served aforetime in the Guards he promised to 'sorrt it' at Alfred's expense.

Alfred went on dourly over-taking the arrears of work on the moor, conscious that he had antagonized his employer's wife. What worried him more than Lobelia Henderson's enmity was that there seemed very few grouse on the moor. The shepherds assured him that there had been too large a stock left in the previous year which a succession of inexperienced shooting-visitors had failed to thin down. In the January snows certain hillsides, blown clear of drifts, had been 'black with birrds' but they had gradually disappeared before the snow went. Neither

Alfred nor the shepherds had come across many dead birds in spring, and it seemed to be one of those cases where there had been not disease but a large scale local movement of grouse to some moor with better feeding. Alfred's predecessor had probably done too little burning in that time, and he had certainly omitted to put down grit. Alfred was now reaping the fruits of earlier neglect. He would have to face an inquisition when his employer turned his attention from the salmon-river to the moor.

All over England and Scotland rich people, who had not seen a grouse since the previous October, were confidently looking forward to shooting them in August and September. They made an orderly migration northwards year after year to do so. Only Alfred who had been 'keeping' grouse faithfully since April, feared the prospect of 'taking the lid off his moors', dreading what he would find on them.

XVIII

BY chance Lady Poynter had come south to attend a wedding and was staying with a marquess who happened to be a cousin. She suddenly decided a day after this conversation to break her journey home and lunch at the Tweedside Hotel.

When she came in and was told that 'larnch' would be in fifteen minutes, Lobelia Henderson happened to be in charge of the ornate bar-parlour. (In this, her guests were always expected to gather before a meal and at any other time when they could be induced to.) 'Lobby' Henderson was not in the best of tempers because in addition to the 'brush-off' she had received from Alfred (and she had derived little satisfaction from relating the incident to Colin), she had had a row with a guest, who pointed out a mistake of £5 in a bill, and another with her head housekeeper.

She summed up the elderly woman in the worn tweed skirt and the old-fashioned hair-do as an impecunious colonel's lady on passage, especially when she ordered tomato-juice in a quiet diffident voice. Lobelia could be exceedingly 'refeened' and patronizing and something made her put her best accent forward. Lady Poynter, sipping her tomato-juice, wondered if this creature's diction came from elocution lessons imposed on the accents of Wigan or was some obscure brand of 'chi chi'. At last she ventured: 'Haven't you a gamekeeper here called Alfred Blowers?' for she was fond of Alfred and wished him well in his new job.

'Oh, Blars, yes, wee have, for ower sins!'

'Really? And how's he getting on?'

'Not up to much,' said Lobby, thinking viciously of that tea-party the night before. Caution forsook her. 'The old fool who gave him his reference must either have been gaga or very anxious to get rid of him!'

Lady Poynter flushed, on the verge of a retort. Then she stubbed out her cigarette firmly and thought, 'This affected ninny hasn't a clue who I am and I won't "pull my rank" on her as most women would.'

The other occupant of the bar saved the situation. Hugo Barnet was a charming inebriate who came to the hotel ostensibly to fish every year, but after about two days, especially if the weather was bad, he spent most of the time in a rather fumbly dream, drinking effortlessly at all hours and recovering upstairs from extra potions out of bottles hidden in his suit-cases. Lobby liked him because, apart from the profits he brought the bar, she had a shrewd idea that he was 'well-connected'. His snippets of gossip about certain great houses of Scotland and their inmates were always illuminating. He now removed his nose from the glass, wiped his moustache, turned, and with difficulty focused the other occupant of the bar. Then his face lit up and he said, 'Marcia! My *dear*, whatever brings *you* here?' The pair shook hands warmly.

'Just passing through, Hugo. I've been to the Latheron wedding. I'm one of the girl's godmothers.'

'Staying at Bowlaw, I imagine? And how's the noble marquess?'

'Bulgy? Broker than ever but in very fair order, considering. Are you lunching with me, Hugo?'

Lobby had listened to this conversation with the keenest attention. Being in some ways stupid, it never occurred to her that this woman might be the wife of the 'old fool' whose keeper she had just been slandering. Only after Lady Poynter had departed she discovered her name from Hugo Barnet and as a result, being the snob she was, she treated Alfred ever after-wards less intolerantly. One remark in particular stuck. Hugo Barnet had said: 'By what Marcia Poynter tells me, the marquess hasn't got many grouse this year. His keeper's un-commonly despondent though it isn't disease. His moors march with yours, don't they?'

Lobby, with a hotel fully booked up with grouse-shooters for August and September, decided to say nothing to Colin about this. Colin would either say he was fully aware of it already or that it was totally irrelevant. Colin was like that.

Alfred plodded on with his butting; so far his employer had asked him nothing about grouse prospects. It came, how-ever, to his ears that Colin Henderson had told fishing visitors that he expected 'a very good grouse-year', as they'd left an 'excellent stock' and May and June had been astonishingly mild. Alfred rarely encountered other keepers. Indeed, on one side was an unkeepered area while the other neighbouring keepers lived miles away. But one evening on his way home, he en-countered on the road an immense red-bearded man with a setter and a Labrador coupled together and keeper written all over him. Alfred was glad to stop.

'I'm Roderick Duncan from Braehills,' said the red-bearded man, scrutinizing him keenly before he shook hands. 'You'll be the new mon at Brinewell? Have you got any groose?'

'A few,' admitted Alfred, 'but nothing like what they told me when I came.'

'Ah, I never see'd the like of this in years! The muir was black with groose in the snow but they've no hungered awa': they've flee'd and I saw them flee. Last autumn the marquess was ill and tho' I told him there was too mony birrds, he only shot ae day in October and never went near the muir after! It's hap-pened before when there's too big a stock for the heather but never as bad as this. There's times when they sicken and dee, and ye can pick them up in spring all ower the muir. And there's times they just gang awa'. The marquess was no pleased when I tellit him he canna shoot mair than three days. And your boss, Henderson, with his Sassenachs and furriners paying big money to shoot, what will *he* do?'

'He'll blame me, I reckon,' said Alfred, with a guardsman's

cynicism. 'He says grouse never move more than a mile from where they're bred.'

'Is the muckle sumph ever on a muir except in the autumn and then the middle o' the day? There was a wee sciencer from Aberdeen veesited me ae year, and to hear him you'd have thocht keepers were a' fou, and blind as well! And he told the marquess later you couldna gang by what ony keeper said and there wasna ony "eevidence" o' this and that. And if ever I saw the groose fleeing off a moor it wasna due to hunger or ony ither urge, but there was an eagle driving them if you looked for it. Eagles! On Tweedside! Eevidence! If you're a sciencer, nae mon can say ye're fou. It's as bad as saying God's fou!'

'I reckon I'll be in trouble come the Twelfth,' said Alfred. By this time both men were sitting on the wall beside the road.

'Aye! It's a' the keepers' fault every time. But with you, mon, who only cam' in April, it'll be Craw Laing's fault. We'll admeet he bauchled his burrnin' and there was nae grit. His birrds used to flee over to my heather or come doon on the roads for grit. But for a' that his birrds went and so did mine. Alan Bothwell on the Low Muir is in despair. I've got a few groose on yon fell' (he pointed across the glen) 'but no what I ocht to have.'

'Nor me,' said Alfred, thinking of the miles he had tramped and the few grouse he had encountered.

Alfred drove on, thinking he had made an ally of long experience in that region whose word might carry weight. Had he known how Hearty Henderson and Roderick Duncan had fought over trifles in the last twenty years, he might have been less optimistic!

Alfred never forgot his first day's shoot on 'the Twelfth'. To the guns assembled from France, America, the Bahamas, and four different English counties, 'the Twelfth' was a social event like Ascot or the Grand National. 'No one who was anyone' would miss it. To Colin Henderson it marked his richest harvest when he could charge a succession of guests three

hundred guineas for eight days' shooting, guests who would
fill his bar with laughter and drink his wines with their dinner
and worry about nothing until their bags were packed, their
cars ready to go and their bills ready for settlement. He could
count on some rich gossip, three or four new stories, and hun-
dres of pounds in the bank. And if the grouse had done badly,
there was always something to blame: bad burning weather
in March, a May frost, torrential rains in July, or disease
spread by neighbouring moors. And the supply of trusting
Southerners, whatever the season's prospects, never went short.
Colin Henderson had been meaning since June to go up to the
moor and have a series of long walks with his dogs, but that
day had never come. It had either rained or the river looked
right for fishing, or he had rheumatism, or someone wrote
from Paris or New York for a gun-dog. (And the selection,
price-fixing and cataloguing of the dog's virtues was a matter
of anxious parley between Colin and his lowland keeper,
George Goddard. There was one good thing about dog-
coping, as opposed to horse-coping. They could not bargain
about prices at several hundred miles range; there was no
warranty of soundness; and if the dog's manners were not all
they might be, you could always blame the journey or the new
owner's dog-handling.)

But this is a digression. The fact remains that Mr Henderson
had no personal knowledge that year of the grouse population
of his four moors. It did not worry him.

Alfred, however, was of a worrying nature, and had never
yet known the tribulations of a responsible grouse-moor keeper.
He woke early after an almost sleepless night, and shaved with
care before putting on his best suit and leather anklets, polished
as the Guards had taught him. He put his nose outside: thank
goodness the weather was fine and the wind right for the
Hopetoun beat! By 7.15 a.m. after breakfast, he drove away
to pick up his team of beaters, led by Jimmy Law, one of the
Hopetoun shepherds, a one-armed ex-keeper who had known
the moor for years. Alfred watched the beaters line out on the
moor, told them to wait till they heard two shots in quick

succession about ten o'clock, and then came back to the stony track where the guns' cars were to assemble.

He waited some time. The hotel party was late in starting because one of the guests had a telephone call from Geneva and it was in this guest's car that Colin Henderson had elected to guide the convoy to the meeting-place. They had been further delayed by stops for petrol, newspapers, and cigarettes. Alfred had expected them to be in their butts by ten with the drive started. He was afraid Jimmy Law, tired of waiting, might start to 'bring it in' before they were ready.

'Morning, Blowers, we're a little late,' said Mr Henderson, 'why aren't your beaters out?'

'They've been waiting an hour, sir,' said Alfred firmly, 'and I said you'd fire two shots when you were ready.' This was Lord Inverarn's method of starting a drive, and Alfred knew that no horn, whistle or flag-signal could reach beaters over two miles away.

Mr Henderson grunted. This new keeper seemed to be taking much too much into his own hands.

Alfred watched the motley collection of guns disembark. There was an American in a yellow cap, a normal safety precaution when deer-hunting on the Great Lakes. There were three women, all luckily unarmed, but one of them wore a natty puce head-scarf and a sheepskin coat with a conspicuous white collar. One, twenty years in advance of her time, wore trousers, which shocked Alfred immeasurably. Their menfolk were almost as variegated in plumage and one was festooned with cartridge-belts like an Albanian bandit. Alfred, leaning on his flag-stick, found his eye resting with approval on the only 'normal' figure in the party, a quiet man in an old deerstalker and dark, much-worn Harris tweeds. *He* at any rate would not show up too conspicuously, and his silence contrasted with the rest, who were as voluble as greylags. The quiet man's eye met Alfred's, and he limped over and shook hands.

'You're the new keeper, are you? What sort of a season has it been? I hear sad stories all round here.' Alfred's heart warmed to him.

'That ain't been up to a sight, sir,' he said in the Suffolk phrase, 'but we'll know more by four o'clock.'

The party very gradually splashed their way across a bog to the butts two hundred yards away. Alfred put the top gun in his butt and strode up the hill to the knoll where Jimmy Law had told him a flanker always lay. Mr Henderson, whose ideas of time were vague and who was hampered by five young dogs and a hangover, was last of all into the butts and Alfred waited for him to give the signal to start the beaters. He waited, but Mr Henderson had clearly forgotten and was absorbed with his dogs, or the pretty lady in the butt. Eventually Alfred had to hurry down and ask the nearest gun to fire two shots in the air.

Back on his heathery knoll, Alfred took his glass from its scratched leather case, turned it towards the beaters (who were still out of sight behind the hill) and then studied the line of butts. Though the day was fine, the breeze blew keenly. One American was dancing up and down in his butt and slapping himself with his arms to keep himself warm. The other had discarded his yellow cap, but was standing bare-headed and bolt upright in his 'blind' and (used to American duck shooting) was continually looking over his shoulder as if he expected grouse to appear high in air behind him. One Englishman was filling a pipe and gazing down into the butt talking to his dog. The man from the Bahamas, shivering, was putting on an extra sweater and a heavy waterproof on top of everything. The Frenchman had turned his back on the drive and was smoking a cigar and talking to his wife and Colin Henderson. No occupant was visible in Number Two butt: he was probably sitting down to get out of the wind. A small covey of grouse appeared from the other flank put up by George Goddard. It flew slowly along three butts unshot at, and as it turned back into the drive, he saw the quiet man shoot and a bird crumpled fifty yards out. Thank goodness, there was something in the bag! Alfred, whose only experience of grouse-driving had been in Angus, and that with a party who to Colin Henderson's gallery would have seemed 'skilled professionals', realized that even if there was an abundance of grouse on his moor, and the wind was right, making a bag was a gamble. He could also see clearly how in the previous year a surplus of birds (far too many for the moor) could occur. In fact that morning taught him more than he had guessed at before.

*   *   *

The day was over at last. The bag was only 21 brace of grouse, of which half at least had been shot by the quiet man who limped. Alfred had actually seen rather more grouse than he had expected, but many late-hatched birds flushed by the beaters had 'gone to ground' in the heather halfway and never reached the butts at all: and the inexperienced 'guns' had failed signally to account for those that did. They had been gossiping, caught unawares, or let the birds 'get on top of them', or had fired stern-chasing shots at fifty yards behind the butts. A team of good guns would have had forty brace but left little for another day. For the opening of the season it was, however, a dismal bag. Worse still, one of Colin Henderson's young dogs, terrified by gunfire and the prospect of being trodden on in the confines of a butt, had slipped its lead and disappeared and was probably hiding, forlorn and frightened, on the moor. Mr Henderson, who had blamed the flanking, the beating and the shooting in turn, grunted a Napoleonic order to Alfred to 'come up after his tea' and recover the dog. To him in certain moods, Time and Space did not exist.

The only balm for Alfred came from the quiet man, who condoled with him after the last drive and thanked him for 'a very well-run day. I was afraid these moors were due for a crash year,' he added, 'and they certainly left far too many birds last year. Your heather doesn't look bad. You may find it fill up later with birds from elsewhere.' Alfred, slightly mollified, drove the beaters home in silence though Jimmy Law consoled him. 'It's no your fault, Alfie. Ye canna' mak' a bag if the groose are no there! And some of them couldna hit a muckle barn, if they was within it!'

They dropped the beaters near their houses, arranged for

the morrow and turned for home. Jimmy insisted on Alfred coming into the Bridge Inn for a dram. 'It'll dae ye no harm, laddie, and it'll stop ye worrying. They'll a' be hame, the gentry, now with twa three drams in their bellies and *they're* no worritin'. Them Americans have a bag leemit in their country and when they've slochtered twa bairds, they canna shoot ony mair. They're happy the nicht! And Frenchies, they tell me a' they shoot in their ain land is craws, larrks, or a wee thrush. And as for the Sassenachs, they've never shot a groose in their lives so they'll be happy slochterin' them again a' nicht in the hotel. There's but ae body I'm sorry for, the wee Major. *He* can shoot!'

'You mean the dark man with the limp?' said Alfred.

'Aye, his father had a muckle place ayont Dumfries and the Major ran it for him, and it was a famous shoot. And then the auld dotterel went fou and marrit on his housekeeper and left the brass to her and none to the Major! All the wee mon can afford now is four days' shooting a year, and he the best shot on the Borrder. A nice gentleman; they put a bayonet in his wame on the Somme the time I lossed my arm. Did he thank you at the end?'

Alfred nodded. Hobnobbing in inns was bad for any keeper and he came away feeling guilty, with the example of Bert Mould before him, but refreshed. As he was driving off, Jimmy Law came to the door and called him back. 'Peter Young in the bar,' he indicated the landlord, 'whispered there was a chap with a gun on the Blue Mary beat a' morning. He cam' on a motor-bike and had a drink here later.'

Alfred thought hard while he made his tea and fed the hungry dogs. He had to get up on the moor again to try for Colin Henderson's missing puppy and there would be little time tomorrow to outwit a poacher who might start operating three miles or more from where his own party was shooting.

He started up at last and on the way shot a rabbit by the roadside for he guessed the puppy would be hungry. A patient spy with his telescope revealed a small dark head peering round the corner of the luncheon cabin. It disappeared as he came nearer and Alfred glimpsed the puppy scurrying down the burn. He paunched the rabbit and spread its remains in the hut and fastened a long piece of binder-twine to the door. Then he crept a hundred yards down-wind to a hollow out of sight.

No need to enlarge on that vigil which lasted nearly till dark. Alfred dozed at intervals in the heather, awoke to think viciously of Mr Henderson's party, flushed and full-fed and garrulous, and crawled twice up the wind till at last he heard munching in the cabin and managed to slam the door before the puppy could escape. No need either to describe his struggles to capture it or the screams of a young dog who thought his last hour had come. But he secured it at last, though it bit him through the hand, helped it to clear up the mess of rabbit on the floor, and tied its forelegs with twine to ensure that it did not escape again. Then Alfred went home.

It was 10.30 by his alarm clock. His telephone was ringing fiercely. 'Blowers? Where the hell have you been? In the pub, eh? I've been ringing you since nine o'clock.'

Alfred bit hard on his reply. As a Grenadier he had learned to suffer in silence the whips and scorns of sergeant-majors.

'I've been on the moor, sir, after your puppy.'

'Did you catch him?'

'Yes.'

'I thought he wouldn't give much trouble.'

Alfred realized that with Colin Henderson one 'simply couldn't win.' He said nothing.

There was a gurgling rumble down the telephone as if the Hearty was clearing his throat and brain simultaneously. 'What about tomorrow, Blowers?'

'You told me we'd do Blue Mary, sir. But . . .'

'But what? Speak *up*!'

'I'm told there was a poacher there all morning. We were busy on Hopetoun, so he was pretty safe.'

More gurgles and rumbles. 'Who was he?'

'That I don't rightly know. He came on a motor-bike. I ain't had no chance to see the police.'

'Why not?'

'You told me to get hold of that puppy. I only just got in.'

'What do you propose to do, Blowers?' At that hour Mr Henderson was in no condition to make a plan, nor did he propose to ring the police himself.

'I thought I'd get Roderick Duncan to give me a hand. The man won't try Hopetoun, and if we're on Blue Mary he'll be on the Allotments or Wanlokelaw.'

'Roderick *Duncan*!'

'The marquess's keeper, if I can get him first thing.'

There was a menacing sound down the telephone as if the Hathi was about to charge. For five minutes Alfred got no chance to say a word. Roderick Duncan was a liar, rude, lazy, and an obstinate braggart, no more to be trusted on a moor than the poacher himself. He had clearly been a thorn in Mr Henderson's pillow for twenty years. Only a marquess, obsessed with keeping up the long traditions of his servantry, would put up with him. Only a half-wit like Alfred would be taken in for a second by Roderick Duncan.

Mr Henderson rumbled off the telephone at last without saying good night, leaving the weary Alfred still uncertain what to do about the poacher, or whether next day on the Blue Mary beat was to be changed. As he turned into bed (with the puppy, no longer forlorn or frightened, sleeping thankfully on a blanket beside it), Alfred recalled Jimmy Law's words: 'There's times your employers will so enrrrage you, that you gang to bed *hoping* they'll have a dam' bad day the morrn with torrents of rain and no groose!'

XIX

THERE is no need to go into Alfred's history at Brinewell.
Like all grouse keepers he had a struggle to keep down the
hill-fox cubs. It meant in spring hours of digging down through
peat slime and knowing that the wretched vixen was watching
him forlornly from the nearest ridge. But it was a necessary
though to him hateful task and kept Jimmy Law and other
shepherds on his side. The poacher from Kelso who came on a
motor-cycle and shot on a neighbouring beat, when Alfred and
his allies were busy elsewhere, was finally nobbled by a ruse in
which Jimmy Law and Roderick Duncan were enlisted. Alfred
'leaked' the news that the shoot on Monday had been changed
to Wanlokelaw. While Roderick watched one moorland track
and Alfred another, Jimmy was collecting the far-flung beaters
and bringing them to the first drive on Lowstone. The poacher
arrived earlier and thuttered past Alfred hiding behind a stone
wall. He concealed his motor-cycle in a sandpit and disappeared into the glen with his gun. Alfred hamstrung the motor-
cycle by letting down the tyres and was waiting grimly on the
track for his return, when the roar of the beaters' lorry

146

alerted the poacher to the fact that he had been 'misinformed'. Long before the guns arrived, Alfred had collared the young man and his gun and was waiting with him by the roadside for Colin Henderson to interview. Unfortunately the Kelso man had no game in his possession, so the prosecution came to nothing but proved Alfred's often-quoted saying that 'prevention of poaching was better than cure'. He was not troubled again.

But all through those seasons at Brinewell, Alfred was feeling either on the verge of giving in his notice or getting the sack. They were not happy years, and he often longed for the atmosphere of Tibberton or the Ross-shire glen he had left, where his employers were gentlefolk, considerate of their servants. One thing was in Alfred's favour. Mr Henderson, acutely suspicious of how Alfred spent his time and ready to criticize, left him largely to his own devices. He sent him young dogs to train and grudgingly doled out to Alfred a commission on those that were later sold as 'finished' gun-dogs. ('Of course, Blowers, we had to put a lot of work into that dog after he came back. He was very stiff on the whistle . . . You want to sharpen your dogs up more.') Alfred suspected this 'sharpening-up' course often involved a beating by Mr Henderson or George Goddard at the first signs of exuberance on the part of the dog. He could not understand otherwise how a keen and friendly puppy, who had been with him for a year, could ever be called 'shy' or 'terrified' by its new owner.

Alfred, single-handed, did a lot of overdue heather-burning on the Brinewell moors, and on Duncan's advice deliberately left unburnt stretches of long heather in certain 'assembly areas'. Here the driven grouse congregated before coming over a rise to the butts. Alfred knew he was likely to be accused of letting this heather grow too high, if his employer ever took the trouble to visit these areas. But Roderick Duncan assured him he had 'convairted the auld marquess' to the need of them. 'It's nae morsel of use,' he would say, 'puttin' three hundred birds all at once over your guns. Some guns are frightened and some just get bewildered, and a' you have at the end is a brace or two down. But if they settle into yon deep heather and get broken up and scattered and hidden awa' on their lane, they'll come ower in sma' lots and *then*'s the time ye'll mak a killing! It's nae bluidy use havin' big packs on the muir, if you canna shoot ony! And my auld marquess has sense. He aye uses double guns, whereas your muckle oaf is afeared his airly guests will shoot too many in August with double guns, and no leave ony for later on. He doesna' ken that if you've got a thousand groose on a muir you'll never shoot mair than five hundred, fufty per cent, however hard you try! I'd sooner have good heather and few birrds in a bad winter, rather than swarrms of groose with no' enough heather to feed them.'

Thus Alfred savoured the frustrations of all keepers on what Duncan called scornfully a 'commaircial' moor, on which the owner was not entertaining friends but paying guests who wanted their 'money's worth'. In that first season, when he had to drive again and again his exiguous stocks of birds, he was glad of bad shooting, or contrary winds, and rain, and even inept flanking, which spared a high proportion of what grouse there were. And when the spring came he watched the grouse which had gone elsewhere (and given certain moors in Roxburghshire a bumper season) come back and stake out their territories again. Their nesting was hampered by May frosts and later still by gales and rain, but the moor was 'recovering' and Alfred, by battling with Colin Henderson down the telephone, saw to it that they did not lack grit.

It was before his third season that the argument about Alfred's truck came to a head. In those days it was not usual to provide keepers with any transport but Mr Henderson blandly assumed that his far-flung beaters were wafted to and from a day's shooting by some supernatural agency. It happened to be a year in which local farming was behind-hand, and Alfred had to trawl for his allies with a wider net than usual. Some said openly that they were unable to beat unless fetched. Alfred explained this on August 4th in a letter giving a list of the men and the scattered farms and cots where they lived, and adding that his own truck would be in 'for servicing and repair' during the first week of the season.

This mild ultimatum brought Alfred's employer over to see him. Colin Henderson was in a thunderous rage, thinking it 'a try-on', and Lobelia accompanied him with the ledgers in which all payments to employees were recorded. Alfred, who had faced Mother Balm, Bert Mould and regimental sergeant-majors of the Grenadiers in his time, was not unnerved before the onslaught, for an unusual reason. He had that week been fortified by a letter from the young merchant-banker who had stalked with him on Ben Bonach, revealing that his four hundred guineas had, by skilful manipulation, grown to nearly a thousand pounds. For the first time Alfred realized the sustaining power of money. Most gamekeepers, living up to every penny they earned, did not dare to be out of a job. Alfred remembered the General's words that 'to run a frontier show you've got to have your resignation in your pocket'. Now he could either resign or endure the sack without fear of immediate consequences.

Mr. Henderson, invited in politely and given Alfred's best chair, lost no time in mounting his attack. 'I've had your letter, Blowers,' he said in a throaty voice like a bishop, 'and I don't like its tone at all. It will be awkward for you if you find yourself out of a job at the start of the season.' He glared.

Alfred was ready for that one. 'Ah, that that would, sir,' his Suffolk dialect was always pronounced when he was moved: 'and more awk'ard for yourself!'

Mr Henderson's warning shot across Alfred's bows had clearly misfired. He rumbled and grunted: 'So you're not prepared to carry on as you've been doing so far?'

'Well, sir, I reckon transport for them beaters cost me very near three weeks' pay in petrol last year alone and I ain't had a penny for it since I came.'

Mr Henderson's vast bulk seemed to swell in a way which reminded Alfred of a sitting duck he had once seen bristle at a grazing cow. 'Well, *that*'s a lie. Lobby, show me the wages ledger!'

Lobelia posed sideways to air her profile, and fiddling with a curl on her forehead said, 'Last year's ledger is with our accountants for the annual tax return. I am sorree it's not available.'

Alfred produced a neat sheaf of papers off the dresser. I've got all my pay-slips here, sir, and you can go through them if so be as you want to. You won't find nothing there for petrol.'

Colin's rage, first with his keeper and now with his wife, was at boiling-point. He gurgled and lit a cigarette. Then a ray of light pierced his brain. '*That* money, of course, was sent not with your wages but with the tip-money at Christmas.'

This time Alfred was genuinely bewildered. 'Why, sir, the only tips I had last year was two five-pound notes what gentle-men gave me on the moor after shooting!' (Privately he reckoned that sixty-five paying guests had been out between August and November.)

'What about *that* one, Lobby?' Mr Henderson's tone made clear that this was another lie and one more easily nailed down.

The explanation took some minutes. Apparently, the tips, added to their bills by hotel guests, had been duly apportioned for distribution among the keepers and ghillies at Christmas, *but* . . . Alfred's share had, it seemed, been handed to George Goddard to 'pass on'. It had never reached him.

Colin Henderson's sole desire at that moment was to get home, and beat Lobelia and George Goddard 'over the head' jointly and severally. He rose with majesty and said, 'We'll go into this later, Blowers.'

But Alfred detained him. 'One moment, sir,' he said. 'Two things ain't settled. First, what about transport for them beaters on the Twelfth?'

'I've told you I'll arrange that!'

'That wasn't clear to me. And you told me twenty minutes back I was under notice.'

The Hathi had forgotten his threat. His peculiar smile, which began and ended at his front teeth, flashed: 'We'll forget all that, Blowers. People get hot in the collar and say things they don't mean.'

'I don't, sir,' said Alfred bluntly. 'And I'd like you to accept my notice come next February. I ain't used to being called a liar. *Good* arternoon!'

Attempts were made in the next months to persuade Alfred to reconsider that decision, and just when he did not care how they went, everything went right for him. The grouse had bred well. Shooting weather day after day was fine and the wind where Alfred wanted it. The driven birds responded to his driving and flanking as if the devil was in them all.

For Mr Henderson, whose own unbridled tongue had caused this trouble, nothing in those months seemed to go right. George Goddard, smarting under a rebuke about the undistributed 'tip-money', took one drink too many on the following Sunday, fell and cracked an ankle. Consequently he was off-duty and Colin had no one to tell him how badly Alfred had handled the drive off Auchnashiel or Wanfell or the misdemeanours of Alfred's young dogs. Instead Colin was told in his own bar by wind-reddened guests: 'That new chap of yours is quite brilliant. The way he turned those birds in! Gave us a fine drive. Pity he's leaving!' And to this the Hathi could only mumble and rumble, 'Obstinate chap! I want a Scotsman who'll get on better with the locals!'

Worst of all was when one of Alfred's young dogs, brought in as a last resort on badly-foiled ground, to look for a grouse which someone insisted was stone-dead, wiped the eye of four of Mr Henderson's most promising pupils. It was a fluke which might happen to any dog but unfortunately it took place under the eyes of guests, and in particular of a Brigadier's wife who had shot tigers in India and was no mean tigress herself. (She had even criticized the *cuisine* to Lobelia, and though Lobelia had won on points the contest had gone the full distance.)

Alfred, sipping his mug of tea in his lonely cottage and occasionally wondering if he had been a fool, could almost have found it in his heart to pity Mr Henderson. For though in his keepering career he had felt a mild feeling of triumph over the downfall of a fox, a poaching cat, a stoat, a crow, or an old buck rat, he felt no triumph in overcoming what a friend of his later described as 'the worst vermin of them all', man.

XX

SO once again Alfred put an advertisement in *The Game-keeper*: 'Able-bodied keeper seeks situation single-handed or good beat. Leaving own accord. Good references.' Alfred was trusting to Sir Jocelyn's testimonial for he doubted if Colin Henderson would give him more than a grudging reference despite his eagerness to keep him on.

Luckily Alfred was saved from sinking himself in the stewpot of the unemployed. A lady handler, Mrs Stewart, stopped at the hotel for a night and heard that Colin was looking for another keeper. She had spent three days picking up on the Brinewell moors in September and had been secretly impressed by Alfred's young dogs, and needed now a handler for her own. Being a dog-lover, she was not fond of other dog-lovers, especially her professional rivals. She had in the past crossed swords with Colin Henderson at field trials, and spoken openly to her friends of the imperfections of his kennel, and of George Goddard's handling. So she said nothing but, on leaving, called at the Brinewell hamlet, and found Alfred at home. He readily accepted the job of looking after her kennel and helping to run her dogs at trials. Alfred in his innocence imagined the competitors at field trials, as at Wimbledon, were all earnest amateurs, concerned only that the best dog should win and that all birds shot should be recovered. He had much to learn.

He found himself in a pleasant stable-flat in Lincolnshire in charge of an excellent range of kennels. The previous incumbent, Ben Mellish, was an old dog-handler but he had had a

heart attack and was forced to retire. He said little to Alfred
for a week while the latter was assimilating the foibles of ten
working dogs and three brood-bitches. (Alfred had once
watched the Tibberton sheepdog summing up four hundred
new sheep. At the end of three days the dog seemed to have
marked down all the 'bloody-minded' and obstinate sheep
which were likely to give trouble, and was effortlessly in command as a sergeant-major is of a mob of recruits.)

Satisfied that Alfred knew how to handle dogs, Ben Mellish
unbent. 'That's a nice little dog,' he would say, 'but he's one
weakness and that's for a hare. He won't look at rabbits but a
hare can be Boodle's undoing.' Or, 'That's Juliet. She came to
us from Brigadier Goodson's kennel, after he died. He always
swore he never put a hand on any dog and that it was all done
by kindness. *But I know better.* When you went round his kennel
it was "Darling" this and "Dearie" that, and keep your voice
low and never raise it to a dog in anger. But one of his lads
worked under me later and told me the old beggar gave every
new dog a hell of a bloody leathering *in its first week.* Most remember that a year, but this bitch *has never forgotten.* She'll do
her work at times beautifully but she's as nervous as a kitten.'

The next three years completed Alfred's education as a
keeper. Mrs Stewart's exercise paddock, bounded by a small
lake, was fitted with numerous gadgets for training dogs. Here
they learned to jump obstacles, to swim, to be steady to the
tame rabbits which swarmed in the bushed enclosure and to
find dummies shot out of a huge catapult from a tower. There
was even a stuffed hare attached by a long cord to a bicycle
frame, a device Mrs Stewart had adopted from whippet-
racing. She would send a young dog for a dummy and suddenly
the hare would flash across his path as Alfred's great forearms
worked the bicycle pedals. And woe betide the dog who
succumbed to this temptation. Few were hardy enough to do so
twice.

Alfred grew accustomed to seeing his name in print on
programmes ('Handler: A. Blowers'). He went to famous
estates on which trials were held, and met peers and baronets

and their wives, and stood behind the most expert shots in the country. (Alfred drew his own shrewd conclusions about their methods of shooting.) And once when his mistress was ill, Mr. A. Blowers, redder than usual with embarrassment, found himself in charge of the winning dog and had to make a speech, a thing he had not done since his wedding. And luckily the resonant voice, which the Grenadiers had taught him, did not desert him when he said: 'I wish this here bitch of mine could be making a speech instead o' me! She knows much better 'n me how lucky we've both been once or twice and I'm none so sure we ought to have won. But thank you kindly, one and all!' And there was applause and laughter for this modest opening while Alfred, the sweat streaming down his forehead, was pulling himself together to recall that he must thank not only the Judges but 'her Ladyship' who had so kindly lent her estate for the trial. It was only thirty years since Alfred had stood, bowler-hat in hand and as tongue-tied as a bird, on the lawn at Tibberton and received the congratulations of the Lady Elizabeth Wenhaston. And that very night in the *Rose and Crown* after he had telephoned Mrs Stewart the glad tidings, and had his supper, a new occupational hazard of his calling came his way. An inebriated lady-handler had been consoling herself ever since Alfred's Juliet had 'wiped her own dog's eye' over a runner. She now made a determined attempt on Alfred himself. But Alfred, after his experience with Mrs Skutz, made some excuse to see to his dog, and locked his bedroom door. So by the time the inebriated lady bumped against it and summoned him in husky whispers to 'open up', Alfred was too sound asleep to hear her.

But in those years Alfred learned how much blind luck governed the results of field trials. It had been the same on the Brinewell moors when a shift of wind, a buzzard, or a big pack of grouse settling near the march, could all make or mar a day's sport. Field trials were as chancy. There were days of no scent at all. There were birds which seemed to fall stone-dead but ran, so that the judge thought the dog must have 'changed on to a hare'. There were birds which fell like runners and then

were brought in so dead that the judge distrusted the dog's
mouth and thought he had 'pinched it'. There were boring
hours spent in kale or high turnips, when the handler knew that
if his dog was sent out, it was 'ten to bloody one' in Ben Mellish's
words, against its coming back with anything. There were guns
who could not shoot, and Alfred had to watch a score of
crippled birds departing into the blue, and judges unable to
mark a falling bird within twenty yards, who ordered the
handler to look in the wrong place.

Alfred came to realize the rivalry behind a field trial. He
saw the acid-drop sweetness which owners displayed to each
other, which later he was to study in its fullest bloom at Crufts.
He heard the cheery 'Hard luck, old man!' uttered by one who
was secretly delighted that his rival had failed to score. He
learned the razor-edge of chance which separated one fallen
bird from another, but which made all the difference to the
dog sent for it. One bird would fall and roll, and was easy to
pick, whereas another fell straight out of the sky and left no
scent. Another runner would be stopped by a rabbit wire fence
whereas his rival's bird had a mile of open woodland before it.
Mrs A. would not run her dogs in a stake because B. was
judging and 'had a down on her'. And Alfred never forgot the
blasphemous abuse uttered by another handler when she
discovered from the programme that Sir C., a judge she
trusted, had at the last moment elected to shoot October
grouse and arranged for a substitute-judge. Alfred, with no
expectation of being a judge, realized dimly that these things
'evened out' in the end, because an owner might be a com-
petitor one week and a judge the next, with the tables neatly
turned. But he did see that 'politics' and personal jealousies
intruded into field trials and so much money hung on the
result, with champion dogs going abroad for several hundred
guineas, that there was bound to be what the Guards had
called 'a bit of fiddling'.

But Alfred's own luck in trials held perhaps because he was
a beginner and expected nothing. Mrs Stewart watched him
carefully in four events and then sent him with her best

'current dogs' to stake after stake. A line of winning 'cards' adorned the roof beams in Alfred's 'office' beside the kennels. And one day in north-west Norfolk Alfred was presented at the day's end to a Royal Princess who said, 'I am so glad your dog won, Mr Blowers. The Judges were being much too kind to that dog of mine, all along! Well done. I understand you were a Grenadier?'

And Alfred, crimson with pride, could just stammer 'Ma'am' and remembered in time to bow and not 'salute with his hat off'. He realized that he had at long last 'walked with kings' or at any rate with one who would be a Queen one day, and that he had come a long way from the days when he was a backhouse boy under Mother Balm.

But two incidents sickened Alfred finally of field trials. His path to success had on occasion crossed that of a little dark gipsy-type called Robert Orby. Orby was Lady Belston's keeper about seven miles away and like Mrs Stewart had both labradors and springers in the kennel. Alfred, who had en-countered Orby on numerous days' shooting when both were picking-up, had good reason for thinking that Orby was 'much too hard' on his dogs. Once, waiting far behind the line before a rise of pheasants, he had seen an erring spaniel picked up by the ears and shaken viciously till it screamed with pain and fear. And on another occasion a wounded partridge, recovered by Orby's dog, had not been mercifully despatched but was thrown back into the grass alive for a young dog to retrieve. And at the end of one shoot an under-keeper confided in him. 'That wee bastard, Orby!' he said. 'I've been looking after a puppy of Lady Belston's this season and I fair *hate* the thought of it going back to him. That dog is *happy* with me now and finding well, but he was terrified of the very sight of a stick when he came to me. I've even offered Orby £30 for the dog (and God knows I can't afford that) but he'll not let the little brute go.'

Robert Orby's dark-haired truculent Spanish face, and the way he looked at his spaniels, reminded Alfred of Bert Mould, who had recited so often with unction long ago the old adage about the woman, the spaniel and the walnut tree. But Alfred guessed that it was safer to interfere between husband and wife than between a dog-handler and his dogs.

One day a Springer Club was holding a one-day novice stake on land which marched with Mrs Stewart's. Alfred was running a dog, as was Orby. Alfred decided it would do his own dog good to walk two miles to the tryst and 'settle down', so he started early and left Mrs Stewart to follow with the car and his game-bag of lunch. The footpath led him under a railway arch set in a high embankment, and round into a narrow lane between a larch wood and the line. As he neared the corner, he heard blows and the shrieking whimpers of a dog in pain. He 'dropped' his own dog and hurried round the corner. Robert Orby, his back to Alfred, had just thrown down his stick and was cursing as he shook the writhing dog by its ears. His face was contorted with menace.

Alfred was on the little man in five swift strides. He gripped his ear in one hand and his coat collar in the other, raised him off the ground and shook him as a terrier does a rat. Orby dropped the spaniel and tried to turn. He was swearing ferociously but Alfred was swearing too, with foul words which the Brigade of Guards had implanted somewhere in his mind. How long the struggle might have lasted it is difficult to say, for Alfred was very angry. But suddenly a firm voice from the larches said, 'Stop that, you two, at once! Put my keeper down please, Blowers!'

Both men turned to see a commanding grey-haired figure standing on a path in the trees and leaning on a thumbstick. Alfred heard the little keeper's gasp of 'M'Lady' and realized it was Lady Belston. She said: 'I know what you were doing, Orby. It's the last time you'll do it in my employment. Go straight up to the farm and tell the Secretary that dog of mine is withdrawn and will not be running today. I should like to report you to the Kennel Club but that would reflect on me.'

Robert Orby slunk up the narrow lane, the spaniel at his heels. Lady Belston stumped out of the larches and looked

Alfred up and down with authority. Alfred, crimson and furious, looked back. Was this old lady actually going to 'give him stick' for taking the part of her own dog. To his surprise she smiled. 'You did quite right, Blowers, and I'm grateful. It's a bad show because I've been suspecting this for a long time, and when I saw him take the dog down that lane I followed him but was too far away to interfere. *But* . . . Blowers, I don't want one word said about this incident to *anyone*. It won't do you or me or the Kennel Club any good, or the dog for that matter. See?'

Alfred said 'Very good, m'lady' and went on up to the farm. He ran second that day, and kept his mask of ignorance when other handlers wondered openly what had happened to 'wee Bob Orby and his dog'. And it was months before Alfred realized the wisdom of Lady Belston's warning. For a friend in a Trial said, 'You know what they're saying, Alfred? That you beat up Orby and scared him into scratching a dog in that novice stake?'

The other incident which convinced Alfred that field trials were 'too like politics' was when a promising dog suddenly changed hands after a stake which it might well have won. The new owner was said to have paid £200 for it and everyone wondered where 'the money had come from'. The mystery was explained months later when its late owner appeared as a judge in an important trial and, in the current jargon, 'made it' a field trial champion. It was then sold for 700 guineas to America. Before the sale it was back in the original owner's kennel, and the temporary owner had only paid a 'token price'.

Alfred realized that this sort of juggling was above him. A simple soul, who genuinely liked animals, his concern was far more for the dog whistled overseas by air and left to find itself in loneliness 'among fresh scenes, new faces, other minds' than for those human money-changers who bought and sold dogs like beef cattle.

When Mrs Stewart married again a rich stockbroker at Sunningdale, and dispersed her kennel, Alfred's heart bled for its occupants, scattered all over the country. She gave him her two most promising puppies, an old bitch, and an excellent testimonial. But Alfred decided to go back to what he called 'keepering proper'.

XXI

ONCE more Alfred had to look for another job. He took
stock of himself and his experience. He had a fair knowledge of an under-stalker's duties though it would be years
before he mastered old Alastair's weather-lore and the tricks
of his highly specialized trade. He had had three seasons on
grouse moors but here again realized that the high moors of
Angus and Banffshire and Aberdeenshire were probably quite
different from those of the Scottish Border or English moors
where you were driving 'on the top' all the time. And though
under Bert Mould Alfred had mastered the old craft of rearing
pheasants, he guessed that even Captain Darty's 'new-fangled'
methods were now outdated, and Mould's stinking carcases on
trestles, and the infinite variety of foods which took so much
time to prepare, even more so. But Alfred had money at his
back and could afford to wait till the right job came along.

Friends hinted that one day there was going to be 'big
money' in trained gun-dogs, and that Alfred, with the quiet
mastery which all dogs instinctively recognized, was a fool not
to 'cash in' on the trend. But queerly enough Alfred was too

fond of his own dogs to like parting with them, when a pur-
chaser came along. Mrs Stewart's dogs knew him and adored
him as a god and he hated the sight of their puzzled anxious
faces when their new owners put a collar and chain on them
and led them away, or Alfred had to cram them in 'a dog-box'
and send them off for ever to squander their heritage of nose
and obedience among strangers. He never got used to the
parting and wondered once if the professional nannies he had
met occasionally at country houses minded parting with their
children.

And the new owners were often so silly! They would pay a
big price for a young dog, take it away in a car, and then
perhaps a hundred miles away, stop at a friend's house 'to
give the new dog a run' and join the friend in admiring it. In
several cases that was the last they saw of the dog for a week,
and occasionally for ever. The puppy, wretchedly sure that it
had been abducted, ran away and hid, and either starved
slowly, or was run over while plodding blindly in the direction
of home, or sometimes, Alfred felt, was caught by dog-thieves
and ended up in a vivisectionists' laboratory. One lost dog he
knew lurked in a marshy copse for days, and was eventually
shot by a keeper who thought it was 'a stray' which might kill
sheep.

Moreover in his last summer with Mrs Stewart, Alfred had
seen something of the telepathy which exists between dog and
man. A young Labrador, fully-trained, was bought by the
agent of an estate in Herefordshire. For a day she seemed to be
settling down, but the first time she accompanied the agent on a
walk she quietly disappeared. The men on the estate were
alerted and the bitch was glimpsed several times near a wood
into which she always vanished. She was clearly famished and
unhappy but neither food nor whistling would tempt her back.

The owner rang up Mrs Stewart and on the fourth night she
said, 'I'll send Blowers over tomorrow morning to catch her if
he can. He'll leave here about 5 a.m. and should be with you
about nine-ish. He'll bring some food for her. The poor thing's
probably starving.'

Alfred started at dawn next day, with half a bucket of rather odorous tripe in the boot. At 7.30, when Alfred was sixty miles away, the bitch was seen two miles from the agent's house. At half-past eight the agent saw her in the stable-yard. He attempted to catch her but she disappeared. He left his car with the door open outside the house. At 9 a.m., as Alfred Blowers' Ford roared up, the bitch was sitting in the agent's car looking round at Alfred as if to say ,'Hullo! I was expecting you.'

'Well there,' said Alfred gruffly, to disguise his extreme gratification as she wriggled all round him, 'I've come a whooly long way for nothing.' The agent said he was damned, but as they watched her in the kennel wolfing the tripe which Alfred had brought they realized that behind the last four days lurked a tragedy of loneliness and bewilderment. Alfred never forgot that lesson.

Thanks to the machinations of the merchant-banker and fairly generous commissions from Mrs Stewart on dogs 'made' by Alfred and sold by her, Alfred was in funds. He bought a second-hand car of his own but the wire-meshed 'dog box', like the modern estate cars, was then unknown. So he left his dogs in charge of the gardener and his wife, who knew them well, and decided to take a holiday. He drove round the Wash to the Suffolk of his boyhood.

Tibberton looked much the same and drowsed in the same mellow October sunshine as of old, but Alfred noticed many changes. Mother Balm was dead, and most of the people Alfred had known at Tibberton too. The windmill on the green was derelict. A garage had sprung up near the gates of the Hall. The trees in the park had been felled and most of the two Big Woods as well. So had the hazel copse by Bert Mould's little bee-skep of a cottage which Alfred had scurried by furtively as a boy. Old Mrs Mould, long widowed, was in the 'almen-housen' and 'on her ninety-two'. The poorer land had gone back to 'breck' in the depression and some heavy land was dense with thorn. There seemed a lot of the black and white cattle about, which once had been known as 'them owd

Dutchmen' and despised as 'furriners' by the farmers who milked Shorthorns. Most of the heaths had disappeared under forests of larch and fir. The little water-splash at Reckford was tar macadam. The farmers still talked of 'being ruined by this here bleedin' Government', as they had in Alfred's boyhood, but now they were also mourning for the genuine prosperity of the lost years before the Kaiser's War, with low wages. The quiet beaches by Misner and Syswell were furred with 'trippers' in the summertime and the tidal mere beside Thorpe Parva had vanished under poplar trees. Alfred did not like what he saw. If he had known that, before his death, a huge nuclear plant would overshadow the whole landscape he would have liked it less.

He went up to Glenovil to stay with his sister-in-law. Ian was now a sturdy boy of nine, with Bessie's eyes and smile, and determined to be a doctor. The young Lord Inverarn promised to keep an eye on him and Alfred forsook at once the idea of taking the boy down to his own comfortless cottage. Janet, the sister-in-law, urged him to marry again: 'Any keeper needs a wife,' she said, as if a wife was like a good pair of boots. But Alfred shook his head. He was old-fashioned enough to believe in a life after death, though he went to church about once a year. But somehow if he had married again he would have been too conscious of Bessie's worried gaze looking down on him.

So Alfred came back, still unmarried, and lodged with the old gardener while he looked around for a job. Whatever made him accept the one he finally selected was a mystery to Alfred's friends and later to himself. Perhaps it was the tail-end of the farming depression, when some estates were cutting down expenses. Perhaps Alfred's conscience pricked him because he had had too secure a life under Mrs Stewart with only dogs to tend, almost no night work and no real 'responsibility'. Perhaps it was that the post he took was not advertised and he heard of it through a friend by accident. 'Joe Mackerel at Loughton Hall wants an under-keeper at once. It's a big shoot. They rear eight thousand pheasants and have a lot of partridges as well. Those rich farmers tip better than anyone, £1 a hundred head, and they like a butcher's bill when they shoot!'

'Never heard of Joe Mackerel.'

'Joe? He was head-keeper for years to Lord Quantock, who thought the world of him! You should see the character he gave him. He's got three under-keepers and the whole show runs like clockwork. Of course it's a syndicate, but they're close friends from Lincoln, who know each other's form and can shoot. Pots of money. They shoot all round the county about four days a week. The under-keepers get two days a week each picking up for other shoots, so they do quite well.'

Alfred saw Mr Joseph Mackerel, the head keeper. He was a huge pale man, running a little to fat but with an imposing presence, piercing dark eyes and a sonorous accent without any obvious local origin. He reminded others of a parson and Alfred found later that he was the son of a head-keeper in Norfolk and had been intended for the Church until an incident with a vicar's daughter had closed this avenue of advancement. He cross-examined Alfred keenly about his past, threw in several references to Lord Quantock, and made sure that Alfred was not afraid of 'really hard work', of which there would be plenty. Just before the interview closed (the subject of keepers' tips had been dismissed as beneath a gentleman's consideration), he said, 'You fully understand, Blowers, that though this is a syndicate shoot of which Mr Denbury is head on shooting days, *I'm in charge of it*? My last under-keeper went because he insisted on going over my head. I don't like that! There are such things as the proper channels, as you know from your life in the Army, and *I* handle everything.' Alfred mumbled his assent with only slight misgivings, and a week later a letter from Lincoln confirmed the details of his pay and the 'perquisites' such as clothes, cartridges, coal and dog food which he could expect. (Again the sordid question of tips was not mentioned.)

By mid-February Alfred had settled down to his routine. The vermin situation on his beat was not bad and there were few arrears to overtake, and Alfred could spend time getting to know the tenant farmers and farm-workers, putting down feed and learning the short cuts about his beat. There seemed to be plenty of partridges but wild pheasants were scarce, as far as Alfred could guess from watching in the rides at feeding-time and listening to the cocks going up to roost. He mentiond this to Joe Mackerel who said: 'Oh, I shouldn't worry about that! We buy five thousand eggs in April and I've got a hundred hens in my pheasantry. It's hard to tell exactly what stock you've got on the ground. Why, Lord Quantock told me the time he shot at Sandringham . . .' and so on.

Joe Mackerel always had a ready excuse for *not* doing anything which involved hard work. When Alfred wanted to long-net some of the rabbits, or have a hare-shoot, it was the wrong time of year or they wouldn't 'fetch a price' in the market. A farmer who had complained to Alfred was a surly 'unco-operative' devil and Alfred ought not to listen to anything *he* said. But one thing Alfred was told firmly: Mr Denbury's brother was a fox-hunting man and the syndicate always liked there to be a fox every time the hounds came. 'This place has never been drawn blank in years.'

The foxhounds came in early March. Alfred stood on the main ride in the Great Wood, and listened to 'the crashing woodland chorus pass'. There was a sudden silence. The group of horsemen behind whom Alfred was standing said: 'They've killed! I'll bet that's one of Holy Joe's three-legged 'uns.' Alfred pricked up his ears. Another farmer put in, 'There harn't been a sound fox killed on this place in three seasons. We used to have some wonderful hunts out of here in the old days.' The speaker turned his head and Alfred saw it was the veteran farmer whom Joe Mackerel had labelled as 'unco-operative', now almost unrecognizable in a bowler-hat, a stock and a long black coat.

'Well, we'd better be getting up along, Tim. I expect they'll draw the Larches.' The knot of riders squelched off up the ride, leaving Alfred wondering a little, for he knew there was not a gin-trap above ground on his beat. He knew also that a three-legged fox was a much greater menace to sitting birds than a sound one, like an injured tiger which turns to man-eating as it finds man the easiest prey. He did not know that it was crippled with a hammer when the cub was small.

The rearing-season was a busy one for Alfred and he had no time to wonder about his own head-keeper. The latter relegated the incessant labour of rearing to his underlings (he was what keepers call 'a gentleman-keeper') but he always had a reasonable excuse for absence. 'The agent wants to see me' or 'I've got to go in to Lincoln and see Mr Denbury about' a score of necessaries; and to show his ubiquity he would suddenly turn up at dusk on Alfred's beat, to know exactly what he had been doing all day. But Alfred put his young pheasants 'to wood' in good order and though he suffered losses from tawny owls (which would 'charge' the young birds on their perches at night and knock their heads off), he was satisfied by August with the stock of game on his own beat.

Joe Mackerel could often put Alfred deftly in the wrong. When Alfred reported partridge-nests missing as a result of a stoat, a cat, a hedgehog or once a rogue badger working a hedgerow, Joe would say, 'Alfred, I *think* you're making a mistake yourself by visiting those nests so often. It makes a path in the grass and that leaves a scent and vermin can tell, as well as a dog can, exactly where you've stopped!' It sounded convincing but Alfred was not sure that it was better to leave nests severely alone during the incubation period, and not know what had happened to them if they failed.

Mr Mackerel was always interfering in minor details with Alfred's methods. When Alfred made a special cat trap with sliding doors on pulleys and baited it with a kipper he caught six village cats in a fortnight. He put a label round their necks before he returned them to their owners, saying, 'Please keep this cat at home. He is poaching and may come to a sad end.' The only villager who complained was the Widow Bowles who had more cats than she could count. She waylaid Joe Mackerel and said if *her* cats disappeared, she would know who to blame.

'You know, Alf,' said Joe with some acerbity, 'you're going the wrong way to work about those pussies. Lord Quantock

always told me to put down any cat I saw but never to admit
I'd seen one on my ground.'

'That,' said Alfred bluntly, 'to my way of thinking causes
as much bad blood, if not more, than what I do. At least I'm
giving the owners a chance to keep their duzzy cats at home.'

There was more trouble in May when Alfred, early one
morning, saw a form swimming out on the little five-acre lake
on his beat. He guessed it was an egg-collector after the nest
of the great crested grebe; and hid the clothes and boots under
a bush twenty yards away. He returned half an hour later to
find the collector, blue with cold but rabid with anger, walking
up and down the lake bank and flapping his arms. There was a
terrible row when Alfred asked him what he was doing and
pointed out that even if the stranger had permission, it was
against the law to take the eggs of the crested grebe.

'I tell you I'm the Reverend Ivo Brown and your head-
keeper gave me leave to come here. I'll report you!'

Another egg-collecting parson! It was many years since
Captain Darty had threatened to let the Reverend 'Soapy'
Blaxall pedal home without his trousers. Later, Alfred reported
the incident to Joe Mackerel, who said, 'Very high-handed!
He's a well-known rural dean, and asked my permission years
ago.' (Mr Mackerel did not add that two pound-notes had
changed hands for the permission.)

Alfred stuck to his guns. 'I knew narthen of that. You told
me yourself no one had permission to be on here. And if he takes
them protected eggs, what's to stop him pinching game-eggs?'

'Don't talk silly, Blowers,' was the only answer he got.

But the first shooting-day convinced Alfred that, whatever
character Mr Mackerel had been given by Lord Quantock,
he was not in any sense a 'keeper's keeper'. It was October and
they were driving partridges. Three of the drives were on
Alfred's ground, and two days before he had pegged out the
stands with Joe himself. Mr Mackerel, spruce as a cock pheasant in his best suit and a new deerstalker, saw the beaters and
his three under-keepers into their lorry and watched them go,
murmuring that he had to remain behind to 'meet the guns and

post them', as if posting was a delicate last-minute operation. He would indicate this moment by blowing a horn. The beaters lined out and Alfred decided to take the downwind flank. In the last field, Alfred from his vantage-point on the flank neared the scattered thorns fringing Thorny Bottom, a grassy hollow of rabbit-cropped grass between two steepish banks. He could see five of the six guns below and beside one on the turf reclined Joe Mackerel, smoking a cigarette with his fat retriever curled beside him. He was patronizing to Alfred afterwards and said he had 'overflanked them a bit', but on the whole had done well. And in subsequent drives he sat with the guns at each drive and barely walked half a mile all day.

The day ended with over sixty brace of partridges and Alfred was pleased to see that over half were young birds. Meeting the agent a few days later he was astounded to hear, 'Mr Mackerel tells me ninety-seven per cent of your bag were old birds.' Alfred bit back any answer and it was several days before he had a chance to speak to the head-keeper. 'I don't understand them game-dealers,' he said, 'making out we had ninety-seven per cent old 'uns that first day. George and I went through them carefully and there was at least seventy young birds apart from what the guns took away with them.'

Mr Mackerel's black eyes flashed. He was clearly annoyed. Then he said, in a voice even more like a bishop's than Colin Henderson's, 'I suppose, Blowers, you're pretending that you know more about the age of partridges than a game-dealer?'

'No, sir, I ain't,' said Alfred, with stubbornness. 'But I know a young partridge when I see one. There's a sight of difference in the colour of the legs *and* the price! It's in the dealer's interest to make out they're mostly old 'uns, du he'd have to pay more money.'

'What we're paid for our game is nothing whatever to do with under-keepers! I don't allow myself to be cheated by any game-dealer.' And Joe Mackerel looked at his semi-gold wristwatch, the parting gift of Lord Quantock, to make clear that the interview was over.

Alfred went away, far from satisfied. He met George Porter

on the boundary of their respective beats next day. George
Porter, a young man from Swaffham, scratched his head. Then
he said, 'It was the same after one of our big days last year. I
heard Mr Denbury complaining that he didn't understand how
so many "damaged" pheasants had been sent in to the dealer.
He'd just seen the receipt.'

'And what did Joe say to that?'

'Oh, whooly a lot but it didn't make sense to me, I'd sorted
them pheasants out in the game-larder and put 'em myself
into the baskets, and put on one side the only damaged birds
there was.'

'Well, that's a masterpiece,' said Alfred, falling back on the
Suffolk phrase for anything beyond his comprehension.

'So the next lot I packed I writ a label on each basket what
said *N.B. There are no damaged birds in this consignment.*' George
Porter grinned.

'And what happened?'

'Holy Joe never see'd them labels when the game-dealer's
lorry came but there was bloody hell for me arterwards! I
thought I was going to get the sack, and I was told never to do
that agen if I valued my job.'

So Alfred learned one more hazard of a keeper's profession.
If you didn't keep an eye on the game-dealer, he 'did you down'
over the proportion of old birds to young ones, or 'averaged
out' the badly shot birds among several neighbouring shoots.
But, if as Joe Mackerel clearly did, you let the game-dealer
go his own sweet way, presumably you were sure of a' present'
at the season's end. To Alfred it was a novel experience to have
to guard not against poachers or trespassers or employers like
Colin Henderson, but *one's own head-keeper.* He said nothing
but did his job as conscientiously as ever.

Both Alfred and George were out night after night on the
watch for poachers before the first pheasant shoot, and covered
a great deal of ground on bicycles, or by listening at vantage
points here and there. But there was no evidence of any raid
on the main coverts. In fact, Joe Mackerel, who always made a
point of knowing everything before anyone, said he had had

'a sure word' that the gang had been on the Pinborough estate that week. 'I have my sources of information and if they intend to come here I shall let you know.'

The syndicate was busy shooting other people's land in the next fortnight but on a certain Saturday shoot they got over four hundred birds. Just as they were tramping home to the stable-yard of the Hall, a lorry drove up and the young driver leaned down and mumbled something to Joe. He turned to Mr Denbury. 'This is the game-dealer's lorry, sir, he has to get away early to meet a train at six. I wonder if the gentlemen would give us a hand to help transfer these birds from the game-cart to this vehicle?'

The gentlemen put down their guns and helped the keepers and the driver to transfer 350 pheasants to the lorry. Alfred and George went into the game-larder and busied themselves tying up the remaining pheasants for the guns and as presents for various tenant-farmers. Mr Mackerel was in the parlour accepting tips, and a dram from the flasks of 'the guns'. Alfred and George tramped home to tea, and spent the Sunday morning as usual picking up.

As they came in about noon with a dozen pheasants on their backs a sergeant of police was in the yard talking to Joe Mackerel. Joe seemed annoyed. He introduced his under-keepers. The wondering Alfred was led away into the harness-room ('I'd sooner examine these two separately, Mr Mackerel'), and gradually Alfred discovered what had happened. Apparently the real game lorry had broken down overnight and arrived about 7 p.m. and the lorry which removed the pheasants had been a privateer, which got away with the greater part of Saturday's bag. Had Alfred noticed the number? was the sergeant's first question. 'No,' said Alfred, 'but I can tell you the letters, because they were my own initials, A.J.B. I did notice that, not the figures.'

'You're sure?' said the sergeant. 'The head-keeper' (he looked at his book) 'said it was A.B.B. or A.O.B.'

'No, I'm sure of that as I am of my own name and the chap's name was "Bob".'

The sergeant wrote this down. 'Now how did you know that?'

'Because when we finished with the loading, Mr Mackerel said to the driver, "Away you go, Bob!" We never thought no more of it, George and me.'

Alfred's recollection of this remark was corroborated by George Porter, who, however, had the vaguest recollection of the lorry's make, letters and number. Mr Mackerel seemed uncommonly annoyed with both under-keepers when asked about these two points. He may have said 'Boy', but never 'Bob', and Alfred was wrong about the lorry's letters.

Altogether it was an unsatisfactory morning. The only definite fact in possession of the police was that 'some person or persons unknown' had got away with 350 pheasants. It was as bad as when Lord Kingscote had his game larder at Welkingham emptied by gipsies while giving a dinner-party after a three-day shoot.

Alfred, who after the episode of the young partridges had been convinced that Joe Mackerel and the game dealer were 'as thick as thieves', was forced to the conclusion that on this occasion they were not. He thought with satisfaction of the highly difficult conversation that Joe and Mr Denbury must be having on the telephone about the missing birds.

XXII

BUT the next fortnight Alfred himself had ample cause to worry. He had spent nights moving about on his beat quietly, and woke every morning tired and short of sleep. On the Friday afternoon Joe Mackerel, coming round with Alfred's wages, had said, 'Take it easy tonight, Alf. Otherwise you'll be worn out before the end of tomorrow. I'll do a patrol myself round your parish but my informant tells me they won't be doing anything near here. They've got other plans.'

But next morning Alfred, feeding his birds at dawn before the shoot, was sure that something was wrong. He was a lot of birds short in every ride including two conspicuously coloured cocks and a whitish hen which Alfred had never known to 'miss a meal'. He had no time to look round under the roosting trees for any signs of poaching but knew that something had 'gone amiss'.

He could not speak to Joe before they started for Joe was too busy 'peacocking it', in his underlings' ribald phrase, on the gravel where the guns parked their cars. Alfred and George and Charlie Hobdyke, the third keeper, had blanked in some kale and a stubble before the signal-horn sounded, and started down a belt towards the waiting guns. And before many minutes, Alfred's old bitch put down her nose and disappeared towards an oak tree. She came back with a dead hen pheasant and while Alfred, puzzled and very angry, was turning the bird over, the bitch disappeared and came back with another hen. Alfred halted his beaters and went to see. He found two more dead birds, piled neatly beside the trunk. There were no cartridge cases or identifiable footmarks. Something had either disturbed the poachers or they had forgotten to pick up this particular pile of birds.

There was all that morning the dearth of pheasants which Alfred had feared. He found no other signs of poaching except some lorry wheel-marks on the grass verge outside a certain wood. He told George Porter but never got a chance to speak to the head-keeper until lunch-time. The latter took it calmly. 'We shall see more this afternoon,' he said. 'We rather thinned 'em out here last time. Where was it you found them dead birds?'

Alfred told him.

'Oh, *that* accounts for it. Last night, when I was on my patrol as I told you, I met Albert Morley slinking home on his bike with no lights. He hadn't a gun and there was nothing in his pockets because I made sure. I expect something scared him and he left them four birds ready to pick up later.'

'That couldn't ha' been Albert working *alone*,' insisted George, 'du he moved about much quicker n' I ever see'd him.' Albert, the village drunkard, poached strictly for his own pot. 'Why, we hardly saw a bird in Scrubbitts and Jordans and there was only about ten in Four Lanes End.'

Joe Mackerel lit a cigarette and blew out a cloud of smoke. 'We'll see a nice show of birds this afternoon,' he said easily. 'Pheasants move about a lot more than some guess. Well, I must be off to my dinner,' and he disappeared into his door leaving Alfred and George still puzzled.

But after a poor morning there was a 'nice show' of birds in the afternoon on the outskirts of George's beat and the guns had plenty of shooting before the day ended. And queerly enough in the next week on Alfred's beat a few more pheasants showed up 'on the feed', which Alfred attributed to the vagaries of pheasants. He too was sure they moved about as natural food became scarcer and reared birds did not have the same hereditary attachment as wild pheasants for the woods where they had been bred. But he still guessed some poaching gang had been on the ground.

The next shoot, a fortnight later, was on a Friday, in order not to clash with a neighbouring estate. Alfred on his nightly vigils had heard and seen nothing. On the Thursday Joe Mackerel arrived at Alfred's cottage just as Alfred was collecting the corn for the afternoon feeds. Joe was in a state of excitement. 'We're on to something at last, Alf,' he said. 'I've got a sure word this time from my spy. I want you and George to be up at The Briff on Charlie Hobdyke's beat at eight o'clock.'

He unfolded a map, which showed the under-keeper's beat boundaries. 'I'd make Charlie watch *here*, and one of you *here* and the third *here*. If they come they'll come along this lane. You'd better all have whistles, so you can call the others. No guns, remember! But you can use your ash-plants.'

Alfred studied the map. 'What time are they coming and from which way?'

Joe Mackerel smiled. 'Well, they've only one way to come, haven't they? And my chap doesn't know everything. But I'd say nine-ish. You and George had better meet up this afternoon at feeding time and arrange where you two'll be hiding. Only, mind, no undue violence! And if nothing's happened by midnight, nothing will.'

'And where will *you* be, sir?' Alfred had not forgotten his training.

Mr Mackerel smiled. 'I'm glad you asked me that, Alf: in support, most probably with the police-sergeant. We've still got a few tricks up our sleeve. But, of course, the beggars *may* never come at all.'

*   *   *

Alfred and George Porter made plans to meet at the Briff, a mile-long belt of hazel coppice and oak trees, at eight o'clock, and George promised to see Charlie Hobdyke. Alfred put on his darkest old shooting-coat and hat, took a torch and a stout stick, and at the last moment a coil of about fifteen feet of cord, which he kept in his car in case it ever needed a tow.

If he knocked a poacher down the cord would come in handy.

Otherwise he would only have his belt or braces to tie him up with, and that would mean his own trousers coming down! He met George and Alfred made certain that they both had whistles and torches and their watches were synchronized. They hid their bicycles on a farm track and took up places above the Briff where the head-keeper had indicated. Alfred was on a rise looking eastwards across the vale. Though carrying out his orders to the letter, he was curiously uneasy as he settled down. His soldiering had taught him that one's enemy usually had two alternatives, A and B. Supposing, having led everyone to think they were going for A, the poachers went for B, the ground George and Alfred would normally be guarding? Then, thought Alfred, part of B was skinned a fortnight ago and the other part shot in the afternoon. A, Charlie's beat, had not been disturbed for a month. It was far more likely.

Alfred sat half-dozing on the slope, for the strain of six consecutive nights watching was telling on him. What a fool a keeper was to do all this for nothing, when a cowman, often on a better wage, got overtime for every hour! He watched the lights of two cars on the road which led past Loughton Hall two miles away, and their red tail-lights as they turned the corner up the hill. Another came along a minute or so later. Suddenly as he watched it turned left and slowed. Then the headlights blinked, and disappeared. Alfred had never overlooked his beat from such a distant point before. Had those lights taken the Cloudshill turning, or had they turned short down the farm track which led to the Great Wood, the Mansion Covert and the centre of Alfred's beat? All had been shot in mid-November but had been spared in the last shoot on Alfred's ground.

Except for an occasional car moving up the main road, there was nothing in sight. If those lights had taken the Cloudshill turning, they ought to have shown up again by now. But would a knowledgeable gang of poachers go for ground already disturbed quite recently? And suddenly the old feeling of unease which had kept him sitting on Ben Bonach, waiting for the Reverend Aubrey Melon, assailed him. He would bicycle down and have a look and could be back here in half an hour. Should he whistle for George? The sound might make Charlie think something was happening on his own beat. Better not! Alfred reached his bicycle and simultaneously a dark figure loomed up alongside.

'Alf?'

'Oh, that's you, George?'

'Ah, I wondered if you'd seen them lights turn off the main road and go out?'

'I see'd them,' said Alfred, 'but I couldn't be rightly sure they'd gone out and not gone behind the trees.'

'Alf,' said George, 'we'd better goo and look. We'd sooner be sure than sorry! I wouldn't put it past them beggars to tell Holy Joe where they was goin' and then goo somewhere else.'

'Well now, George, that's right exactly what I was a-thinkin'.' The two had fallen easily into the comfortable rising intonation of East Anglia.

They reached the Cloudshill road but there was nothing there and nothing on the way. They came on to the main road and turned down the rough track which skirted the Great Wood. Two hundred yards down was a six-foot gate leading into a ride. It stood open. 'Ah!' breathed Alfred and the sigh was replete with satisfaction and a touch of menace. Twenty yards up the ride was the dark mass of a vehicle. 'A.J.B.' he murmured delightedly, shielding his torch in his fist. 'That's the one what had my initials what took all our pheasants from the Hall after the shoot. Write that down, George 'bor, before Mr Mackerel can say we ha' got it wrong! A.J.B. Alfred John Blowers. One-oh-nine.'

They went slowly round the lorry, made certain it had the same number back and front, and George, a lithe monkey of a man, disappeared over the tailboard.

'There's a sack in here,' he whispered, 'that's got pheasants in it by the feel of it. I reckon them b——s went somewhere else a-poachen' before they comed here!'

Alfred had not commanded a headquarter platoon for

nothing. 'Cop us here that sack, George 'bor. We'll put that under the lorry in case they knock us oover and run. Have you got a potato?'

'I always hev,' said the man from Swaffham, 'a master good cure agin the rheumatics.' And Alfred stuffed it up One-oh-nine's exhaust pipe. He remembered the rope on his handle-bars and had an inspiration. He lashed one end round an elder bush, and paid out the rope across the ride. He motioned George Porter to his side and they hid in the lee of a hawthorn bush. 'If you hear anyone acomen down the ride, pull that rope right tight to trip them,' said Alfred. 'Oh ah,' said George who was enjoying himself.

There had not been a sound in the wood above them and Alfred was puzzled. They were certainly not using shot-guns. Were they using airguns, catapults, wire-snares on long poles, sulphur, or acetylene, or what?

George gave an excited hiss and dug Alfred in the ribs. 'Here a' be suthun a-comen' ' and there was no possible doubt as to his county of origin. Where the ride crested the hill, there was something dark and moving. The object sank out of sight, and both men could hear footsteps approaching. Alfred, his hat drawn low, peeped very slowly round the bush. A man was coming, bent nearly double under the weight of a heavy sack. He panted a little as he came. Alfred felt the cord tighten in George's grasp. The man tripped heavily over it and with the sack weighing him down, fell with a crash against the tail-board.

Alfred and George were on the recumbent form in an instant and Alfred made three swift turns of the rope-end round his legs. The prone figure did not make a sound. Alfred flashed his torch and could see blood welling freely from a flattened nose and a big graze on the forehead.

'Christ A'mighty!' said George in awe. 'Hev he killed himself? He hit the owd lorry good tidily.'

Alfred picked up a limp hand and felt for the man's pulse. In the torch-gleam he suddenly recognized the ornate wrist-watch on the man's wrist. 'Love my bloody heart alive, George 'bor,' he said, 'if we ain't copped Holy Joe hisself!' In that blinding moment, Alfred found himself wondering if any under-keeper in history had caught his own head-keeper poaching game.

XXIII

THE alarm clock which every good keeper carries inside his vitals awoke Alfred at four. He shaved, made tea, and meticulously cleaned his boots and anklets. At five, still in the frosty dark, he was feeding his pheasants or rather putting out the food which they would find when they left their trees at dawn. At six-thirty he sought the two keepers and enjoined them very firmly to secrecy.

'That 'ont du us, nor the shute, no good if this tale gets about. I reckon it shows up an under-keeper if his head man is caught apoachen'. We ought to have got on to him before.' Though Alfred later admitted to George that 'never in all his life had he imagined such a thing could be'.

Then Alfred, very stern, knocked at the head-keeper's door. Mr Mackerel was in bed; his swollen nose, lips, and forehead, looked obscene. His comely wife, whom Alfred had always respected, wept when he came downstairs. 'Can't we hush this up *somehow*, Mr Blowers? I feel so dreadful!'

'I've told your husband, ma'am,' said Alfred, 'none of us 'ont say a word beyond that he's "indisposed" today but . . .

he's got to give in his notice. I made that clear. Otherwise we'll all leave and the story of them 350 pheasants will come out in court.'

'What's that about three hundred and fifty pheasants?' asked Mrs Mackerel. Alfred told her. 'It was the same chap, Bob Hawke, who druv that van last night. We've let him go but we know all about him.' Mrs Mackerel stared tearfully into the future.

'Your husband,' said Alfred, not unkindly, 'got a master good character out of Lord Quantock. He should get a job on that, but not round here. Now do you write out his notice for him, Mrs Mackerel, and see he signs it today.'

At nine-fifteen, Alfred was pacing the gravel on which Joe had long paraded. Mr Denbury's car drew up.

'Morning, Blowers, where's Mr Mackerel?'

'Indisposed, sir. I'm afraid I'll be in charge today. The others have gone with the beaters. We had to make some changes. With this wind I thought we'd begin with the kale and then . . .' Alfred outlined the programme with an authority which surprised him. Mr Denbury was full of curiosity but the arrival of the other guns precluded questions.

Alfred's first day as head-keeper was a good one. The birds flew well in the frosty air and there seemed plenty of them. Alfred found himself wondering at midday, as he often did later, whether with wild pheasants there was an untapped mysterious reservoir of birds, birds which usually never showed up until the season was over, or lurked just outside the area beaten, or which hid at the first sound of a gun. Pheasants were not like partridges which were always on the same fields.

In after years Alfred used to contrast his dreams about becoming a head-keeper with that day's reality. You usually became a head-keeper by the lapse of years. They appointed you in February and you had nine months in which to rear your birds and perfect your plans, and to get to know your underlings and auxiliaries before the opening day. Nine months of waiting and Alfred had had nine hours, though, thank the Lord, it was on ground he knew well.

That day ended with a spectacular flush of very wild, very high-flying pheasants coming out of kale. Alfred had thought this 'rise' was a gamble, but everything had gone so well, that he decided, as eminent generals had done, to 'reinforce success'. Mr Denbury was pleased. 'A wonderful stand!' he said, 'never saw a better. We must do it again. Come in when you've counted the bag and have a dram.'

So Alfred came in, like a bandmaster on a guest night, and in return for a card which showed '297 phts, 6 woodcock, 15 hares, 1 teal, 14 woodpigeons, 2 rabbits', received a number of congratulations, a larger number of Treasury notes (based on £1 a hundred for 350 head) and many inquiries about Joe.

Alfred insisted that Mr Mackerel was 'indisposed' and would be all right next week, but Mr Denbury was looking hard at him. When the other guns had gone, he stayed behind.

'I want to know what happened last night?'

'Sir, you'd better ask Mr Mackerel.'

'He's sent me his notice, to take immediate effect. You're acting head-keeper.'

'Ah.'

'I'm still wanting to know.'

'He ain't given a reason, sir?'

'No. I'm asking *you*.'

'Sir,' said Alfred, 'if Mr Mackerel 'ont tell you, that ain't my place, as his under-keeper. There was a bit of poaching. George and meself intercepted 'em. You had a good day today, I reckon?'

'Very good.'

'Well, sir, if I may make so bold, why not let sleeping dogs and sleeping head-keepers lie?'

'Damn it, Blowers, it might make the difference between my making you head-keeper here and someone else getting it!'

'Well, sir, begging your pardon, I'm not one for tales. I said I wouldn't say a word. One thing I promise: the poaching's stopped what was worrying me.'

And with this Mr Denbury had to be content. Secretly he respected Alfred's firm refusal to say. Everyone else assumed

that Joe had had a row with the under-keepers who had beaten
him up. Alfred did not mind when this tale reached his ears.
He was busy re-organizing the shoot and a hundred minor
improvements testified to the guns that Alfred was firmly in
control.

XXIV

ALFRED was fifty-two when the Second War broke out and had been six seasons as head-keeper to Mr Denbury's syndicate. But all through those seasons the shoot had improved until it became famous far beyond Lincolnshire and many people would have given good money for 'a gun' in it. Field trials were held there, game-farmers competed eagerly for its custom, and research bodies interested in game tried out new ideas on its ground. Alfred found himself known, and even deferred to, by several hundred people, some eminent and all interested in shooting or dogs.

Alfred, in his quiet woodlands, had been more aware of the change of seasons than of the events of 1938 and 1939. The new War took him by surprise, but he did not hesitate.

At Wellington Barracks and the Caterham Depot, most of his old lawgivers were dead. The rest were busy and he like the Lotus-eaters in Tennyson was only coming 'as a ghost to trouble joy'. They took down Alfred's name and age and address but could promise him nothing except as an instructor 'on the square'. He returned, worried and annoyed, to Lincolnshire where nobody seemed to be taking the Phoney War seriously. It was not like 1914 when Kitchener had pointed an accusing finger at you from hoardings and there had been a mad rush to get into uniform and then 'under fire'.

Then came Dunkirk and Churchill took over. All Alfred knew about him was that Mr Churchill had once been attached to the Grenadiers 'for instruction', but everything got a new impetus. The close seasons and even the game laws went by the board. One could actually shoot a pheasant in September! Rearing had stopped; petrol, cartridges and beaters became harder and harder to obtain. Mr Denbury went to a 'ground job' in the Royal Air Force and the young underkeepers faded away.

Ex-Sergeant Blowers, D.C.M., M.M., was left forlorn, until a Colonel, who had shot several times with the syndicate, drove round to his cottage. He had, it seemed, been instructed to form a battalion of Auxiliary Military Pioneers, then called 'Amps', and he wanted ex-Sergeant Blowers as a sergeant-major. 'They're mostly old lags, specially released from clink for the duration, but they've nearly all served in the Kaiser's War and there's a sprinkling of chaps with the same decorations as yourself. It'll be a tougher job than with ordinary recruits, but I'd be very glad to have you.'

Alfred did not hesitate. He had no dependents except young Ian who was now reading medicine in Edinburgh, after a career at Fettes. Alfred Blowers sometimes wondered if Ian was secretly ashamed of his father but he had grown into a sturdy youth with Bessie's eyes and smile, who spent his autumn holiday along with others of his kind helping to drive grouse on the Angus moors. Alfred was very proud of him, and had been touched to discover that Lady Poynter, after the General's death, had made herself partly responsible for Ian's schooling. 'It was the least we could do,' she said in reply to Alfred's thanks conveyed on one of his annual Christmas cards. 'We were very fond of Bessie and the boy will be a credit to you, when he qualifies.'

So Alfred, untouched by domestic cares, went to the Pioneers and speedily became a sergeant-major. The troops under him were a mixed bag and many had been released from His Majesty's Prisons, but had had good war records before turning to crime.

But on them Alfred managed to impose a measure of discipline and though Guards sergeant-majors whom he encountered said, 'I wouldn't have your mob for all the tea in

China', the unit emerged from the war with quite a good record of work put through in the Middle East and Europe.

Alfred came back to a changed world. There had been a revolution. The countryside had been cleared of game by the hordes of troops waiting in East Anglia for D-Day. There had been no rearing for five seasons, carrion crows and magpies abounded, and it was almost impossible to get feed for birds. A few elderly keepers in the neighbourhood collected the seed of 'fat hen', a pestilent weed, into sacks to try and keep their few remaining birds 'together'. There were still partridges, for they were normally too wild to poach. Prices had soared, and the farmers, whom Alfred had heard grumbling about 'this here Government which was agoin' to ruin us', were now at the zenith of their prosperity. Money and the social status that went with money had changed hands. Dennis Sole, whom Alfred had known as a small cattle-dealer in Lincoln market, was now a landowner, said to be worth £300,000. A gipsy type whom Alfred had known in boyhood as a 'tit-puller' on his father's dairy-farm at Kelsall had migrated to Lincolnshire and become a big sand and gravel contractor worth nearly a million, men said. The guns that came into Mr Denbury's syndicate, and others where Alfred helped to 'pick up', were nearly all large farmers and prosperous men to whom the urgent needs of agriculture had been a sound reason for avoiding war. Nearly everyone among the returning troops wanted to 'go into farming', in order to evade controls, and Alfred with the money saved from his sergeant-major's pay was tempted to follow suit. But he knew his place, as he had known it all his life, and the same feeling which had made him refuse a commission twice, kept him still keepering on little more than the agricultural wage.

He now had five men under him but was sensible enough to delegate and not 'breathe down the necks of his underlings'. But he usually knew what was going on, on his distant beats. The old days had gone for ever, when game was paramount and a farmer who complained of damage done by game could be given notice. Now the farming community traded on their security and pre-eminence. A tactless keeper beyond Alfred's boundary, who had annoyed a tenant farmer's son, soon realized which had the whip-hand. After a day's partridge-driving the young man would take out a Land-Rover and traverse field after field with a spotlight and a gun, saying that it was the only way to keep down the rabbits; and the keeper had to endure new wire fences being erected along his nesting banks in May. Alfred spent much time in what he called 'politics', fraternizing with farmers and farm workers, but he found it paid a dividend; by timely presents of game and invitations to shoot, he managed to keep the peace.

Neighbouring head-keepers envied him. 'Of course, you've got a third of the place in hand,' one said, 'and that makes a difference, and I wish we had a tenant like your old Margery. I reckon half the game off one of my beats walks into Lincoln on its feet or is hanging in old Albert Heyter's deep freeze at this moment, but what can I do? He's been there thirty years too long.'

'I don't whooly trust that young keeper of yours,' said Alfred slowly. 'My chap says he's seen him twice shooting at partridges on the ground.'

'You couldn't mistrust the beggar worser'n I do, Alfred. He's picked up every damn fiddle in the Army but if I was to sack him, I couldn't get the bastard out of his cottage unless he wanted to go. Things ain't what they used to be.' Alfred understood at last why Mr Henderson had been so suspicious of his own good 'character' given long ago by a Lord Lieutenant. Nokes, the keeper, sighed. 'There's two head-cowmen in this part of the world who are so bad that they can put any bloody herd back a hundred gallons a cow, but to judge by their testymoanials they're the best in all Lincolnshire! I reckon whoever writ them was only too anxious to get 'em away from their herds and off the farm.'

'Joe Mackerel had a wonderful one out of Lord Quantock,' said Alfred. 'Did he write that for the same reason?'

'Oh, no, he was sucked in proper by Joe. Joe had some useful under-keepers then and very good seasons for weather.

He couldn't go wrong! And he was courting then and watching his step.'

'Well, Jim, 'bor,' Alfred rose, 'here are we a-talkin' scandal like two owd wimmen on a 'bus. We'd best get back to work. By the way, where's Joe now?'

'He's in north Lincolnsheer as valet and loader for a wee Scotchman, who made a lot of money in the war. It ain't a keeper's job but Joe will always fall on his feet. D'you know what the story is round here?'

'No.'

'That you and George Porter beat him up and threatened him with worse if he didn't resign.'

Alfred's weather-beaten face flushed deeper. He spat on the road. 'That's what always comes of hushing up the trewth. Has Joe been spreading that yarn?'

'Someone has. One of my under-keepers heard it in Louth before ever he came to me.'

'Well,' said Alfred savagely, 'it's a bloody lie and I'll knock his teeth down the throat of anyone who hints that to me.'

XXV

ALFRED found himself slowing down a little after the war. He was 'on his sixty' now and though to keepers age meant little, he was content to leave more work to younger men. A great Field-Marshal, who knew Mr Denbury, came down several times to photograph birds on the shoot. Alfred and he became close friends, and often had tea together in Alfred's cottage. Once, to settle some argument about birds, Alfred got out the notebook in its stout cloth cover which Bessie had bought him in Dingwall. He still kept it up with notes on badgers, hedgehogs, squirrels, frogs and moles, partridges, kingfishers and owls, crows, woodpigeons and jays and it now contained a mass of material. The Field-Marshal asked leave to study it. He took it away in his car and brought it back next day.

'Look here, Blowers,' he said abruptly. 'Do you realize the value of what you've got here?'

'I don't reckon that's of much use to anyone. You're the first what's ever looked at it, sir. That ain't up to a sight.'

'It's unique.'

'That's the word Lady Poynter used to my wife long agoo, but then we was in a wild part of Ross-shire and had opportunities. What I see, thousands of others can.'

'Ah, but they don't and that makes all the difference! Or if they see a thing they don't write it down. And it may be forty years before they see it again. I tell you, there's stuff in here which has probably never been published before, and it *ought* to be. D' you get me?'

'Ah!'

'Now I've got a friend in publishing who'd take it and I know a young artist who'd simply jump at the chance of doing some sketches for this. He'll have to come and see you. It'll want an index of course, but that's easy. Would you trust me with this book for a week?'

'Why yes, Field-Marshal, of course, but I never had no education except in the Grenadiers. I never in all my life thought of book-writing.'

'Nor did a lot of famous writers. Someone once said that there was nothing to equal "the plain and simple testimony of men living in the open air". There's too many half-baked writers nowadays who never leave a house and the stuff they put on paper isn't worth a damn. They've seen *nothing*. You have.'

Over a dinner in the Tower of London, Alfred's book was born. It was called simply '*A Keeper's Notebook*', by Alfred Blowers, but the Field-Marshal himself contributed a foreword which made Alfred blush to read even worse than Lord Inverarn's speech at his wedding had done. The young artist enjoyed himself with the illustrations and spent days in Alfred's cottage asking eternal questions: 'Did it look like *this*, or like *that*? And I don't mind how many times I re-draw these sketches as long as *you're* satisfied,' which is not always the way with book-illustrators.

The volume emerged some years after the war, costing 15/-, clad in a green jacket on the front of which was a picture of Alfred's cottage under snow, taken by the Field-Marshal, and

on the back a blurb which made Alfred wriggle with embarrassment and turn 'as red as a ferret's eyes'. Alfred was,
like other authors, deeply ashamed of his offspring and
was more astonished to receive a cheque for £75 as 'advance
royalties' on publication. The Field-Marshal wrote at Christmas that the first impression had been sold out. Alfred did
not know what to do with his six presentation copies but
sent one to his son, Ian, and gave one to George Porter and
one to Mr Denbury to whom he said defiantly, 'This ain't
been narthen to do with me. That's all *your* friend, his lordship!'

But Alfred received several letters, addressed to 'Alfred
Blowers Esq.' c/o his publishers which said how lucky he had
been to see as much as he had, and he realized that he had given
genuine pleasure to unknown people in faraway places. And,
not reading the newspapers, he was spared the reviews. Indeed, one by a long-haired young intellectual (who wrote on
country subjects for *The Dictator* and innately disliked all
field sports) was so acid and *de haut en bas* that the Field-Marshal,
an ex-gunner, brought his heaviest artillery to bear in support
of Alfred in a letter to the Editor. The Field-Marshal had held
his own with Prime Ministers, and Admirals, and other
belligerents in his time, so the young reviewer stood no chance
at all, especially as he had once when a subaltern met the Field-
Marshal at Larkhill and had in his presence misidentified a
carrion crow as a raven.

Alfred, of course, lost caste with George Porter and his
fellow gamekeepers who thought that no keeper 'what wrote
books' could be doing his job properly, but the members of
Mr Denbury's syndicate looked at him with interest when
he stumped in at the end of lunch with 'the bag'. Then he
would be asked to drink a ceremonial glass of port, as Mould
and Joe Mackerel had done so often, and discuss what had
gone wrong in the morning and what all hoped would go right
in the afternoon. And the 'guest guns' would tell their wives
and cronies: 'We had a goodish day. I met Alfred Blowers who's
head-keeper there and wrote *A Keeper's Notebook*. Interesting

chap and he knows how to run a day's shooting.' So Alfred's book went on selling for years which was more than happened to most others. The shepherd boy who had eaten raw turnips in 1899 had indeed come a long way.

XXVI

DURING the years that Alfred was at Loughton there were several changes in the syndicate, for it had never been a 'cheap' one and costs were going up steadily every year. Certain people found they could no longer afford 'a gun'. Alfred himself felt as embarrassed as they were when this happened. They would look wistfully at a late January sunset, and hear the clatter of cock pheasants going up to roost and mutter, 'Well, Blowers, I shan't be here next year, more's the pity. Wish I could be but . . . Thank you for all you've done and the best of luck.'

Thus Alfred had seen many shooters come and go. He had acquired the keeper's unerring eye for a gun's weaknesses, guns noisy and guns quiet, guns dangerous and guns safe, guns useless and guns reliable, and worst of all, a gun who was excitable, brilliant (in patches) and dangerous (again in patches). It never ceased to astonish Alfred and George, who usually held a *post-mortem* when picking up the day after, that so many gentlemen were shooting, and had been for years, who could at moments be palpably dangerous. No one knew when that moment would occur. The older flankers got to know these men and had an uncanny knack of taking evasive action. But there they were, year after year, and in George's words, 'However rich them beggars are, they hadn't ought to *be* here.' Indeed, Mr Denbury, witness of a bad accident on a grouse-moor years before, had made it a rule of his syndicate that if anyone fired a palpably dangerous shot, or injured someone,

home he went *for the rest of the season*, and forfeited what he had
paid. This drastic rule was rarely invoked but the syndicate
knew of its existence and behaved themselves accordingly. As
a result, the shoot's reputation was high. 'They don't stand
any dam' nonsense at Loughton,' people said. 'I sometimes
wish we had the same rule here.'

But one year when money was short, two new guns joined
the syndicate. One was a brigadier from Eastern Command,
who seemed to Alfred harmless except for a badly trained dog,
and the other was a small man who arrived on the first day
in a chauffeur-driven car of sumptuous opulence and was
dressed in rather loud tweeds. He was accompanied by a lithe
blonde tabby of a woman in a sheepskin coat with a puce scarf
and a long cigarette-holder. Alfred had not troubled to ask
beforehand the name of this gun : in fact Mr Denbury had said
he was 'a stranger from the north' who had a gun already in
another syndicate not far away.

The tiny stranger, led up to be introduced formally to
'Blowers, our head-keeper', seemed a bit offhand. He shook
hands convulsively, did not look up at Alfred, and said, 'Good
morning, er, keeper, my, er, man will see to my guns' and
turned away. Alfred, whom little could surprise, discovered
that the 'man', who was having difficulty in parking the huge
car, was none other than Joe Mackerel. Others might have
been diffident in Alfred's presence, but not Mr Mackerel. His
episcopal eye rolled over Alfred and he said : 'Well, Alfred, I
hear you've been lucky this year and had a good season.
What number's my boss drawn?'

'That's nothing to do with me. Mr Denbury does that,' and
Alfred turned away. In Joe's day there had been a certain
amount of quiet 'fudging' of the draw for places by the head-
keeper, so that his favourites could be sure of a 'good number'
at the hottest stands. He used to say 'Mr So-and-So said he
might be late. So I've drawn for him.'

But after two seasons Mr Denbury had stopped this practice
firmly. Now he always conducted the draw himself, with
playing cards, after all the guns had assembled.

At the first drive of a new season, Alfred always made a point of standing with the line of guns. This was not laziness, as in Joe's case, it enabled him to sum up newcomers, to see if they 'swung through' the line, or chattered, or could not keep in their places, or had dogs which whined or ran in. He was thus in a position to drop a hint later to Mr Denbury who would 'keep his eyes open' in later drives.

Alfred knelt now behind one of the other guns whom he knew well. The drive was off rising ground downwind, to hurdles on the edge of some mangolds. It was early October and Alfred expected a fair number of partridges and some wild pheasants. The new brigadier, at the next peg, seemed alert and neither he nor his soldier-loader were too conspicuous. His dog was firmly lashed to a spike driven into the ground. But two butts further down, 'the little man' and Joe were lighting cigarettes and talking with their heads together, while five full yards behind both the blonde lady sat on a shooting-seat, hatless, with a puce fillet in her gorgeous hair and talking loudly. She was so far out of line as to be highly conspicuous and not concealed in any way by the hurdle, and her position would embarrass any gun who took a bird behind the line. Well, thought Alfred, this is the only drive we've got today over hurdles and we'll see. No good worrying before it's time!

It was a gorgeous morning with the sky ballooned with cotton-puffs of clouds and the leaves had just begun to turn after an early frost. It was, though Alfred did not realize it, the start of his fiftieth season, and if he had been given to retrospection, he would have looked back on the road he had travelled since he had waited with Harry Clarke beside the laurels of Tibberton Grange for the dog-carts bringing 'the guns' to his first 'First'. He had his own car now, and was well-known half over Lincolnshire, and on friendly terms with Field-Marshals and Admirals, and had been presented to a Queen. He knelt and savoured the peerless morning. His two dogs lay next him, the old grey-muzzled bitch half asleep, the young dog trembling quietly with excitement, and taking everything in.

Faintly Alfred heard George's whistle and saw six brown

dots slide over the fence on the crest, and settle in the beet. He looked along the line. Most of the guns seemed vigilant but the 'little man' had propped his first gun against the hurdle and was talking with the lady. Joe, still puffing a cigarette, was holding his second gun in the loader's favourite, most convenient and most dangerous position in the crook of his left arm, its muzzle pointing down the line. Alfred hoped Mr Denbury would notice this and save himself from admonishing his predecessor. The whistle sounded again and sixteen partridges topped the distant fence and swept down the slope of the field. To the waiting guns they were 'a big lot', well grown, new and exciting in their imminence. To Alfred and George they were an 'old' covey which they had known ever since they hatched on June the tenth. The hen had weathered a vixen, a cat, a shocking thunderstorm, a drove of heifers which had broken out, a wandering dog, a rogue badger, at least one stoat and later, after she had hatched fifteen chicks from seventeen eggs, a motor-car which obliterated the smallest in a lane. They were now the best-grown covey on George's beat and Alfred expected them to settle in the mangolds and go back when the beaters came on. But to his surprise they skimmed steadily on the wind down the slope, apparently intending to pitch in the grassy 'bottom' where the guns were waiting. The other guns crouched intent behind their hurdles at the covey came on. But the little man, his gun still propped against the hurdle, was lighting another cigarette with Joe's hands cupped round a match. The lady on her shooting-seat was contemplating her own slender ankles. In the dead stillness Alfred could hear the startled chuckles as the covey realized the 'presences' behind each hurdle and rose as sharply as it accelerated. The little man picked up his gun, spat out his cigarette, swept the muzzle through the line and then fired one shot almost over his girl-friend's shapely head. Alfred heard the clash of barrels as Joe and he changed guns, and the girl-friend ducked and swore.

Well, blow-my-life, thought Alfred, if that ain't a masterpiece. The 'gun' in front of him, James Yelberton, embraced

Alfred and his own loader with a grin: 'Talk about little Lord Ripon,' he said, 'I wonder he didn't blow the ruddy girl's head off! But better *his* girl-friend than mine.'

Alfred was busy for the rest of the drive, marking wounded birds which fell behind the line and generally seeing how the drive was being brought in by George. There were a nice lot of partridges in it and Alfred thought there always would be. He little visualized a day when the grey partridge would unaccountably decline to a fraction of its former numbers.

At the day's end he counted the bag and brought it in on a card, so many young birds, so many old, so many pheasants and hares and woodpigeons.

'There's two brace of partridges over,' he told Mr Denbury.

'Who hasn't had any?'

'The little gentleman Joe was loading for.'

'Oh, Mr MacBean! He had to get off early to meet a train. Put 'em in my car and I'll see he gets them tomorrow. And then come back and have a dram!'

Alfred went out, wondering vaguely why the 'little gentleman's' name, MacBean, seemed to 'ring a bell'. Where had he heard MacBean before?

He put the partridges in Mr Denbury's car, spoke to the waiting loader, and came back to the cottage. As he did so, and knocked ceremoniously at the door of his own parlour, he heard the cheerful voice of James Yelberton say, 'I'm a bit scared of Wee Hamish, as you keep calling him. I was looking down his bloody gun-muzzles far too often today.'

The banter ceased suddenly as Mr Denbury called 'Come in!' and Alfred strode in majestically.

'Sit down, Alfred, and help yourself.' Mr Denbury pushed across a whisky bottle.

'Thank you, sir.' Alfred sat with a wooden face, wondering why the words 'Wee Hamish' which must have been applied to the absent gun, Mr MacBean, roused in him so much curiosity. 'Wee Hamish', he had heard that sobriquet before, but where? He poured himself a tot and diluted it with water.

'Alfred,' said Mr Denbury again, 'how did things go from

your end?' It was one of John Denbury's endearing foibles to look at a day's shooting from two conflicting standpoints, that of the keeper and that of the guns. 'We saw a lot more partridges than I expected!'

Alfred dragged his mind back from reverie. 'Ah, sir, but there was four big droves on the Southacre side what properly bid George defiance! We didn't see not half the birds what should have been in that drive but of course we was driving it across the wind.' And as Alfred discussed such details he was thinking 'Wee Hamish MacBean? Now where the devil have I heard that name before?'

The other guns rose one by one and wished Alfred and Mr Denbury goodnight. At last when they were alone, Mr Denbury looked at his watch and said, 'I must be getting along. Anything to tell me, Alfred? You and George ran a very good day.'

Nice of him to add that 'and George' which so many would have forgotten! Alfred said, 'Well, sir, there ain't much. We had a couple of noisy young beaters but they 'ont holler again. And George did whooly well . . . But . . .'

'But what?'

'I ain't happy about that little gentleman what went early . . .'

'Mr MacBean. What about him?'

'In the first drive he swung right through the line twice and he nearly blew his wife's head off . . .'

'She isn't his wife, but never mind.'

'And Bill Green what was flanking he said he'd been shot at, accidental like, by Generals and Admirals and Cabinet Ministers in the forty years but that little' (Alfred corrected himself) 'feller had shot at him twice knowing he was there and Bill had to shout at him in the latter end. And one of my buoys said he shot a hare coming through the fence when the beaters was just the t'other side. And that lady of his, if she carries on like today in them clothes and shows up as much, later in the season when my birds are a bit butt-shy, why, she'll put a whole drive wrong!'

Alfred stopped. He had said too much but Mr Denbury said, 'Thank you, Alfred, I'm not surprised to hear what you say. Mr MacBean is from Inverness, where he's made a lot of money and he's new to partridge-driving and the way we run things here. I'll speak to him this week.'

'Wee Hamish MacBean' from Inverness! Suddenly Alfred's wonderings swam into focus. He remembered a Dingwall inn adorned by stags' heads just after Bessie's death and the bar-man saying that 'wee Hamish had never been the same mon since last month'; and how the police inspector had told the factor that it was one Hamish MacBean who had almost cer-tainly shot Bessie but 'they could pin nothing on him'. Alfred had badly wanted to pin a curse on him, but the curse ob-viously had not taken effect. Wee Hamish had prospered only too mightily since that episode if his clothes and guns and car were anything to go by. So many skulkers had made fortunes out of Hitler's War as their forebears had from the Kaiser's.

Alfred was thinking as intently about the little Highlander as if he had just come across the 'fresh work' of a marauding stoat or cat or fox. With vermin one knew exactly what to do. But with a paying gun, it was not so easy. He had hushed up the incident of Joe Mackerel's poaching, because it would have done the syndicate no good. And it would do no good and probably earn Alfred the sack if he, as head-keeper, took reprisals against 'a paying gun'.

For the first time in fifty seasons Alfred found himself worry-ing about the future at the season's very start.

He might have been still more worried if he had overheard a conversation which took place over Mr Denbury's supper table. There were only two other people in the room, John Denbury's wife and the gun behind whom Alfred had knelt in the first drive, James Yelberton. They had been discussing Hamish MacBean. 'I thought he was a bit naughty swinging through the line. And the first shot of the day he was caught napping without a gun and by the time he'd finished he nearly blew the head off that blonde floozy of his. But do you know what he told me about Alfred? He said his loader, Joe Mackerel, left here because Alfred beat him up one night when Joe was lying out for poachers!'

Mr Denbury looked interested. 'I never could get out of Alfred what happened that night. I tried and George Porter wouldn't squeak either. All *we* know is that Joe had a face like corned beef next day and sent his resignation in from his bed. But I can't believe he or his wife would have let an under-keeper get away with that nonsense. Joe would have taken out a summons, instead of slinking off the way he did! Damn it, he was out of work for months.'

James Yelberton nodded. 'Of course Alfred was a Guards sergeant and they learn to be pretty brutal there and what's more, he was afterwards sergeant-major in a unit recruited sixty per cent from prisons. A chap in those jobs must use his fists, like they do in a glasshouse.'

'Whatever,' put in Mr Denbury, 'happened that night, the poaching's stopped and Alfred's done a lot to improve things here.'

James Yelberton was thinking. 'Wee Hamish asked me today if I knew where Alfred had been keepering in the past. He said there was a stalker of that name near Wyvis who was supposed to have shot his own wife by accident one night. Alfred's a widower, isn't he?'

'Yes, and that's another thing I've never drawn him out on. I know he lost his wife up in the North.'

Mrs Denbury liked Alfred and had often been to his cottage blackberrying or mushroom picking. 'I'm *sure* there's nothing like that, John. I've seen her photograph and he was very proud of her. All he would say about her death was "I don't like to talk of it, ma'am, even now. Lady Poynter knows the whole story". But she's living up on the Halladale now and we're never likely to bump into her.'

So that was that. But a story once started has a momentum of its own, and mud, once spattered, sticks.

'Well, you never know,' said James Yelberton. He always claimed that there was no smoke without fire. 'I was shooting at a spaniel trial last season and met old Lady Belston. When

I told her I had a gun here, she was interested and asked me how Alfred Blowers was getting on. She told me that years ago she had a handler called Orby, who, unbeknownst to her, gave all her spaniels hell before he ran them! And Alfred, who was handling for Clarice Stewart at the time, caught him doing so, and nearly killed him!'

He looked at the Denburys defiantly.

John said, 'Well, anyway we couldn't have a better keeper here!' and his wife added, 'I'm fond of Alfred and *I* could half-kill anyone ill-treating a dog!'

Which left the question of Alfred's innocence much as before.

XXVII

FOR Alfred, full of hatred and suspicion of 'wee Hamish', it was a season of growing annoyance. Joe Mackerel, ensconced now as loader-chauffeur and some said butler, seemed to take pride in being off-hand with Alfred and in breaking as many unwritten laws of the shoot as he could. Alfred sensed Joe had 'put about' the story that Alfred had beaten him up one night to make him resign; but was too proud to go round making inquiries.

As for Mr Hamish MacBean, he gloried in making remarks which were meant for Alfred to overhear about the way the day was run or the keepering. As George put it: 'If I had a spannle dawg with as many vices as that little b—— I'd hang him to a tree and walk away.' For Mr MacBean was noisy, disobedient and trigger-happy. When he shot something and it had fallen, well, it was someone else's job to pick it up. He would light a cigarette and resume his endless conversation. Luckily he was an erratic shot and missed as often as he hit. But there was one shoot when Alfred picked up *next day* four hares which Hamish had shot coming over a grass brow and had forgotten to tell anyone about. And after a partridge drive it was always round Mr MacBean's butt that Alfred searched, sure that he had either miscounted what was down or 'not bothered'. Most of the farmer guns who shot at Loughton, either as 'guest-guns' or paying guns, were only too anxious to pick up everything they could, for they felt it was a reflection on their marksmanship, if they did not surpass their neighbours. But as long as Mr MacBean blazed off a lot of 'squibs', the bag was immaterial and if he wounded a hare or tinkered a pheasant, well, that was just too bad. Such things obviously did not cause him any loss of sleep.

His manners, both with keepers and beaters, were bad and those of the blonde Mrs Abney worse. Most of the guns were at pains to cultivate friendly relations with what John Denbury called his 'auxiliaries' but MacBean went through a day as if they did not exist and was disliked accordingly. Indeed no one realized how acutely those silent witnesses had summed up each gun before the season was half over, his manners, his means, his marksmanship, above all where his money came from. A. was 'just a foundryman' from Yorkshire. B. had made a fortune out of toothpaste or cinemas or fried fish. C. was in cut-price insurance and would probably not last the season. D. and E. were farmers of varying capacity and means. F's father had been a knacker but he himself was a 'fertilizer king' based on the same end-product. As for the 'wee beggar', Hamish MacBean, with his Rolls and fine clothes and new Purdey guns, he had avoided the war, and made a packet out of potted venison on the Moray Firth. Into this went, in season and out, tons of red-deer flesh, much of it, so George swore, poached. It was there converted into dogmeat, and sent abroad. Nobody knew how George had found all this out but his sister had 'married on a Scotchman' from Nairn, and Mr and Mrs Porter spent a week with them every year. When the story reached Alfred, he was tempted to ask if they had heard about Alfred's own domestic tragedy but decided that it was beneath the dignity of a head-keeper to do so.

But along with Alfred's obsessional dislike of Mr MacBean

went the realization that this trigger-happy little man would one day cause an accident. Mr Denbury feared so too and twice referred at luncheon to accidents he had witnessed and reminded everyone of the syndicate rule that an accident meant forfeiture of rights for the rest of the season. But just as no one will believe that they themselves suffer from body-odour and halitosis, so no shooting man will ever believe, until an accident occurs, that he himself could ever cause one. At the other syndicate of which Hamish was a member, an accident had involved someone's eye. The injured man had sued for damages. Apparently six guns had been walking abreast through some kale, a cock pheasant came sailing down the line and five shots were fired at it, one of which caused the injury. Mr Denbury had talked to a member of this syndicate after the case was over. . . . 'It was dam' queer,' he said. 'I don't believe either of the two guns sued could possibly have fired that shot, unless it boomeranged, which I don't believe. And the Judge, who was a shooting man, in finding for the defendants, hinted strongly that the shot must have been fired *by a third party, and the bastard never came forward to give evidence.*' 'And who was the bastard?' asked John Denbury. The other man closed an eye. 'No *names, no pack drill* and no slander actions, *but, John, your guess is probably better than mine!*' And that was as far as Mr Denbury got, though he shared Alfred's disquiet.

Alfred was hoping that, as guns come and go, the only one he disliked would last but one season. But Hamish MacBean was back again next year full of the little man's unquashable bounce, flamboyant and noisy and trigger-happy as ever.

Alfred swore under his breath when the guns assembled for the first day. The brigadier and James Yelberton were also there but there were three new guns. Worst of all, Mr Denbury, who shot grouse every year in Durham, had fallen into a grass-covered hole in a gully, and sprained so badly a knee already injured in the War that he was often absent. His young nephew took his place and James Yelberton ran the day but with no wish to exert close discipline over the other guns. By the end of that day, what has been called 'the unconquerable enmity

which exists between the Huntsman and his Field', which
exists also between the Gamekeeper and his Guns, had been
focused in Alfred's case on Hamish and Mrs Abney.

Alfred began the second day's shooting in late October in a
doubtful temper. The beaters' lorry would not start and 'Buffer'
Stinson, the driver, who was no mechanic, had to rope in
George and Alfred to push it. Alfred felt sure this was due to
careless maintenance, but it had made him hot and bothered.
And though there was only a threat of rain, the all-important
wind was wrong for the beat. However, Alfred, as usual, made
his last-minute plans with George and went to breakfast. He
was frying some bacon and mushrooms when the telephone
rang. It was John Denbury. 'Well, Alfred, all set?'

'Yes, sir.'

'I've got some bad news for you, Major Yelberton has to go
south for a funeral, so you'll have to run the day.'

'Me, sir?'

'You.'

'But, sir, can't the Brigadier . . . ?'

'No, he'll only get himself in a tangle and upset your arrange-
ments. What's the trouble? You can run it as easy as kiss-me-
hand.'

'Yessir, but . . .'

'I know what you're thinking but you needn't stand any dam'
nonsense from *him*. You're in charge and you can tell him so,
or if there's a dangerous shot fired, he knows the penalty like
all of us. I'll back you up whatever you do, Alfred. Go and give
'em a good day.'

'Sir,' said Alfred, replacing the receiver and hurrying back
to the frying-pan. He ate his breakfast morosely. He would
have liked nothing better than to tell Wee Hamish and Joe
plainly what he thought of both, but no such chance seemed
likely to occur and it meant extra worry and pinpricks to put
up with. However, a keeper's job, he thought, was just one
long worry and if it weren't one thing it was another. Alfred
suddenly remembered old Danfer, the rat-catcher from Snape,
kneeling in his great leather kneecaps fifty years before, and

ejecting a yard-long squirt of tobacco juice into a rat-hole, the while he said, '*I* doon't know a ratcatcher what doon't swear tremendious. There's so many bloody things to annoy them.'

The morning went well but the drive off the hill over the hurdles was a failure. The partridges were packed and wild, and the wind had shifted several points so that the drive was almost in its teeth and Mrs Abney, conspicuous in a scrubbed white mackintosh, made no attempt to conceal herself behind her hurdle. George and Alfred could force the partridges in that drive just so far and no farther. There were no mangolds that season, though the field had been thinly broadcast with 'hungry-gap' kale. Alfred on the downwind flank could see birds settling in the kale, then continually getting up and going down again, and their harsh chirping calls showed that they knew the danger. Alfred thought there must be nearly two hundred birds in the field, but few came over the guns. When the beaters reached the fence at the hilltop they rose and swirled high over the heads of the downwind flankers and back to the stubbles from which they had come. Alfred closed his beaters in gloomily, knowing that few partridges had been shot at and fewer still were down.

'Lot of birds there, Blowers,' boomed the brigadier. 'What put 'em all wrong?'

Alfred was in no mood to mince his words. He pointed with his stick. 'Well, Brigadier,' he said, 'that lady's mackintosh for one thing. That showed up like a duzzy lighthouse from the top of the hill. That *and* the wind was enough to put any drive wrong.'

'What *is* the creature saying?' said Mrs Abney haughtily.

'Not to worry,' said Wee Hamish in a voice which he meant to reach Alfred, 'it was a dam' silly drive to attempt in any case.'

For the first drive after lunch Alfred changed his plans. Normally they swept eighty acres of stubble and clover eastwards over a low fir-belt on to a grass down but with the wind as it was, Alfred proposed to drive it at right angles to the normal line over a high belt of thorns interspersed with oak and elm trees. He sent Jimmy Porter, George's twelve-year-old son, up on his bicycle before lunch was half over to 'change the pegs', in fact to put out a new drive. Knowing his team, he could not be sure of their being in their right places if he left it to chance, and there would be enough noise and confusion to 'put wrong' the cock pheasants he hoped were in the stubble.

The lorry decanted the guns in the corner where the fir-belt and thorn-belt joined. Jimmy Porter, munching a sandwich, was waiting.

'Well done, buoy,' murmured Alfred. 'I want you to stand right *there*' (he pointed) 'just to turn any birds what try to break out this corner. And who's left-hand gun?'

This took longer to settle than you might think as no ordinary gun has ever mastered the elementary arithmetic of 'moving two' after each drive. However after much loud talk (which Alfred feared would send all the wary old cocks scuttling to the horizon) it was agreed that the left-hand gun was Mr MacBean. Alfred led the party through the corner and in a whisper pointed out Mr MacBean's peg. He added, 'It's cocks only, here, gentlemen, please,' and looking wee Hamish between the eyes, 'and there'll be that boy flanking, sir, where you can see him.'

Mr MacBean acknowledged these instructions with a nod, and Joe and the lady stalked past Alfred as if he was not there. 'What absurd nonsense,' Mrs Abney's voice floated to Alfred as he led on the rest of the guns, 'why cocks only at *this* time of year? Is he *trying* to be bloody-minded?'

It was understood at Loughton that except in special circumstances, the usual custom was reversed. Instead of 'cocks only' being shot towards the end of the season when they were at their wildest and most cunning, the Loughton rule was 'cocks only' in October partridge-driving and 'the first time through' the main coverts in November. John Denbury thought that in the long run more cocks were accounted for by this method, and sport was evened up throughout the season. Alfred assumed this had been explained to the guns before the season, and he did not intend to have more noise and delay in explaining now. He dropped the other guns at their pegs, blew his horn as loudly as he could in the teeth of the wind, and posted himself and his dogs as flankers in the belt.

Far away Alfred could see the tiny black dots of his beaters advancing across the huge expanse of stubble, preceded by smaller dots of birds. Pheasants and hares kept scurrying towards him along the belt and scurrying back, and there was a lot of shooting on the leeward side of the belt, mostly at pheasants streaming high on the wind.

'They 'ont hit much in this,' Alfred grunted to himself, with the game-keeper's invincible distrust of the guns' marksmanship. To him it seemed that he was putting a lot of 'good birds' over people unqualified to compete with them. Then suddenly as the beaters neared the belt, he heard a double shot, a shriek and then another shot, followed by another shriek and a babble of shouting. He peered out of the belt. The beaters were near the belt and all looking towards the right of their line, away from Alfred. Then without a word they started marching towards one spot. 'Damn my bleeding heart alive,' thought Alfred, 'someone's been shot.' That would bloody well happen, when neither Mr Denbury nor James Yelberton were there to help him. He strode masterfully into the field and along the stubble to the far end.

XXVIII

ANGER hurried Alfred along the barley stubble but he kept the wooden policeman's mask on as he approached the crowd clustering round Jimmy Porter (Alfred could see who it was now) from both sides of the belt. Alfred thought savagely: This would be my luck, but Mr Denbury said I was in charge. Hope the buoy ain't blinded. He also hoped the culprit was not the brigadier.

George and a boy-beater were bending solicitously over Jimmy, who was bleeding, in melodramatic quantities, from the cheek, ear and legs, blood mixed with tears coursing down his crimson face. Beside him knelt Mr MacBean, his gun on the ground. George was regarding him with unmistakable hatred. Guns, loaders and beaters formed a ring round the injured Jimmy.

Alfred, towering over the press, and still wearing his wooden mask, said, 'Who was it, Jimmy?' Both Porters pointed at Mr MacBean. Then George burst out, his temper adding a rising squeak to his words: 'He had two barrels at a hare gooing back right straight towards young Jimmy, and then changed guns and fired a third!'

Alfred swung round. Joe was standing behind him, one of Mr MacBean's guns held in the crook of his elbow and pointing at the brigadier's soldier-servant. 'Is that true, Joe?' he thundered.

'How should I know?'

'Christ Almighty, man, aren't you his bloody loader?'

No one had ever seen Alfred so angry before. 'And hold that gun, as it should be held, du you'll blow some poor beggar's head off.'

Alfred's angry eye swept round the scene. The 'little man's' other gun lay on the stubble beside him, its muzzle pointing at George Porter's boots as he squatted.

Alfred, conscious that everyone was looking at himself, strode forward, took up the gun, noting that it was not on safe, and opened it. A spent cartridge flew out of the right-hand barrel. The left was loaded. Alfred removed the cartridge, feeling curiously satisfied. Then he said, 'All right, George. We'll whistle Jimmy in to the doctor.' He hailed the lorry driver. 'Du you take Jimmy in to Dr Stranger right quick. George, du you get your beaters over there,' he pointed, 'for the next drive.' The beaters drifted away reluctantly as Buffer surged up with the lorry. Alfred turned on Hamish MacBean. 'And as for you, you can goo right straight home! We've had enough of you, surelie.' Never in his life, thought Alfred, had any keeper addressed a gun in such a tone.

Hamish, to do him justice, attempted to stand on his dignity. 'Don't you *dare* talk to me like that, Blowers! In any case, I don't take orders from you. It wasn't my fault: that young blighter moved from where you posted him.'

'That's correct,' said Joe with unction.

Alfred looked at the bloodstained stubble. 'And that's a bloody lie from both of you. He's where I put him *and* warned you he was there.'

'Well, anyway,' the little man was unexpectedly defiant, 'I'll discuss this with Mr Denbury when I see him. I'm not going home now.'

'That's the stuff, Hamish,' put in Mrs Abney. 'Don't argue with a man who not only shot his own wife but beat up his own head-keeper.'

The blonde tabby looked down at her shapely finger-nails and ankles. There was, she implied, no more to be said. The beaters stood irresolute. Everybody seemed waiting for Alfred.

Alfred blew his whistle and raised his hand. He had once

seen a Master of Foxhounds check an unruly field before he took his hounds home. 'Sit you down, you lads, where you are. I ain't agoin' on with the shute till this here gentleman is on his way home.'

The beaters waited. Mr MacBean did not lack bravado. He actually took out a cigarette, tapped it on a gold case and said, 'Got a match, Joe?'

Alfred's temper went suddenly. He lost it once in five years. 'God damn my heart alive,' he roared as the Grenadiers had taught him thirty years before, 'I told you to goo. Now goo! Mr Denbury put me in charge today and told me what to do if you shot anyone. Goo, you little b——. Du I'll put my stick across your back.'

Hamish MacBean went, like Alfred's temper, very suddenly. He threw away his cigarette and hurried downhill. Alfred was towering over the lady. His face was crimson, but his voice was very quiet. 'It's quite true, madam, that my poor wife was shot dead. But you can ask that little owd' – he checked himself – 'pipsqueak *who* did it. And if he denies it, you go to the Ross-shire police. They know all about him.' This was a bow at a venture but Alfred was past caring. His sergeant-major's eye swept on to Joe, who looked startled and outraged, like a bishop lured into a casino and surprised there. 'And you be off, too, Joe, and tell 'em what happened to your face that night. And if ever I see you on this place agin,' his stick swished alarmingly.

Altogether it was a most unseemly encounter, such as Loughton, for centuries the family seat of the Earls of Louth, had never witnessed. Alfred was too savage to mind. He would resign that evening before anybody sacked him, but that could wait. They had three drives, all short ones, to get through.

*   *   *

John Denbury, his injured knee resting on a cushion, listened that evening to the shocking tale poured into his ear by Hamish MacBean and Mrs Abney. Both had clearly been dining and drowning care before they arrived, but John

Denbury gave each a stiffish whisky to crown the edifice of garrulity. He puffed his pipe, with a hand to his ear.

'And so, John,' Hamish concluded, 'by sheer bad luck . . .'

'On the contrary, Hamish, you were wonderfully lucky!'

'Lucky? How?'

'In not blinding the boy. The doctor tells me one pellet was an inch below his right eye, and he had two in the ear.'

Hamish suddenly realized that John Denbury had received other versions of the outrage. John went on softly: 'And is it true you actually changed guns and shot him again?'

'I told you I was firing at a wounded hare.'

'If you'd been sued for Jimmy Porter's injuries that wouldn't have gone down with any jury.'

Hamish MacBean changed the axis of his attack. 'But to be shouted off the field as if Blowers was a bloody referee! in front of everyone.'

'I'm sorry, Hamish. You knew our rule when you joined the syndicate, and it's not for want of reminding since. Alfred didn't wish to run today because we both realized you were the most likely candidate . . .'

'Me? Why?'

'General style. You *are* a bit trigger-happy, you must admit.'

Mrs Abney thought it time to come up in support. 'It's a harsh and silly rule.'

'Perhaps, ma'am, but my predecessor brought it in after a bad accident to a beater. And three seasons later he himself shot someone and, though he was not altogether to blame, he very sportingly gave up his gun for the season.'

'But to be cursed and threatened by a man who *shot his own wife* . . .' Her lovely eyes were turned on John Denbury, pleading for the iniquity to be understood.

'Did Alfred tell you that?'

'Of course not, but they all say . . .'

'Exactly. Well, *I've* taken the trouble to nail that yarn about Alfred down ever since I heard it. The Chief Constable of Ross-shire says there was no question of it. Alfred's wife was shot by a gang of deer-poachers when Alfred was out on the hill trying to intercept them.'

Mrs Abney flushed with annoyance. 'So they *say* . . . Even supposing Blowers didn't kill his own wife, to shout at Hamish as he did . . .' She let the sentence trail off into thin air.

John Denbury dropped his remote air of listening. 'It depends what deer-poacher shot his wife . . .'

'What *has* that to do with it, pray?'

Doris Abney had not noticed that during this conversation Hamish MacBean had gulped and turned paler, his eyes as pronounced as those of a rabbit. He obviously wanted to kick the lady tactfully under the table but there was no table. Mr Denbury thought the conversation had gone on long enough. 'Actually, Mrs Abney, the police were looking for a small red-headed man from Ardfin, who queerly enough had the same names as Hamish here.'

Mrs Abney knew she had missed but she fired a quick second barrel. 'And what about Blowers beating up Hamish's loader in order to get his job?'

'Did Joe tell you that?'

'Yes.'

'Have you asked him about it since this incident?'

'No.'

'Well, do so! I know *exactly* what happened.'

John Denbury had only known it from Alfred's own lips that evening, after Alfred had put in his resignation, had been given three whiskies, but refused point-blank to reconsider it. 'As long as I was head-keeper here, sir, I felt I ought not to tell you, But now I ain't . . . you may as well hear the truth.'

'Anyway,' said Mrs Abney viciously, 'I hope you'll sack Blowers.'

'I can't. Unfortunately he's resigned.'

'A good thing too. And you won't give him a character, I presume?'

'On the contrary, I shall say he's one of the best keepers I've come across and the most reliable we've had at Loughton.'

'You're not going to tell us what Alfred did to Joe?'

'Ask Joe.'

It was a most unsatisfactory evening for all concerned. The outraged pair swept out, the lady with dignity, though Hamish was clearly anxious to go. Mr Denbury, who had been tele-phoning before their arrival, took up the receiver to get some encouragement from his friend James Yelberton. And far away at Loughton, Alfred sat lonely in his cottage with the glow of three whiskies dying out of him. He patted the adoring head of the young dog who sat between his knees. He was savage. He was out of a good job, all because he couldn't keep his temper! The wraith of Bessie seemed to reproach him. No need, Alfie, she would have told him, to keep anger in your heart over the years. After all, Hamish had forfeited some ten days shooting at £40 a day by one unguarded moment of carelessness and he would be a marked man in his other syndicate if the story got round. He had suffered enough. Had he? Alfred was not so sure. Perhaps he should have 'throshed' the little man down the hill and then gone to jail for assault. But that would have been an inadequate revenge for Bessie's death.

The lamp on the table spluttered and went out, for Alfred in the stress of the evening had not filled it as he always did on Fridays. He sat in darkness, fondling the dog's silky ears. Alfred had not been inside a church for years, but as a small boy at Tibberton and a Guardsman later, church had been a com-pulsory parade. He had loathed 'the polyphanalia' of dressing up for it, but phrases he had heard there had stuck in his retentive memory. And now he suddenly found himself mut-tering words, long-forgotten, out of a Psalm:

> *such as sit in darkness and in the shadow of death: being fast bound in misery and iron.*

How often had Alfred thought that when he was visiting his traps! An old Norfolk keeper, Reuben Tye, had gone off his head after years of keepering because of the inhumanity trapping entailed. He used to kneel in his great calico night-shirt praying resonantly a litany, not for women, who could

look after themselves, but 'for all varmin labouring in traps'.
He had been a joke in East Anglia but Alfred often thought of
Reuben Tye on a soft spring night when everything was brim-
ming with life, all except those luckless creatures who had been
trapped and now, racked with agony, waited, struggling im-
potently, until Alfred or some other keeper gave them the
release of death in the morning.

All Alfred's traps were sprung; but Alfred also knew George,
what with his son and all, would not visit any of his traps until
the morning. Alfred knew where most of them were and George
would not mind even a resigned head-keeper visiting his beat
in the dead of night to shorten the sufferings of vermin who
were 'fast bound in misery and iron'.

Alfred took his torch and put on his rubber boots. It was
better than sitting in darkness with only a dog to fondle, and
even less future than a trapped animal.

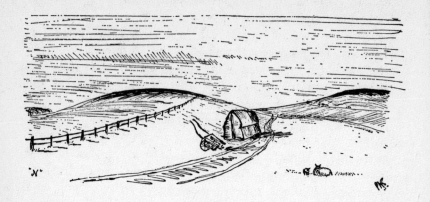

XXIX

THAT is nearly the end of Alfred Blowers' life-story. It led to his coming to Salisbury Plain where we first encountered him. Up till then he had hardly heard of a place called Wiltshire and did not know if it had a coastline or not.

But there Alfred spent fourteen years. Certainly neither he nor Sir Harry Westleton would have agreed that Alfred as a game-keeper had 'never had to think or worry himself, same as a cow'. But whatever the reason, he had somehow retained his looks, those on which Charles Turner, the artist, had commented.

* * *

Alfred had come home, angry and worried, at two in the morning after visiting those traps of George's. It was a dark and windy morning; he was tired as a dog and nothing mattered any more. He had sacked himself and could not in decency 'withdraw his notice'. The dogs on their blankets thumped their tails as though in sympathy, while Alfred climbed the steep and narrow stairs to bed. He slept for a few hours 'in a dream untroubled of hope' and about 6 a.m. awoke in a sweat, dreaming that he had kicked 'Wee Hamish' in a graceful arc clean over the heads of a circle of beaters. Alfred got up, shaved, made breakfast, and suddenly realized that, what with going over to see Mr Denbury overnight he had eaten nothing since lunch the day before. He was out later than usual feeding his pheasants, and at nine o'clock drove his truck to meet George and the other under-keepers for the task of 'picking up'.

The three underlings greeted Alfred with the ceremonial 'Morning, Mr Blowers'. Nothing was said about the previous day (though all three were bursting with curiosity), beyond a remark from Alfred himself, 'How's young Jimmy?' George Porter explained that Jimmy was 'fine' and had had seventeen pellets extracted from various portions of him overnight and would be home 'by dinner-time'.

Then they split up to the business of the morning, with seven dogs hunting free in front of them and the keepers searching in line around and for three hundred yards behind each stand.

They converged on Alfred's truck with a dozen birds. Alfred said, 'George, you come along o' me' and sent the other two keepers away. Alfred always made a point after partridge-drives of cruising at random in his truck over certain stubbles where his partridges fed. This often resulted in the capture of runners which had rejoined their coveys overnight.

Once alone in the truck George burst out, 'I'm whooly grateful to you, Mr Blowers, about yesterday. I was very near taking my ashen stick to that little sod's backside, blow-my-life if I wasn't! If he'd ha' been allowed to go on shuting . . .'

Alfred cut him short: 'That's all right, George boy, I'm glad you didn't. One keeper makin' a fule of hisself in a day is enough. That might ha' stopped you taking on as head keeper here.'

George gaped. 'But you ain't agooen', Mr Blowers, surelie?'

'Ah. And they'll want a new head-man at once. So keep calm and your mouth shut!'

That was all that Alfred would say, as George, bursting with curiosity, hurried home to tell his wife.

Alfred let himself morosely into his house. A letter in an

unfamiliar hand, pushed by the postman under the door, ran:

Dear Blowers,

   I am sorry indeed to learn that you have decided to leave us, but if you are looking for a head-keeper's job, my old aunt's head-man in Wiltshire has just died on her suddenly. I would be only too pleased to recommend you. It's a good little shoot and they used to get 1000 brace of partridges there before the war. Let me know.

Yours sincerely,

Jimmy Yelberton

Mr Alfred Blowers, D.C.M., M.M.,
Head Keeper, Loughton.

Mr Alfred Blowers scratched his head. He had never thought of Wiltshire, but this offer would enable him to get away quietly from the scene of what he still thought was his 'shame' and start afresh where no one knew him. It was nice of 'Major Jimmy' to write like that. People said the Major was too fond of the bottle (as his handwriting suggested) but he was a safe shot, always had a joke with the underlings on a shooting day, and Alfred had met worse gentlemen in his time. He had also a useful dog and could mark birds, which was more than most of them could! Alfred put the letter thoughtfully in his coat-pocket. Just as a keeper's work was never finished, so, if one kept on doggedly, there was always something new to think about and take your mind off the past. The class from which Alfred sprang never had enough money to look forward, to plan their own lives or change their jobs 'between one day and the next'. But thanks to the merchant-banker whom Alfred had taken out stalking years before, he had enough money behind him to be idle for a month if necessary; and there should be at least a fortnight's wages due in royalties from his book, come November. Alfred ate some bread and cheese, threw a handful of biscuit to the dogs to 'stay their stomachs' till it was time for their evening feed, sat down in his tattered armchair, and slept dreamlessly for hours. It was the first time in forty years that he had spent an afternoon in such a way.

Even for Alfred who had 'been about' more than most keepers, a migration to Wiltshire was almost as distant a journey as when he had journeyed from Tibberton to Glenovil with his cab-sick dogs, or later from Caterham to Ross-shire. But now he travelled south comfortably, with both dogs in his own car, stopping a night with Rex Dale, whom he had met at field trials, and who was reputed to have been sacked for knocking down his employer after Rex's favourite spaniel had been wantonly shot. Rex had now migrated from Suffolk to Hampshire, where he trained young dogs or kept them at what horse owners called 'livery'. He was enthralled by Alfred's tale, gave him whisky to make sure it all emerged, and strongly advised Alfred, if the prospective job at Hanging Compton fell through, to telephone him.

But there was no need. Alfred was interviewed in a stone house behind clipped yew hedges by an elderly lady who asked a lot of very shrewd questions as to Alfred's past, and seemed interested in the fact that he had no wife. The puzzled Alfred explained about Bessie, adding, that it was a suggestion from a gentleman about the manner of her death that had caused him to 'forget himself' and resign. It was an hour before Alfred knew he had 'got the job' and five years before he knew the reason for the questions. He was that rare bird, a bachelor keeper! Most keepers were married. If so, their wives were often a nuisance, slatternly, nagging, quarrelsome with their neighbours, dissatisfied with loneliness or their houses. The only bachelor keeper James Yelberton's aunt had encountered had been found by her late husband one Sunday afternoon embracing Lady Westleton's French maid on the grass of the sacred pheasant pen.

The incident had created a local sensation and led to the sudden promotion of Bill Sound to head-keeper. He had lasted ten seasons before his heart-attack but had not been a success. Years of under-keepering, starting as a boy, had given him an inferiority complex, purged by rudeness to guests, and an outspoken contempt for the opinions of others. He preferred to give a shooting party a moderate day's sport rather than a good one and Sir Henry Westleton, across the valley, had nick-named him 'The Gloomy Dean'.

At length, after many inquiries into Alfred's matrimonial past, and a few into his knowledge of keepering, the old lady gave him Bill Sound's job, and actually had his house repainted before he moved in. Alfred soon realized that he was starting from scratch, whether in the matter of grit, the feeding of partridges in winter, the catching-up of hen pheasants, the provision of dusting places, tunnel-traps and later a host of details of pheasant-rearing which at Loughton had been taken for granted.

Alfred found himself re-organizing in the middle of the season every detail of the shoot. For years Bill Sound had done things 'my way', the most convenient way, and had intimidated all who argued. One covert, for example, had never been driven eastwards over certain tall beeches lest the birds which were not shot should cross the river on to Sir Harry Westleton's land. Bill Sound was sure that if any drive near a boundary was taken in the obvious way or with the prevailing wind, his rivals would steal his birds for ever. There was, in short, no liaison with the staff of neighbouring estates, who all 'ganged up', in Alfred's words, against this stranger from Lincolnshire.

Alfred studied these barriers for weeks and then called, formally, on a Sunday morning, not on the head-keepers but on their employers. In his best clothes and with his bowler hat between his knees, he explained his difficulties. 'But of course, Blowers,' said Sir Harry, 'I never knew why old Sound didn't do that drive in the obvious way. And if you think my keeper's going to pinch your birds, well damn it, you can pinch ours back!'

Lord Nettleton was equally decisive. 'My keepers and your predecessor fought bitterly for years. I never could think why. Tell me, weren't you a Grenadier?'

'Sir,' said Alfred, 'but only war-time.'

'I've heard of you. We're full of Grenadiers in these parts. But we stick together. I'll do all I can to help. Ask her Lady-ship if you can come and pick up for me tomorrow and start getting to know *my* keepers! No, don't bother to ask: I'll telephone.'

So things improved and Alfred settled down to enjoy the unending rolling sweep of the Plain, with its sea-like air, its distances, its beech clumps on a dozen heights; and the chalk river-valleys, with their duck-haunted side-streams and back-waters. There were still a lot of partridges then (they disappeared later) and Alfred soon mastered the art of driving them (though never as far as he had driven the Brinewell grouse) over lynchetts and 'bottoms', sometimes with forty or fifty birds in the air at once, and the companion art of showing pheasants in a country where you needed more stops than guns. And he loaded or 'picked up' here and there, at Warrendon and Quilton, Burnford, and Nettleton and Celtic Lodge and Tamington, places where they had as much game as he had and all in an incomparable setting.

James Yelberton came down to shoot with his aunt and to compliment Alfred on what he had done. One evening he brought round a bottle of whisky and insisted on Alfred sharing it in his own parlour.

'You're a legend at Loughton now, Alfred,' he grinned. 'It's six years since you left. In another ten years they'll be telling how you walloped that little MacBean chap down the hill with your stick, and made him take to his bed for a month. Actually I hear from a friend in the Highlands that little MacB's in trouble. Too much poached venison going into that dog-meat cannery of his! And his restaurant's suspect ever since an inspector found fifteen empty tins of 'Doggo' or 'Catto' or whatever he makes, in the kitchen swill-tub.'

Other visitors descended on him. The Field-Marshal who had photographed birds at Loughton came down to study stone-curlews and woodlarks and hobbies. And when Alfred retired, Charles Turner, the artist who had seen him leaning over a gate that evening, invaded his cottage and went to great lengths to induce Alfred to sit, or rather stand, for him, in his best suit of keeper's broadcloth and with his dogs beside him. The resulting picture, 'A Game Keeper', showing Alfred as 'large as life' against a rolling background of Salisbury Plain, hung on the line and aroused much comment at Burlington House. And later it was reproduced as a frontispiece to a new and illustrated edition of *A Keeper's Notebook*, of which Alfred was heartily ashamed.

Alfred, in fact, was in danger of becoming a legend, not only in Lincolnshire and Suffolk, but in Wiltshire. When he showed up, people said, 'That's the keeper who wrote a book', or 'That's the chap that caught his own head-keeper poaching and smashed his face in', or 'He once caught a parson stealing rare birds' eggs and made him bicycle home without any trousers', or '*He's* the feller that walloped the hide off a dangerous shot and packed him home.'

They were mainly stories of superhuman violence and most were untrue. One, which was probably started by Mrs Skutz's boy-friend and reached an American gossip-column, shortly after Alfred's portrait was exhibited at The Academy, was that Alfred had been the original lover of *Lady Chatterley*.

Alfred heard few of these legends. His boy Ian was now well launched on a surgical career and thank goodness did not despise his father's calling. And the old man busy with his household chores and garden was content. At times he thought sadly of the cruelty which any keeper, year in, year out, has to employ to keep vermin at bay. And then he would think of the thousands of song-birds and other forms of wild life which survived each year because the crows and magpies and rats were killed down. The years had taught him the paradox that man can be the worst vermin of all, the only species capable of exterminating another species for its own amusement or gain.

But Alfred Blowers, ex-backhouse boy, ex-sergeant of Grenadiers, ex-stalker, ex-keeper and author of *A Keeper's Notebook*, found all his life an abiding joy in the world of the wind and sunlight and if he had 'spilt the wine that God the Maker gave', he had at any rate enjoyed the spilling.